WITHDRAWN

NAPIER'S BONES
DERRYL MURPHY

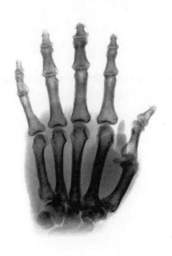

ChiZine Publications

FIRST EDITION

Napier's Bones © 2011 by Derryl Murphy
Cover artwork © 2011 by Erik Mohr
Cover design © 2011 by Corey Beep
All Rights Reserved.

LIBRARY AND ARCHIVES CANADA CATALOGUING IN PUBLICATION

Murphy, Derryl
      Napier's bones / Derryl Murphy.

ISBN 978-1-926851-09-9

      I. Title.

PS8626.U7515N36 2011   C813'.6   C2010-907280-4

CHIZINE PUBLICATIONS
Toronto, Canada
www.chizinepub.com
info@chizinepub.com

Edited and copyedited by Sandra Kasturi
Proofread by Samantha Beiko

Canada Council   **Conseil des Arts**
for the Arts   **du Canada**

We acknowledge the support of the Canada Council for the Arts which last year invested $20.1 million in writing and publishing throughout Canada.

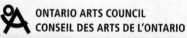

ONTARIO ARTS COUNCIL
CONSEIL DES ARTS DE L'ONTARIO

Published with the generous assistance of the Ontario Arts Council.

Printed in Canada

This one is for my wife JoAnn. Her patience, her support, and her enduring love are all reasons you hold this in your hands. Her belief in me through the few highs and many lows of writing this book is what kept me going.

NAPIER'S BONES

DERRYL MURPHY

The good Christian should beware the mathematician and all those who make empty prophecies. The danger already exists that the mathematicians have made a covenant with the devil to darken the spirit and to confine man in the bonds of hell.
— St. Augustine of Hippo

PART ONE

For as Old Sinners have all poynts
o'th Compass in their Bones and Joynts
Can by their Pangs and Aches find
All turns and Changes of the wind;
And better than by Napier's Bones
Feel in their own the Age of Moons

—Samuel Butler

Dom paused at the bottom of the hill, took a swig of warm water and wiped the sweat from his forehead. Above him the sun blasted down through the hard blue sky, harsh and yellow and hotter than anything he'd ever felt. Below him the desert sand and red rock told him nothing he needed to know, so he closed his eyes and rubbed the baseball in his pocket, muttering multiplication tables under his breath as he traced the stitching.

Fire streaked across the darkness inside his eyelids, slowly refining itself to a sequence of numbers and formulae. He opened his eyes and watched the direction they pointed, caught the path before they faded away in the angry, greedy light; up the hill, switching back and forth to handle the steep incline.

He climbed, cursing the heat, cursing his lack of preparedness, cursing the luck that had led his search to here in the Utah desert. Near the top he stopped and took another swallow of water, trying hard to conserve the tiny amount that remained in the bottle, wondering if he was going to be forced to turn back before he reached his target.

There was a rustling sound from overhead, and he looked up to see a series of logarithms flapping by like wiry bats, dipping and diving through the air before breaking up into their constituent numbers and, with nothing left to hold them together, quickly fading away. There were more sounds now, a distant clicking that quickly segued into a great ripping and grinding sound, like a giant's zipper that somehow controlled all seismic activity, and then all colour above Dom was washed away, formulae and numbers and sequences exploding across the dome of the sky, sure sign of backlash of some sort. Dom flashed his fingers, frantically counting primes in ascending order, using binary as a shorthand, hoping to hell that it would be enough to keep attention from being fixed on him.

It wasn't. A grey mass, pulsing with unclear integers, fuzzy and indistinct against the now-screaming numbers in the sky above, launched itself over the edge of the ridge, dropped through the air and pierced his body. Dom was flung backwards, blackness overtaking him, his last awareness of the rumbling and shrieking suddenly cutting off, and the pure Silence that for one sudden moment ruled the world around him.

New patterns slowly floated into focus, more numbers flying across his vision, except this time he was sure they were trying to tell him something. Dom made an effort to squint and make it out, but before he could define what they were saying everything faded away, the fire in his eyes drifting from red to orange to pale yellow before finally disappearing altogether; the blackness fading to grey, and finally jumping to brown. He stared at the brown, then started as his view broadened, saw that it was the hair on the back of someone's head. He was on a bus.

He gingerly turned his head and looked out the window, wincing at the now-apparent headache. He was in a large town or, more likely, a small city, seeing how this appeared to be a transit bus, not something like a Greyhound. Buildings drifted by, none taller than three or four floors; the streets were wide, and there was also that overwhelming sense of easy-going that he could see in all the pedestrians. Not too distant were some small mountains, their foliage mostly dried-up brown with small green punctuation marks.

So how the hell did he get here?

"And where the fuck am I?" he murmured to himself, loud enough that the guy in front of him turned around and fixed him with a quick glare.

Dom rang the bell and jumped off the bus at the next stop, crossed the street against the light and found himself a bench in a small park behind a restaurant, confused and scared. Where he'd been in the desert was a good long distance away from any city this size, a few hours in a car at least, and yet he had no recollection of making his way here. He felt inside his pocket, found the baseball still there, and pulled it out to toss it while he thought.

One toss in the air with it, though, and he froze, then stabbed out his hand and caught it at the last second. The ball was badly scorched along one seam, blackened enough to be pretty much worthless to him now, to say nothing of any collector. He flipped it around in his hand, rubbed it and looked for the numbers to shine, but they were few and very weak.

"Jesus Christ."

"Profanity seems to be your strong suit."

Dom dropped the ball to the ground and stood bolt upright, looking around for the owner of the voice. There was no one else in the park. "Who's there?"

"Are you sure you want to know?"

Dom grabbed the ball and sat back down on the bench, shocked. His own lips had moved, the voice had issued from his mouth, but it hadn't been his voice, in tone or accent.

"I've read about you," he finally said. "Or your type, anyway."

"Indeed. We had sensed you earlier that day," said the voice. "You were tracking the same treasure we were."

"*You* were out there as well?" Dom raised an eyebrow at this news. He'd been sure he was the only one who'd been onto it. But if he'd stumbled onto a duel, obviously someone else had to have put it all together as well.

"For six years now." The voice stopped for a moment as a young woman with four children in tow walked by. Dom smiled politely at her, sure that he looked a wreck. She smiled back, although the effort to override a frown was obvious on her face, and then hurried her kids along.

Once she was out of range, he continued. "You were saying?"

"You were *numerate*, it was obvious to us early on. And even though we could tell you were still quite raw, you did an admirable job damping down your own numbers. It was only because we had the same target that we were able to see you coming."

"If you could see me coming, how come the guy you went up against couldn't?" He didn't know this, not for certain, but the fact that he had gone unmolested before the duel made him feel pretty sure.

"We saw you because you were using the same search numbers we were. The problem is, your numbers weren't as close to the ground as our own; he would have eventually been able to spot you, but found us first. Bad luck. I guess he must have thought we were the ones kicking up those numbers."

Dom rubbed his eyes and then ran his hand through his hair, which was feeling somewhat greasy despite its short length. "You weren't able to handle him head-to-head, were you?"

"I said he, but in fact it was a she. Sort of. We expected to be able to take her by surprise, as you likely did." There was a pause. "We didn't. A duel was the last thing we wanted; her numbers and formulae were far beyond anything my host had ever seen before."

"So what happened?" asked Dom, afraid he already knew the answer.

"My host was killed, while our foe was seemingly incapacitated. My host's last act," here the voice broke, "was to cut me loose. I had not quite a twenty-three second window before I would have fractioned, and I knew where you were."

"So you came to me."

"I did. I've invested generations of myself in this search, and I'm not about to go to fraction when I'm so close."

Dom's stomach rumbled. He stood and pulled his wallet out.

"You had enough money to take us on the bus to this city."

"Which is?" Indeed, there were no more bills.

"Logan, Utah. The transit system here is free, so I was riding you around, waiting for you to awaken after the co-option shock."

Next Dom pulled out his credit cards. It looked as if a scratch-and-win lottery fanatic had taken a coin to all the magstripes, and the raised numbers on all of them had been reduced to blackened smears. "Backwash from the duel," said the voice. "I already checked. Everything you had with numbers has been zeroed; I hope this wasn't all your worldly mojo."

Dom shook his head. "I have safe deposit boxes all over the place, things I've been caching ever since I became a part of the sequence. Nothing else in Utah, though." He crossed the park, heading for the street. There was a bank just a block away.

"You've never carried an adjunct, have you?"

Dom shook his head. "Nope. Read about it, but that's all. Never expected I'd ever find someone to co-opt; never even thought about looking." There were several people on the sidewalk, so he stopped talking for the moment, waited for the light to change so he could cross the street.

When it did change and cars and trucks started up, he took advantage of the momentary roar to mutter, "Who the hell are you, anyway?"

"I don't know." There was a pause. "The numbers failed somehow along the way. I've been travelling in this form for decades, maybe longer. My hosts have all called me Billy."

Dom looked at the numbers coming from his mouth as the name was spoken, saw that they added up. "I'd say that's your name, all right. No other clues?"

"We'll discuss it later," said Billy. "First do what you must, and then we'll find somewhere private to talk."

Dom nodded and opened the door, walked into the air-conditioned coolness of the bank. There was no ATM, so he turned to a younger woman sitting behind a desk and asked for one.

"We have a drive-through banking machine behind the building," she said, gesturing over her shoulder.

Dom thanked her and walked out, cursing under his breath. A quick walk around the corner showed that the machines were indeed out in the open on the pavement. He dashed across the street and kept walking, looking for a store that might have a privately owned ATM, something easier to deal with.

The first machine he came across was in a gas station, but there was an overhead security camera inside. He stood to the side of the ATM for a few seconds, letting an older man go ahead of him, while he collected his thoughts and tried to decide the best way to circumvent everything. He had a standard routine whenever he needed to plunder a bank machine, but the incidental damage he'd taken from the duel had for the moment left him less sure of his abilities.

Finally he just bore down and concentrated, watched the numbers as they swarmed the air above the ATM, looked for a pattern he could use. It wouldn't be the old man's, that was for sure; his account balance fluttered up for the briefest of moments before sinking through the floor, barely enough to give the guy a week of mac and cheese.

There, near the ceiling in one corner, hovered some numbers that were interconnected, from a recent customer with a big enough balance that Dom's conscience wouldn't take too hard a hit, and the string was easy enough to lay out in proper order with a few simple equations. Dom pulled his bank card from his wallet and fed it into the slot, watched the numbers slide in after it, all the while muttering more primes to keep the camera from being able to focus on him. He held his hand above the PIN pad and pretended to use it, listened as the numbers beeped and the machine clunked and clicked.

The money slot opened but nothing came out.

"Sonofabitch," he whispered. Sweat was beading up on his forehead and there were now three people lined up behind him. He thought for a few seconds more, then typed a sequence a girlfriend who'd been a teller at a bank had taught him.

"Tricky," muttered Billy, as the money slot opened and closed several times, eventually putting three thousand dollars in twenties into Dom's hands. "I've never seen those particular numbers before."

He pocketed the money and his card, now reconstituted with new numbers and a fresh magstripe, and shoved his way past a fat woman wearing powder blue sweats and a stained white t-shirt who held her hand up to her breast and said "Oh my heck!" in a stern fashion. He ignored her and crossed the parking lot for the grocery store, at the same time eyeing the motel across the street, wanting to fill his empty stomach and then sleep and wash up.

"I'll grab a few things and then get a room," he said. "We can talk then."

"Good idea," replied Billy.

He picked up a BBQ chicken and fries meal from the deli in the grocery store, as well as a cold six-pack of Bud and apples and bananas.

As he paid with two of the bills, he rubbed at their serial numbers and silently muttered primes as he did so, ignoring the look the cashier, a sweet young blonde with glasses, gave him. For a brief second as he did so he seemed to jump outside of his body, looking at himself from the viewpoint of the cashier, but he blinked and was back in his own body; the girl gave him a strange look as she gave him his change, and he hurried away.

He paid the same way at the motel, rubbing away the numbers. Little things like that made it harder to track him down, and now that Dom was carrying an adjunct, just after Billy had fled his host on the losing side of a duel, the winner of that fight might be hunting for either one of them. After he staggered up to his room, he ran the bath, stripping down and taking a long piss before climbing into the steaming water. The first thing he did once in the tub was take a deep breath and dip his head underwater. It was too hot to open his eyes, but he could do this sort of thing by feel, no problem. With his right index finger he inscribed a little curlicue followed by *1049* on the underside of the water, then slid back up, gasping for air and relishing the coolness on his face.

Surface tension kept the numbers in place, and when he sat back up they'd slid to the opposite end of the tub, upside down, bumping up against each other as they counted down, the amount of seconds a good prime number to add to his cover. When they reached zero the water would quickly chill, chasing him out before he became viewable from a distance. This sort of thing was needed when he wasn't wearing his clothes, loaded as they normally were with all sorts of numeric talismans—his mojo—to keep him invisible to numerate eyes prying from a distance.

"God, this feels good." He leaned his head back and closed his eyes, let the heat just open his pores and flush the dirt and crap from days on the road from his body.

"You should eat before you fall asleep," said Billy.

"Well, I won't be falling asleep in here." Dom sat up and leaned forward, looked at his indistinct reflection in the tall mirror that was fogging up on the inside of the door. "Anything special I'm going to need to know? Seeing this is the first time I've ever carried an adjunct."

He watched as his head shook, an action that was definitely not under his own control. "Well, with practice we might be able to communicate just by thinking at each other, although I've only had two hosts who were able to do that."

Dom blinked. Even through the condensation on the mirror, watching his mouth move and hearing the words come out in a different voice with an English accent of sorts was more than strange. "Maybe it's something we can work on," he finally said. "This talking to myself is likely to attract more attention than I want."

"Patrick . . ." There was a pause. "My last host, the two of us would often use a note pad, write down our thoughts in a kind of shorthand. I could teach it to you if you like."

"Maybe so." Dom grabbed the little shampoo bottle and lathered up his hair, then dipped his head back underwater for a moment. When he came back up, he said, "But I think I'd rather be able to talk as quickly as possible." He rubbed water from his eyes and then grabbed the soap and started scrubbing. "I didn't come looking for you. Did this Patrick?"

Billy nodded his head for him. "My previous host had found him, taught him everything he could, because he was dying. He prepared himself to be an adjunct as well, but his numbers must have been bad; the addition never happened, and Patrick ended up carrying only me."

"So Patrick was ready for you, knew how to deal with you and everything else he needed to know." He nodded at himself. "Me, I only know what little I've heard and the few hints I've managed to find in dusty old books I've peeked at in libraries." Dom took a breath and dipped under the water one more time, then waited for the time to count down. As the last digit faded away the water went from still hot to ice cold, and with a childlike squeak and a shudder he stood and jumped onto the towel on the floor, testicles shrivelling and goose bumps rising everywhere.

He towelled down and then quickly pulled on his shirt and ran straight to the bed, climbed under the covers and shivered uncontrollably for almost a minute. When he was finally feeling warm again he sat up, still trying to keep as much of himself covered as possible, turned on the TV with the remote and popped open a can of beer. After a long drink he dug into the now-lukewarm chicken and fries, relishing every bite and surfing the channels in between swallows.

When he finished the one beer he casually smeared away the UPC on the can with his thumb, then opened another, drinking this one more slowly. There was a ball game on, Cubs hosting the Dodgers, which he watched with mild interest. On the screen numbers constantly floated by, pitchers and fielders and batters all doing their unconscious calculations, digits doing battle with each other as simple formulae fought to come out on top; baseball players, even those who had been idiots in school, were among the strongest in latent ability. Only snooker and pool players showed more talent, but since baseball was a team game, and one that welcomed fanaticism about stats and figures, many more of its artefacts could be made useful.

Finished with his food and second beer, he put the garbage on the table beside the bed and leaned back against his pillow. Numbers quietly fluttered through the air above his head, some of them bumping against the lampshade like lost moths at night. He closed his eyes.

W e won't be able to fly out of here," said Dom. He had finished off a fine breakfast at a local greasy spoon, and was now walking across a large park that surrounded the local Mormon tabernacle. Expanses of green and healthy grass were punctuated by large leafy trees, everything pleasant and orderly, enough so that Dom almost felt guilty for walking on the grass instead of on one of the paved paths.

"I agree," said Billy. "You'd only succeed in lighting up the sky. Perhaps if we went south again, to Salt Lake. The flights are large and anonymous enough from a big city."

Dom shook his head. "South is where we came from, and I'm not interested in heading back to whatever it was that woman had until I'm ready for it."

"You could purchase an automobile."

Dom shrugged and sat in a shaded patch of grass. Still fairly early in the morning and already it was getting hot. "My license got fried with all my other cards, and I don't have anything nearby to replace it. With a little work I could probably reconstitute some of it, but I don't really want to have to worry about insurance. I'm not from these parts."

He actually felt his body sigh and then his head shook. Obviously Billy was trying to make a point.

"What?"

"How long have you been actively numerate?" asked Billy.

"Close to fifteen years." Dom scrunched up his face, thinking.

"Yeah. About that. I could always see numbers and make them work for me, but the breakthrough happened about then."

"And you've been on your own all that time?"

Dom nodded. "The closest contact I've had is in some anonymous chat rooms online with some folks."

There was a pause. "Chat rooms? Online?"

"Uh, yeah. I found some ciphers left on a website that directed me to them. So far the times have all been random; I'd say there's probably about a half-dozen of us who stop by, now and again."

"You're saying that someone has taken the time to set up a numerate presence on the web? Has anyone discovered you there?"

Dom shrugged. "I dunno. I imagine that they wouldn't be too successful if they did. We talk to each other in coded binary."

Billy closed Dom's eyes and pinched the bridge of his nose. It felt very peculiar, like he was being frustrated with himself.

"What is it?"

He shook his head. "All that time that Patrick thought the two of us were alone, just cryptic hints about lives lived in dusty old university library books, mysterious numbers fluttering away just at the edge of the horizon, but nobody to confide in, no way he could find anyone. It was pure luck my previous host had found him, and it looked unlikely any others would ever crop up." He fell on his back, lying in the grass and looking up at the green trees and blue sky. "It can be a lonely life, especially since you're almost always competing with the other guy. Trust is difficult to come by, difficult to even fathom. It took forever for Anders to convince Patrick that he was sincere about handing me over."

"No family, no friends, just a never-ending search," said Dom. "It's still like that, even with a lousy hour chatting online every month or so." He laughed, a sharp bark that turned heads twenty yards away. "Hell, this is the most conversation I've had since I started this loony trip."

He felt his mouth grin in response. "We should—" started Billy, but he stopped short as suddenly he caught a glimpse of himself from nearby. Just as suddenly he was back in his own body, confused as all hell, and above them a girl was leaning over and looking down, hair lit up like a halo by the hot sun behind her.

"Go on," she said, sitting down on the grass beside Dom. He sat up and squinted at her, finally recognized her as the cute cashier from the grocery store. She was about twenty, he figured, not skin and bones, but with a pleasant bit of heft to her. Her glasses were different than the ones she'd had on at work, round spectacles like John Lennon used to wear instead of those heavy black rims. She wore shorts and a loose-fitting white t-shirt and sports sandals, and her blonde hair was tied back in a ponytail.

"Um, what do you mean, go on?" He picked at the grass, pulling up blades and rolling them between his fingers before tossing them to the negligible breeze, avoiding her eyes and instead reading the pseudo-patterns of chaos they made as they fell back to the ground.

"Whatever your friend was saying," she replied, and he looked up at her so suddenly he felt his neck crack. She tried to smile, but he could see that she was feeling uncomfortable.

"Friend?" Dom looked around, trying his best to act in the dark. He wiped fresh sweat from his forehead.

"It's like a blurry shadow, hard to tell exactly what it is," she said. "But I see it slide in and out of you, and I can see even from a distance when it's the one doing the talking."

Dom fixed her with a stare. "Look," he said, "I don't know what it is you think you're seeing or hearing, but I'm just mumbling to myself, going over some ideas about where I want to visit next. Nothing else."

"My mother used to tell me that when she was a kid in school," she said, seemingly ignoring him, "that if they wanted to show movies they actually had to get out a big old projector and thread the film in and feed it through the reels, and then sometimes the projector made such a noisy clackety-clack sound that she could barely hear what was coming from the speaker."

Dom blinked at this sudden change in conversational direction. "And I should care how?"

"But when I was in school, we always watched movies on video, even back in elementary. I guess that makes me pretty young compared to you."

Still unsure of where this was going, Dom shook his head. "I'm not that much older than you."

She shrugged. "I don't mean you, I mean the other you. But anyway, I remember watching one movie that Mom had told me about before she disappeared. I was in fifth grade—when I watched the movie, not when she disappeared—and then I knew what she had been talking about." She paused again and picked some grass of her own, rolled it between her fingers and tossed it into the air. "When you were a kid, did you ever see that short movie with Donald Duck called *Donald in Mathmagic Land*?"

Dom nodded, suddenly struck dumb.

"My life is sort of like that," she said. For a second she turned her gaze to the tabernacle, then back to him. "There are these patterns that I see all the time, floating through the air, patterns that my mind finally realized were numbers. It sometimes feels like I should be able to control them, although every time I try weird things happen. But I've never in all my life seen numbers do something for someone else."

"The money in the store," whispered Billy.

She frowned. "You have an accent now."

Dom waved his hand in the air. "That's the blurry shadow you say you can see. Get on with it."

She nodded, and the look on her face was a cross between confusion and excitement. "It was the money. I don't know exactly what it was you were doing, but I could see the numbers float away when you were paying for your food. Like the money had never even been there in the first place, and you kept fading in and out of view, like you were there but my eyes didn't want to look at you." The girl stared hard at him. "I see those numbers all the time, but they've always been random, confused, sometimes just in the corner of my vision. Like they were trying to avoid me. Until yesterday. The numbers I saw moving around you and, and, even through you, those were numbers moving with a sense of *purpose*."

Dom pursed his lips. Suddenly he thought he could see where this was going, and he didn't like it.

"I want you to teach me. I want to learn everything I can about how to use numbers like you can. To use them the way I know my mother could."

"I don't think—" Dom started, but then the sky exploded in a bright flash of integers, logarithms, algebraic formulae, more. Entire sequences plummeted from the sky, dropping and screaming like Nazi Stukas, twisting and pulling up at the last second to avoid hitting the ground, ripping through people, cars, buildings, trees and birds, before climbing hard back into the sky and breaking up in lightning-bright explosions. And even though Dom knew they were invisible to everyone else in the park and on the street, the numbers were so powerful that people were flinching and waving at them like they were especially pesky mosquitoes and flies.

"Search numbers!" shouted Billy over the din, but Dom was already ahead of him, up and running across the grass, reeling off primes and grabbing them before they got away, smearing them against his skin and clothes.

But that would only help for a few minutes, he was sure. He'd *never* seen any patterns so strong, so large.

The girl was running beside him now. "What's wrong? What are those numbers doing?" She sounded breathless, panicked.

"Someone we're not prepared to meet right now is looking for us," said Billy, squeezing in words over Dom's desperate counting. Dom ducked as an especially loud sequence screeched through the air, sailing just barely over his head and bumping off some already frazzled primes. "We won't get away," said Dom, panting.

The girl grabbed his arm and pulled him to the right, pointing to the street. "My car!"

He nodded and they both ran madly, Dom stutter-stepping twice to avoid more numbers. She reached the little red Subaru wagon first, flung the door open and jumped in, Dom jumping in right after her. Before he had the door shut she was peeling out of her parking spot, forcing an oversize RV with Arizona plates to slam on the brakes.

"Where to?" she yelled. Even with the windows rolled up, the screaming of the numbers as they dived was overwhelming, crashing against their ears in deafening waves.

Dom scratched more primes on his window. "North!" yelled Billy.

The girl turned a hard left, followed the block, then left again. Directly ahead there were more numbers plummeting from the sky and with a brief muttered curse she turned right, followed a one-way road that curved up a hill.

"We're leaving them behind," she said, voice cracking. There were tears in the corners of her eyes.

Dom looked back, saw that the sky above the tabernacle was still thick with numbers, a flock of insane numerate crows circling as they searched for prey. But many were now streaking high into the air and flying north. Looking that way, he saw that they were gathering, circling like a low storm cloud, probably readying for another search.

"We can't go north now. She's trying to squeeze off our escape route."

The girl leaned forward against the steering wheel, looked up and ahead. "I see nothing towards the canyon. We'll go that way."

"How long until we're in the canyon?"

She passed a slow-moving car, ignoring the horns from oncoming traffic. "Five minutes. Maybe ten."

"The primes won't last that long," said Billy. "We're bound to show up before we reach it."

Dom spun around, saw that the back seat was loaded with junk and papers. "What do you have back here?"

She glanced around quickly. "Stuff. Stuff to help me with numbers." She managed to force a wry smile. "A little obsession that guarantees I don't ever get to keep a boyfriend."

Kneeling on the seat and leaning over the back, Dom started rifling through things. "Have you got a . . ."

"A what?"

"Fucking great!" he yelled, turning back around. In his hands he held what looked to be almost twenty feet of tape from an adding machine, random numbers cooing softly at him.

"I was looking for patterns," she said. "But I couldn't find any with that roll."

"Ideal," said Dom. He started wrapping the tape around his waist and right arm and as quickly as he could brought it up towards his head. Ignoring the looks he was getting from the people in the car beside him, he started wrapping it around his neck and head, a numerate mummy preparing to meet his own version of Osiris. The harsh glare of the sun was now softened as it shone through the paper and ink, and the smell of sun-baked paper was thick in his nostrils. It was small mojo, but better than the makeshift stuff he'd been running with.

Finished, at least as best as he could be, he then leaned down, put his head on the girl's lap as she drove. "Just keep driving," he said, voice sounding hollow inside his makeshift wrap of numbers. "We don't want to be stuck in town waiting for them to find us."

"There are some skimming the streets not too far behind me," she said, fear raising the pitch of her voice. He felt the car accelerate more.

"Are they coming our way?"

"Sorta." He felt the road dip; they were going downhill now, a fairly steep drop. There was a long pause, and when the road levelled out again she breathed a heavy sigh. "No. I don't think they're following us anymore."

"I'll give it a few more minutes, I think." He closed his eyes, relief starting to sink in, the roll of paper rustling loudly in his ears. "I hope you don't mind me being down here like this."

She tried to laugh. "I just hope the Highway Patrol doesn't decide to pull me over. This would look bad enough anywhere else, but in Utah . . ." Her voice trailed off.

After another couple of minutes, Dom asked, "What's your name?"

"Jenna. Yours?"

"Dom."

"Billy," said the shadow.

"Okay, I'm feeling a bit weirded out," said Jenna. "One guy wrapped in paper with his head in my lap is bad enough, but two in the same body is too much."

The car slowed down, and the steady whine of tires on pavement was joined by the rumble and pop of rocks underneath. Dom sat up and peeled the paper off his body, then opened the door and stepped out. They were in a half-full parking lot on the side of the highway; down below people fished at a small lake surrounded by trees, and above and around him there were steep grey cliffs and mountains, as close as the other side of the highway. A semi rattled by, four cars and minivans jostling anxiously behind it. "This is part of the canyon?"

Jenna climbed out as well, nodded. "Logan Canyon."

"Where does this take us?"

"Does that mean you'll take me with you?"

Dom frowned. "Give me a minute, will you?" He walked over to the far side of the lot. "So what do we do?" he asked, and immediately noticed how easy it was to say *we* instead of *I*.

Billy scratched his head for him, and he turned and looked back at Jenna, who was standing watching the traffic go by. "I've already figured out that you aren't the type to just kill her and leave her at the side of the road." Dom flinched at this; the thought would never have occurred to him, but he knew there were numerates out there who wouldn't hesitate. "Take her along. We have no real idea of what the landscape is like, how far we are from anything, and no transportation other than her automobile."

Dom nodded. "I guess I can teach her some stuff."

"But keep it elementary, Dom. Don't give up too much information; you don't want her to end up knowing all your secrets and stealing some mojo."

"Right. And maybe I can get rid of her when we know we're in the clear." He paused, scratched his chin. "Have you noticed something weird about her?"

"How so?"

"Like a couple of times it felt like I was looking at things from Jenna's eyes. Just for a tiny second each time."

Billy shook his head. "No, I haven't." He smiled. "Don't go getting all infatuated with this girl."

"That ain't the problem," muttered Dom. He turned and walked back to the car. "Okay, here's the deal," he told Jenna. "I need your wheels, and you need my expertise, right?"

She nodded.

"Then we get in and drive. Let's get away from here, then I'll take the time and teach you a few things, all right?"

Jenna smiled. "All right."

"But in the meantime," he said as they got back in the car, "I have some other things I'm doing. So the stuff you learn will be from following along and paying attention, not from me pretending I'm up at the front of the class."

Jenna backed out, waited for two trucks to go by, then pulled back out onto the highway. "Is my first lesson knowing when to run away?"

"Damn straight it is." Dom turned his head and looked back, one last check for stray numbers. "I still don't know the name of that woman, but I do know that I don't want to take her on face-to-face, *especially* not right now."

"That would be your second lesson," said Billy, sounding dry. "Never attack a problem straight on when you can sneak around the back way."

Jenna did a slight double-take, looking at Dom for a few seconds before the road twisted and forced her attention back to driving. "Right. You told me your name is Billy, shadow guy. Let's make that my third lesson. Exactly who or what are you?"

Dom felt his shoulders shrug. It was a gesture he didn't often make, but it seemed that his new adjunct liked to use it quite regularly. "My name's Billy. I don't know much else about myself, except that I've probably been dead for at least a hundred years, probably more."

Jenna gasped, but kept her attention on the road. "I'd say you were feeding me a line, but maybe those screaming numbers have opened my mind a bit."

"Dead is a relative term," continued Billy. "This form of immortality takes an odd shape, I know, and is tenuous at best; I thus partake in a search for the means to make this a permanent state, one that would also return to me a corporeal form." He grinned. "I'm also constantly searching, with the aid of whoever is my current host, to find clues to my lost past."

"Corporeal form would mean your own body, right?" asked Jenna. "Would this be like something out of a horror movie, where you take over someone else's body?" She looked pointedly over at Dom.

"Not at all. Dom is only my most recent host. My experience can be useful to him, as his body is to me. But our goal is essentially a common one."

"You both want to live forever?"

Dom shook his head. "Later on in the learning curve, Jenna. As it is right now, everything Billy says about his history is as new to me as it is to you. Okay?"

Jenna nodded. "Not like I really have a choice."

"Shall I continue then?" asked Billy. "Or is my storytelling ability not so captivating?"

Jenna slowed down and inched over towards the shoulder to make sure that an oncoming tractor-trailer would go by without sideswiping the car. "Sorry. Go on."

"Secrets for the numerate have been handed down, often somewhat begrudgingly, over the centuries, perhaps even over millennia. Numeracy is the life-blood of power for a lucky few, and the ability to find the items—what numerates like Dom these days call the *mojo*—that help contain and build that power, is one of the biggest factors in how successful you are.

"An even greater power, and one that most numerates are never able to develop, is the ability to fashion mojo that can hold your numerical shadow."

"Shadow?"

"Essence, if you like."

"What, like a soul?" Jenna made a rather sour face. "I had to put up with enough of that crap when I was little and forced to go to church."

Dom shrugged and said, "I know, it all sounds like goofy metaphysical shit. Don't think of it as a soul, though. From what I've read, template might be a better word. Or avatar. But 'shadow' is what most of us use, or else 'adjunct.' Sometimes 'co-opt,' as well, but that isn't as common a term."

Now Billy nodded. "This much I know: a long time ago, when I was still alive, I set my life's essence into something of numerical significance. But somehow something went wrong with what I laid out, or perhaps something happened later on, during a transfer from one host to another. I remember enough to know some of my name, and I still retain my numerate abilities, even though those of my host will always supersede them." He rolled down the window and leaned back, let the mountain air, cooler by far than the heat in Logan, wash over his face.

"The numbers that I put in place did their duty, although it still took a long time for my first host to find it and to unlock the secret. So long, in fact, that we wasted some time while I learned to handle new slang and vernacular. I can only imagine the difficulties Napier might have had with Archimedes."

Dom sat bolt upright, eyes open. "Holy shit! John Napier hosted Archimedes?"

Billy shrugged Dom's shoulders again. "I think so." Suddenly he smiled and slapped Dom's knee. "By damn, a memory! A previous host and I were acquainted with someone who knew someone, if you understand what I mean. From what we gathered, all the evidence seemed to point to his hosting the Greek." He scratched his chin, thinking for a moment longer. "I wonder if the shock of joining up with you has unearthed any other old memories."

"I've heard of Archimedes," interrupted Jenna. "But who was John Napier?"

"He was a Scottish mathematician and inventor," replied Dom. "He's one of two men who separately invented logarithms. There have always been whispers that he managed to leave his shadow in all sorts of artefacts, although I've seen no sign that he's actually been brought forth. I think the gal who's after us might have been able to lay her hands on one of the artefacts. I'm pretty sure, even."

"And so you were, what, trying to steal it from her?"

Dom grinned. "If I'd known she was there, then damn straight. She could either cough it up happily, unlikely in the best of circumstances, or with a fight. She wasn't the reason I was down there in the first place, but the shit storm that came out of my trip to the desert is why Billy and me are together like this, and why this woman is now on my ass instead."

They had left the canyon behind some time ago, although the mountains still surrounded them, although at more of a distance. Now they were coming out of trees after having crested the top of the pass. Jenna signalled and pulled into a viewpoint overlooking a big lake, a gorgeous blue that reminded Dom of pictures he'd seen of the Mediterranean. Dozens of sailboats dotted the lake, and cabins were spread across the brown, desiccated hills that led down to the water. "Judging by what happened back in Logan, she was a little too much for you."

Dom climbed out of the car and pushed hard against its roof, stretched his back and legs. "I was sitting in your hometown without any of my own mojo," he said to Jenna as she also got out of the car. "I took a bad hit when I was hunting for my quarry, but that's because I got backlash from a fight between two experienced and powerful numerates, both of whom were hosting pretty powerful shadows. That's a lot to fend off when you're caught by surprise."

Jenna pointed down to the water. "That's Bear Lake down there. The left side is north. About one-third of it is in Idaho, the rest still in Utah. If we go south around the lake and then over those hills," she pointed to brown hills on the other side of the water, "we'll end up in Wyoming. You need to tell me now where we're going."

Dom scratched his head, thinking. In the meantime, Billy asked, "Is there anyone you need to tell that you've left home?"

"I'll phone my roommate and tell her she can keep all my stuff. My Dad died a couple of years ago, and I gave up on the church when I was a teen, so I tend not to have contact with any other relatives." She shook her head. "So the short answer is no, there's no one out there that really cares."

"Can we get lunch down the hill?" asked Dom. When Jenna nodded, he said, "Great. We'll do that first, and then on to Bozeman." They got back in the car. "The university there has a mathematical sciences department, and when I last visited a couple years ago I found something in the library that no one had cottoned onto yet. As long as the protections I laid out are fine, it should still be where I left it. Plus, I have a little stash there, some mojo safe for pickup in case of emergency."

Jenna steered them back onto the highway and started down the long twisty path that led to the lake. Dozens of cabins peppered the dry scrub and grass that covered the hills; she slowed down to take a good curve on a steep portion, and six Harleys thundered by from behind, the last one leaning back into their lane just ahead of an approaching SUV.

Dom pulled the baseball from his pocket and looked at it, worried that the backlash may have even travelled as far as Bozeman, maybe further, wiping out any hope he had of protecting himself. Staring out the window, he started to flip the ball in the air, giving it a backhand spin and then catching it with a small downward swipe of his hand.

Anyone with the slightest awareness of the provenance of the ball would have a conniption, seeing him do this with it. It was Mark McGwire's sixty-first home run ball, hit on the day McGwire's father had turned sixty-one. Mojo enough, but the fact that Roger Maris had hit his own sixty-one in 1961 added that much more to its power. He hadn't known for sure that the ball was going to be hit that day, but the numbers available made the time spent well worth it. Harder still was getting it in contact with McGwire and his father that day, while their numerate mojo still raged from the fantastic series of coincidences, but he had managed, fighting through crowds of fans and reporters and security and lawyers and agents, fending them off with previously prepared formulae, holing out a path through everyone and then calling forth their mutual mojos, tied together by virtue of family and proximity, only a few hours shy of their peak.

The ball had been one of his strongest artefacts, a confluence of dates and times and numerical events that so rarely happened. And he had been the one to get it done, had beaten four other numerates that he'd known of, perhaps even frightened off others, smaller players in a big game of numbers.

He'd gone through much the same with number 62, which had the advantage of being hit on 9/8/98. That one, not quite as powerful, was stored in a safe deposit box in Edmonton. But it was better than what he was holding in his hand right now, the backlash having made it completely worthless, just so much seared leather and rubber, all of its mojo lost doing its job. Which was good, he knew, but it still hurt to lose something this powerful.

He leaned out and tossed the ball into the scrub on the side of the road. Maybe some kid from one of these cabins would find it and use it as intended, to toss and catch and hit.

Lunch was a burger and fries and an excellent raspberry milkshake at a little joint on the side of the road, sitting on picnic tables in the shade of trees that seemed barely capable of defying the heat. Dom paid for the food as well as gas for the car from his thick roll of bills. Then, after stocking up on junk food and drinks for the long drive, Jenna grabbed some change and ran over to the pay phone.

"Time for lesson two," said Dom, jogging up behind her. "First off, I'm glad to see you're not using a mobile phone. Those things are easy for everyone to track, numerates and analogs alike. Second, for the pay phone, something with numbers like this, you should never have to pay. That, plus we don't want any trail showing where we've been, just in case we're still being hunted. Any change you use will light up like fireworks at night to the right kind of eye."

She put her hands on her hips. "So what do I do?"

Dom frowned, sticking his tongue slightly out of his mouth while he thought. It was an outside phone, which meant that numbers didn't stick around long enough for lifting. Not that pay phones were that easy for it these days, with everyone using mobiles instead. Eventually these things were probably bound to go extinct.

"Look here. See this number?" He tapped the phone number on the little label sitting above the keypad.

Jenna leaned forward, squinting. Obviously her glasses weren't just cosmetic. "946-8668."

"Right on. So what you need to do now is concentrate real hard, see if a pattern emerges from that."

"W-e-ll," she said, drawing out the word, "8668 is a pattern, right?"

Dom nodded. "And one a child could see. Instead, you need to look for the numbers you've been seeing since you were a kid, look for how those relate to the entire number that's on here."

Frowning, Jenna crossed her arms and stared hard at the numbers. Then her face lit up. "Oh! I see something!"

"And?"

She frowned again. "No, I don't. I thought I saw a cube root in there, but I was wrong."

"You're still thinking along elementary lines," said Dom. "Don't look so hard for conventional formulae; rather, just see what the numbers can do for you. Watch them, stroke them, make them come out. Hell, do you think I went to university and studied math and even *learned* how to write and read a formula of *any* type?" He shook his head. "And I may be talking out of school here, but it's a good possibility that Billy here was anything *but* a mathematician."

"You're probably right," responded Billy.

Jenna looked up, watched a passenger jet cutting across the sky high overhead. "I see circles," she said. "Triangles, other shapes. Some numbers are squeezing their way in, filling gaps between them."

"Good," said Dom. "From what I've heard, it works, or at least looks, different for everybody who does it. Does it seem complete?"

She looked back at the phone, waved a finger in the air and whispered to herself. "They don't want to cooperate," she said, frowning. She reached out a hand, and Dom watched as a small cloud of numbers tried to break away from her, but with an effort she managed to get them under control. "Okay. Got them. I've just added my home phone number. Wow!" She broke into a huge smile. "Everything just fell into place!"

Dom frowned. The numbers were still bouncing in the air around Jenna, but seemed to be doing their level best to keep away from her. But he nodded his head and said, "One more thing to add, then. Pick up the phone and punch in whatever numbers work with the pattern you just made. Then add a series of eleven primes, starting with . . ."

"Seventeen," said Billy.

"Seventeen. And jump two when you get to the fifth and the seventh."

Jenna screwed up her face, concentrating. Then she punched in a bunch of numbers, finishing off with the set of primes, the last one seventy-three. This last number Dom seemed to see from her eyes, one blink there and one blink back in his own body. "It's ringing!" she said.

Dom shook off the momentary shift and smiled at Jenna. "You did good," he said. "Elegant, actually, for someone who's just starting."

She pointed at the phone and whispered, "There's no one home." After pausing a few seconds, she started to speak. "Cindy, it's Jenna. No time to explain, honey, but I'm leaving town. I don't know how long. You can keep my stuff if you want, or give it to Deseret Industries, or sell it to help with the rent. Sorry to leave you in a lurch like this. I'll call when I can. Love you. Bye." She hung up. "Answering machine."

Almost immediately, the phone rang. Startled, Jenna reached for it.

"Don't pick it up!" yelled Dom, voice sounding of panic. He reached out and grabbed her hand.

It rang again. Jenna looked at Dom, fear in her eyes. He didn't feel too good himself.

There was a riff he knew from a Charlie Mingus piece. With phones like they were nowadays, playing music on the keypad was just one note, although if you had a good beat, and remembered where the notes used to be on earlier telephones, then the tune could do the job. He started to play the riff before he picked up the handset, hoping that it would be enough to keep prying eyes from finding him.

"Yeah?" Beep-beep-a-beep-beep.

The voice was quiet, a woman's voice, hoarse, and the beeping of the Mingus tune did nothing to tune it out of his head. "I don't know who you are, boy, but believe me, I'll find you."

Beep-a-beep-a-beep-beep-a-beep.

"We'll find you," said another voice, a male voice—how the hell did that work? His accent was different from Billy's, but definitely present.

"And after you're dead, we'll strip your body of all its mojo and wave an ever-so-sorrowful goodbye as your shadow fractions away." The woman's voice again, soft and deadly but still hoarse, almost strangled, raising goose bumps on his neck and arms.

"You won't catch me by surprise again, bitch!" said Dom, showing more grit than he felt. Beep-a-beep-a-beep-a-beep-beep-beep. "In the meantime, wipe away a little tear over the fact that you couldn't even get me when I was stripped to the bone." He slammed down the phone, hands shaking, then with a yell pulled the handset from the box, threw it to the ground, where it clattered across the pavement, metal cord and wires dragging behind.

"Fuck!" he yelled. He ran over and kicked the handset across the pavement. "Fuck fuck fuck fuck fuck!"

Jenna ran over and put a hand on his shoulder. "Dom, *hush*. There are people watching!"

Dom pushed her hand away and marched back to the car, Jenna in pursuit. "I don't give a rat's ass. Let's get the hell out of this state; I need to be on the open road and well away from that freak." Before climbing in he leaned over the back and gave the numbers on the license plate a quick swipe, glaring at the strangers watching as he did so. Everyone turned their gazes elsewhere when he was done.

"How did she find us?" asked Jenna, once they were back on the highway headed north.

"She didn't," answered Billy. "She must have gotten the scent of you and figured out where you lived, but the best she could do was introduce a formula to dial back; there's no way it could have told her where we were, though. Not that fast." He sounded like he was trying to convince himself.

Dom laughed, a short, bitter sound. "So we can hope. In the meantime, we worry about just how strong this person is."

"But you told her back there," said Jenna, glancing over at him. "The only reason she almost caught you was because you didn't have anything with you."

Eyes closed, Dom leaned his head back against the seat. "It's looking like this person is capable of shit I can only dream of, Jenna. I'd say we were lucky to get out. Lucky you showed up and had a car."

"We were hunting the same thing she was," continued Billy, "Dom by himself and me with my earlier host, and she was faster off the mark, seems to have found what we were all after." He cocked open his left eye and looked over at her. "And now she's hunting *us*."

"You wanted to learn." Dom forced the eye closed again. "You're in now, like it or not, and school it ain't. This is going to be a trial by fire."

Jenna tapped the steering wheel in a familiar pattern. "Since I'm learning, maybe it's time for another lesson. What was that you were doing with the phone's keypad?"

Dom nodded. She was tapping the same beat that he had kept when he'd faked up the Mingus tune. "Time was," he said, "you could play musical notes on a phone's buttons. Not anymore, but there's still a residual numeracy there. I was playing a rough estimation of a piece by Charlie Mingus."

"Why him?"

"The same day that Mingus died in Mexico at age 56, 56 sperm whales beached themselves nearby."

Jenna blinked, then glanced at Dom with her right eyebrow raised. "So?"

"So there are some hints in numerate literature that whenever whales beach themselves it's because they've come to collect the shadow of a person who has died," said Billy. "Of course, we can't talk to whales, so we can't say for sure, but they are numerate creatures. Whether or not you need to die by the sea, well, nobody knows." Billy shrugged. "But it does seem that it's always the same number of whales as it is years the person, or even persons, has lived."

"What's also interesting is that sometimes they seem to take shadows that want to go, and sometimes they take them against their will. Mingus, I think he was voluntary." Dom leaned his seat back, turned his head to the right, feeling exhausted from the heat and all the action. "Wake me up when you want me to spell you for driving."

Jenna turned on the radio. A distant classic rock station was tuned in, ELO's "Telephone Line" playing, accompanied by the hiss and static of interference, and, Dom could swear, harmony by the man from the phone call. But before he could say anything, Jenna slipped a CD into the stereo, and he drifted off to the sounds of Coltrane.

Jenna woke Dom a few hours later and he drove on until he came to a town with a store big enough to outfit the both of them. Again, he decided to bankroll her, and an hour later they walked out with a couple days worth of clothes, toiletries, and two small wheeled suitcases to carry everything. Jenna also bought some new sneakers, having noted that she was finding the long drive in her sandals uncomfortable.

He gassed up the car again, nervously listening for ringing pay phones, then drove on. They stopped for supper, and when they were back in the car Jenna fell asleep, Dom insisting that he had plenty of energy and that she should bank her sleep now, in case it was suddenly in short supply.

After a search showed that Jenna listened mostly to pop and hip hop with a sprinkling of house music, he kept the Coltrane disc on, volume low and in the background, but enjoying the numbers that wafted from the player with each note. He'd never listened much to the jazz performer before, having focused most of his energy on discerning the mojo that Mingus was able to give, but he was pleased to find there was a lot of numerate subtlety here as well.

Jazz musicians, like baseball players, also had it. In spades. Classical composers too, and of course musicians who played other styles, like rock and bluegrass and reggae. But the intricacies of good jazz worked well in Dom's world, and knowledge of how a musician had constructed a tune, not by notes, but by numbers, was a handy tool to have when working through that world.

Billy was silent, probably aware that Dom was feeling quiet himself. So he just sat back and let himself enjoy the drive, once again able to relax, even though his ass was being ridden by someone with numerate ability he'd never dreamed possible.

And that was the biggest problem he had. Dom was strong, even if he was relatively new at this. Until this latest stretch of fear and bad luck, he had felt pretty confident that he was the strongest numerate around, maybe not in the world, but at least in the circles he had travelled. He had plenty of natural talent, and not only was he a quick study, he worked hard at learning what he needed, and once the world of numbers had changed for him, opened up beyond his confused youthful awareness of numbers and formulae and algorithms that floated through his everyday life, he had been able to grab hold of every treasured piece of mojo he had sought.

Sometimes he was given a bit of a fight, but even so, the hardest time he'd had retrieving an item had really been simple. He had talent, he used it well, if selfishly, and life up until the past few days had gone fairly well, if a bit lonely. He'd been on a smooth ride to the top, and the trip down to the desert had been another step on the way to his ultimate target, a goal that was likely shared by every numerate person on Earth. He knew that he would have some trouble if someone got there first, but had frankly been unprepared for just how much power would be involved.

Just as obvious, Billy and his former host had also been unprepared; while they had carried more experience into their duel, Dom felt sure from the numbers he'd seen that he held more innate ability. With some new mojo and perhaps a bit more research, and with Billy along for the ride to give solid advice, he'd be able to figure out this mystery person and get what he was after.

The thought made him smile.

"What?" asked Billy.

"Hmmph. Just thinking about this gal and the shadow she carries. Do you suppose she was this strong before she got to whatever was sitting in the desert?"

Billy shrugged; it was funny how natural the motion now felt. "I don't know. She would already have had to be very good, just making out the trail like we did. But to have that much power before she got there, and for us not to have had any idea that he existed, it seems a bit of a reach."

"What if it was the big gun itself?"

Billy shook his head. "If she had held that, we would not be sitting here talking to each other."

Dom nodded and chewed on his lower lip. "I guess it's not like it would have been in the middle of the fucking desert, either."

"True enough, although all sorts of powerful artefacts have somehow slipped the bonds of the British Isles."

"Well, there were plenty that started out away from Britain in the first place, right?"

Billy nodded his head. "Yes, but by far the majority came from there. Something there has always been conducive to the creation of all this mojo." In the passenger seat Jenna snorted in her sleep and turned her head. Billy chuckled. "There are plenty of items still sprinkled throughout the world, Dom. As a matter of fact, the way I've seen things play out in the time I can remember, I'm pretty sure that there are still a dozen or more of my own still lying around, even, ones without my essence, but still fairly powerful artefacts."

Dom cocked an eyebrow. "If you found one do you suppose it would kick-start your memory?"

Billy made a face, scrunched up his mouth as he cocked an eyebrow. The feeling Dom got from the face was *consternation*, even though he wasn't looking in a mirror. "I hadn't thought about that. The odds would be extremely long against finding anything, but it might be a reason to go looking some day."

Dom blinked. "Must be hell knowing more about your host than yourself."

Billy shrugged again. "I live with it. And in the meantime, I even have a theory about why I'm like this."

"Which is?"

"Being numerate doesn't preclude anyone making a tiny mistake in the numbers, Dom." Billy turned the music down to a distant background whisper. "Think of the numbers I laid out as the equivalent of DNA."

"Um, okay." It occurred to Dom that he was now having a discussion about genetics with someone who had died long before that particular science had come into existence.

"When Watson and Crick first announced their discovery, my host did a fair amount of reading on the subject, searching for more numerate possibilities in the building blocks of life. Since then I have made an effort to keep up with the field, as a layman, in case anything rears its head.

"Not long ago it struck me that perhaps the reason I can't remember who I am is the same reason some people are born with genetic defects; a switch is thrown in the wrong place or, more aptly, information is translated incorrectly. It's there, but for whatever reason it does not come across as intended. A birth defect, a handicap, or in my case, numbers that either mean nothing or else mean something other than intended."

Dom chewed on this for a minute. "So what you're saying is that it's possible that other people made the same mistake in processing their numbers."

"Probable, even."

"Okay, probable. And so there's lots of shit lying around that no one has any idea where it is."

"Indeed," replied Billy. "Certainly some of it has been destroyed over the decades or centuries or even millennia, in wars, even in hunts for witches, but much of it has just been . . . misplaced. And there's no accounting for those unfortunate souls whose numbers were wrong and whose shadows ended up either lost forever or else mistranslated worse than my own were."

"What happens then?"

Billy grimaced. "Empty husk without a spark is the description that has been used."

Dom shuddered, then squinted his eyes at an upcoming sign. Bozeman was soon. He leaned over and tapped Jenna on the shoulder. "Hey. Time to wake up."

She grunted and stretched her arms as best she could in the car. "There yet?"

"Soon. I just wanna stop and gas up in case we have to blow town as fast as last time." He signalled and hit an exit way too fast, kicking up rocks and grabbing hard at the steering wheel to correct as he tapped the brakes. "Plus, I have to make a call, considering how early we are. See if we can get in before things open."

"I'll fill it up," said Jenna as they pulled up to the gas pumps. "You make the call."

"Right." Dom got out, thought about pocketing the keys to keep Jenna from suddenly getting cold feet and booking while he still needed her and her wheels, but then just sprinkled a few numbers over the hood to keep the thing from starting until he came back. He headed for the pay phone, arms folded across his chest against the cold.

"I don't think you want to risk using your own change," said Billy.

Dom stood and looked at the phone for a few seconds, thinking, then said, "Yeah. I don't know if I can cover up anything that's been on my person when I haven't been carrying mojo."

"But you may also not want to use numbers to make the call."

Dom rolled his eyes. "Look, Billy, we were found last time because it was Jenna who made the call. I'm a hell of a lot better at this than she is, especially right now."

In answer, Billy leaned against the phone and reached behind, came out with change for the call. "Old traveller's trick," he said. "Leave money behind when you can, take it when you need it."

Dom blinked. "Jesus. Can't believe I've never seen that before."

"It doesn't always work, my friend. Especially when times are tough."

Dom dropped the money into the slot, blew on his finger, then dialled the number. "It's not even five in the fucking morning," said the voice on the other end; it had taken eight rings before the phone had been picked up.

"I know. Sorry about the time, Sy."

There was some shuffling and grunting. "Dom? That you?"

"Is too. Sorry to do this to you, man, but I'm in urgent need of some stuff. Are you able to meet me down at the library?"

"No can do, Dom. Got a circular yesterday telling us that you're a suspected book thief."

Dom closed his eyes. "Sonofabitch. Sy, you know that isn't true. Hell, *I'm* the guy who made it pretty much impossible for anyone to walk out from your area with anything."

There was the click of a lighter on the other end of the line, followed by a deep breath and coughing. "Jesus," said Sy. "I've gotta shake this nasty habit. Can't even keep myself from grabbing a puff at five a.m."

"Sy."

"I know, I know. Dom, I trust you completely. But you know we have cameras everywhere, and the memo said that you might be headed this way, so there are gonna be people watching specifically for you."

"I can take care of the cameras, Sy."

There was a sharp laugh, followed by more coughing. "Listen, I don't pretend to understand everything there is to know about this special ability you have, but just the fact that word has gotten out about you, right or wrong, tells me that you've gone and gotten yourself good and fucked."

Dom took a breath, unsure what to say. Sy remained quiet on the other end, except for the distant sounds of sucking on his cigarette. Finally, Dom just shook his head. "Don't believe any of the shit you might end up hearing, okay?"

"Oh, no doubt about that, Dom. I hope you manage to get out of whatever scrape you're in, and I know that *I'll* always trust you, but you'll have to take it somewhere where you don't put me or my books in any danger."

"Right. Take it easy."

"Done. You too."

Dom hung up and leaned against the wall. "Well, it looks like this fucker is getting ahead of us now."

"I don't think so," replied Billy. "If he or she really was, then they would have responded to our presence here in town with more than just a piece of paper. No, I think that perhaps they managed to pick up some numerical spoor that you left behind, maybe when you were unconscious, and is just sending out small packets of search numbers wherever that scent leads. One of those packets found an old scent of you here and created an alert that it had been programmed for."

Dom thought about this for a moment. "Makes sense. Let's go get breakfast and then hope that my other stop in town remains unsullied." He walked over to the booth to pay for the gas, then back to the car. Before climbing back in he brushed the numbers from the hood, then drove off.

"Couldn't trust me?" asked Jenna.

"What?"

"The numbers on the hood. Were you afraid I was going to drive off and leave you standing in the middle of nowhere?"

Dom grinned, a little sheepishly. "Too late for you to get cold feet now, Jenna. I need your wheels, and you're in deep enough that you need to stick with me. So to preclude rash decisions, I did it for both of us."

"All three of us," interjected Billy.

"Right. All three of us. Let's find us a Denny's."

Both had a large breakfast, although where Dom consumed several cups of black coffee, Jenna got by with only orange juice. "I don't belong to the church anymore," she said, when he asked her about this, "but sometimes I think parts of it still belong to me."

When they were finished, and after two trips to the toilet for each of them, Dom settled the bill and they walked out into the day, thin high clouds beginning to slide in and blank out the blue sky and sun. "Where to now?" asked Jenna, as they climbed back into the car.

Dom checked his watch. "A mailbox about five blocks away from here, and then the bank. Here's hoping that my trail there had better cover than the one to the library."

At the mailbox he told Jenna to wait in the car and ran across the street, waving his fingers in the air and watching where the numbers fell. It had been a long time since he'd been here, and he was hoping to hell that things were still in place. Happily, the numbers eventually and casually drifted in a small cloud over to the box, which shook violently for several seconds after they covered it. Dom opened the little door, pulled out an envelope and ran back to the car, the numbers behind him falling to the sidewalk and slipping in between the cracks or drifting down the gutter towards the sewer.

"What's that?"

Dom ripped open the envelope and shook out a small key, which he pocketed, a passport, and a Montana driver's license with his picture and the name *Eric Wood* on it. "ID."

Jenna made a face. "Now how did you do *that*?"

He tucked the license into his wallet and the passport into a pocket and then shrugged. "Not hard, really. I have stuff like this seeded all around the continent, in places I've already been or else in places where I have a friend willing to do the mail drop." He held out the envelope and let Jenna take it. "See how it only has a one-cent stamp? I pilfered a few hundred of those from the home of a mildly numerate fat guy."

"A what?"

"A fat guy. Shoulda seen him, he was fucking huge. When he died he weighed 733 pounds, and they had to cut a hole in the wall of his apartment building to get his body out and into a truck, since a hearse wasn't big enough. Had to use a crane to get him down, too."

Jenna shook her head. "What does him being so large have to do with anything?"

"I find myself rather curious as well," said Billy.

Dom grinned. He realized he rather liked telling tales like this, after so many years of keeping to himself. "His name was Randall Morgenstern, and he lived in upstate New York. The best I could figure out, when whatever part of his mind that does the job realized his numeracy, he'd been gaining so much weight already that it just kept pushing him up until it found a nice prime number where his weight could hover. He was actually pretty happy with that, the last couple of years he was alive; he couldn't lose any weight, but he could eat as much as he wanted and not gain any, also."

"The stamps, Dom," pleaded Jenna. "Please tell us what this has to do with the stamps."

"Oh. Yeah. Randall, I met him when I was in New York for the 9/11 attacks, and I decided even *I* couldn't stomach picking through the detritus like a ghoul, looking for all the mojo that rained down out of the sky that day." Jenna looked stricken at this, and Dom reached out and put a hand on her arm. "You asked to get into this. I could tell you stories that would *really* raise the hairs on the back of your neck, but I won't. At least not right now. In the meantime, I should finish, right?"

She nodded.

"Anyhow, it took two days, but once I managed to get out of the city I drove north, and while on the road I spotted numbers on the horizon. Not really strong, but weird enough to get my attention. I followed them and they led me to Randall's place. And then they faded away. I think that the events around then had flipped a switch somewhere in Randall's brain; he was panicked enough about the terrorist attacks and about his own life right then that he subconsciously cast out numbers as a call for help, and I happened to be the numerate in the right place and the right time, probably the only one not paying attention to the attacks."

Dom started up the car and pulled out. "Need to get to the bank," he explained, before continuing. "Randall lived on the second floor, and the doors just popped open for me as I approached, both the front entrance and then the one to his apartment. I didn't have to do anything with my own numbers." He signalled left and, instead of racing to beat a light just turning yellow, waved his fingers and mumbled a string of numbers instead. The light reverted to green. "When I walked into his apartment, Randall had no idea who the hell I was, and I didn't know squat about him, either. But neither one of us was terribly surprised, either."

"He was expecting you," said Jenna.

"He was expecting someone," replied Billy. "Dom just happened to be that someone."

Dom nodded his head. "Right. He was lying there in bed, enormous, like a fucking hippo, covered with a sheet. His TV was blaring away, a cable news channel, talking heads alternating with pictures of the towers collapsing over and over and over again, and beside him, on a small wooden chair, was a full and rather smelly bedpan."

"Ew." Jenna wrinkled her nose. "That's disgusting."

"Tell me about it." Dom pulled out into oncoming traffic to pass an especially slow driver, dipped back into his lane just in time to avoid a dump truck that was about to swerve out of the way. "It's funny," continued Dom, "but I didn't even pay attention to those things. Didn't even know they were there until after I'd left. Then the pictures of everything in the apartment dropped into my brain like a slide popping into a projector and shining on the screen."

"Why not?" asked Billy.

"Because when I walked into that apartment I almost collapsed. My knees just about buckled, I could barely lift my feet to walk or my hands to lift my suddenly weighty hair out of my eyes. Hell, I could barely catch a breath. Turns out old Randall's weight thing was being passed on to everything in his localized area. He couldn't control his own numbers, but they sure could control him, and his own little world. Any visitors to his apartment felt the sudden weight gain, but also all of his crap. It was all fucking heavy, from the bedpan that could probably only be lifted with a forklift—"

"To the stamps sitting in a drawer somewhere," finished Jenna.

"Well, not in a drawer. Sitting on the kitchen table. But yeah, that's right. Heavy as shit. And probably worse at that time because he was so freaked out."

"So you stole them? Is this how you get *all* of your mojo?"

Dom rolled his eyes. "Let me finish the story, Jenna. Think of this as one of your lessons."

She nodded, lips pursed.

"So Randall looked me in the eye, the end of the fucking world playing and replaying on his TV, and he asks me, 'Am I going to be all right?' His voice was high and whiny like a scared little kid. I pause for a second, then realize what it is he's asking, and I nod and say, 'Yeah, you're going to be fine.' He stares at me for a couple of seconds more, looks back to the news, and then this huge blast of sequences comes storming out of his chest and hits me full on, an immense gigantic pressure wave that combines with the extra weight in the room to finally knock me to the floor, like I imagine it feels being caught in the blowback of some huge explosion. I'm lying there gasping for breath, side of my face pressed into the floor, and it's all I can do to pull myself back up onto my knees."

"What happened?" asked Jenna.

"Heart attack. He got his reassurance and then he died. All of the numbers he'd accumulated in his short and bizarre life were rushing out of his body, out of pores and orifices and combining over the bed in this huge vortex, some of them bleeding off and adding even more weight to everything in the apartment—me included—and the rest pounding through the ceiling above and snaking off into the atmosphere, looking to fall I don't know where. I staggered over to the door, still on my knees, got the door open and rolled out into the hallway, where my weight returned to normal. Once out there that picture of the apartment wormed its way into my memory, and I remembered seeing the stamps sitting on the table; since they had numbers right on them they were the only things in there I could immediately picture how to use, so I decided to grab them. I worked up some numbers that kept the weight from affecting me too much and crawled back in, grabbed them, then left the building and called an ambulance from a phone down the street. Then I went and got a burger and sat in the car and watched the cops and firefighters and paramedics do their little dance, trying to get big Randall's body out of his apartment. It was probably tougher since I'm betting the events from the other day had taken a lot of them down to New York City. Later on I put the stamps on envelopes, sealing in some numbers I'd woven into the thread of the envelopes so that not only would they sink to the bottom of the mailboxes and stay there, they'd be invisible to anyone who wasn't looking for them. Instant emergency ID in eighty-three cities across the continent."

"Then why even bother with stamps?" asked Jenna. "If you can make stuff go invisible with a few simple numbers, then why not just do it all without having to rob a dead fat guy of eighty-three cents worth of stamps? Even more curious, why not just create these driver's licenses and passports as you need them?"

"I'll answer that if I might," replied Billy. Dom nodded his head. "There is an interconnectedness to the numerate world, Jenna, and while Dom likely *could* do what you asked, it would shine like a spotlight at a Hollywood movie premiere; any envelopes he left behind with nothing but his own numbers would be a beacon that would attract every other numerate from hundreds of miles around.

Then they get their hands on stuff that he's created and it's suddenly powerful mojo for them, sometimes mojo that can be used against him. Also, using your own numbers takes a lot out of you. Anytime you can find numbers that have been created by someone else, on purpose or, more often, via happenstance, you use them. The personal cost is almost nil, and if the benefits aren't immediate, I think we've seen today that there might come a time when they are felt."

"It's sorta the same reason I don't just go to Vegas and try to make an easy buck," continued Dom. "The place is crawling with numbers, but it's also crawling with numerates who don't know any better, and the casinos wised up to that long ago and hired pretty strong numerates of their own. If I went there wanting to use any of those numbers, it would be way more effort than it was worth, with every two-bit hick who thinks he has a lick of number sense crawling around looking for the angles and guys I don't want to tangle with watching for the slightest sign that I'm using the numbers to my advantage. *And*, I've heard rumours they don't just escort numerates to the edge of town, but that sometimes numerates are known to disappear."

"They *kill* them?"

Dom tilted his head as he rounded another corner. "Dunno. With that much money involved, maybe so. All I know is, I'm not interested in finding out."

5
6
7
8
9

Traffic was still light, and they arrived fifteen minutes before the bank was to open. Dom drove around the block twice, looking for signs and numbers, anything to tell him that they were being watched or hunted. Nothing showed itself, though, so he parked on the street and they got out. He gave the car's license plates another swipe with his hand, smearing the numbers enough to keep any long-distance snooping from getting a fix on them, in case the bank was now being watched. "Why didn't you do that at the Denny's?" asked Jenna.

"Because I wouldn't have stored any mojo there," said Dom. "If this gal's still looking for us, and it seems pretty obvious she is, it's gotta be taking a lot out of her to do it from such a distance and to so many places. But she'll naturally think that banks are smart places to be looking, so even if my numbers work better here than they did at the library, I'm still not going to take chances right now."

They sat on the hood of the car and watched the workers in the bank go about their business behind locked doors, counting down the minutes until opening time. "So why do you think the numbers will work better here than they did at the library?"

"I can answer that one," said Billy. "Or rather, I think I can make a good guess."

"Go ahead," replied Dom.

"The human factor," said the shadow. "Here at the bank, all anyone knows is that Dom has a box, likely not under his own name. At the university, I gathered that the librarian he was dealing with not only knew who he was, but had dealt with him in the past. Correct?"

Dom nodded his head. "Sy's an old friend of mine. Absolutely no numerate abilities at all, which is the best type of friend. You know they're never gonna try to step on you on the way to get something, and you're never second-guessing yourself, wondering when you're gonna try the same on them. He'd sent me a message a couple of months ago telling me that the library had acquired some new manuscripts in special collections, and I was hopeful they would have something for me to use. No good if I'm expected, though. They think I'm a book thief."

"Another good lesson to learn," said Billy. "A librarian, especially one who works in special collections in a reputable university, can be an excellent friend to have."

"Oh, yeah," agreed Dom. "There's a lot of mojo out there we may never see, because it's stored away in private collections, owned by rich fucks who have no idea what it is they're sitting on. But every once in awhile something hot and new shows up, and if you have the right connections, you can often get the jump on whatever competition is floating around in the neighbourhood."

"How much competition is there?" asked Jenna.

Dom shrugged. "Don't know. I've only run into about twenty people in the time I've been numerate, and not all of them were in person. Some online, some with just the scent of their numbers showing that they'd been in a place a few days before me, and of course the person who's making this trip so necessary." He pushed himself off the hood of the car and walked to the bank doors, which were just being opened by an older woman in a dark blue business suit. "Your name is Lisbeth while we're here," he said over his shoulder to Jenna, then he turned to greet the woman at the door. "Sandra, good to see you again."

The woman blinked, obviously trying to remember his face, then smiled. "Mr. Wood. What a pleasant surprise! Back from your business trip so soon?" Her voice sounded of a lifetime of cigarettes, her face was weathered and filled with deep lines, and her teeth when she smiled flashed yellow and brown. Dom had never thought about it before, having always been in Bozeman alone, but both people he knew well here—Sy and Sandra—were heavy smokers. He wondered if there was a numerical reason for it.

Dom shook the hand she offered, nodding his head. "Yup. And off on another one right away. Sandra, this is my . . . trainee, Lisbeth."

For a second Jenna stood there, staring blankly at the two of them, but she quickly recovered and also shook the banker's hand. "Nice to meet you."

"Why don't you have a seat, Lisbeth. This shouldn't take too long." He turned back to the banker. "Sandra, I need to get into my safe deposit box." He pulled out his wallet and handed her his license as they walked to the back of the bank. "Proof that I'm still me," he said, grinning.

They exchanged a little more small talk on the way to the back room, and then Sandra excused herself and went to get the box. After she delivered it to Dom she thanked him for remaining such a good customer and then left the room. Dom fished the key out of his pocket.

"Quite chatty," said Billy, keeping his voice low.

"Small town born and raised," replied Dom. "It's why I chose this branch; she keeps on top of things for her customers, and watches out for them as well."

As he inserted the key into the box's lock and twisted it there was a hollow whooshing sound and a flash of light from inside the box. "Shit shit shit shit shit!" said Dom, lifting the lid and waving at the smoke that was rising up from inside.

"What happened?" asked Billy. "Did they get us again?"

Dom stood on the chair and wove some numbers around the smoke alarm so that it wouldn't go off, then pulled some more numbers and formulae into a ball and raced it around the room, chasing the remaining fragments of smoke and scooping them up like a Pac-Man trying to get a cheap high. That done, he compressed the ball into a hard little marble and tossed it to the corner, where it landed with a soft click against the baseboard; it was temporary, would probably last only ten minutes at best before it evaporated and released the smoke again, but it would have to do. And there was no way he wanted to carry anything on his person that could track back to the numbers being used by their pursuer. "Last thing I want is for the alarm to go off and have to stick around and explain why to the fire department and the cops, especially if word about me is starting to spread." He turned his attention back to the box, reached inside but quickly pulled his hand out again. "Guess I'll give it a minute to cool down."

"This was Them again," said Billy, and this time Dom could both feel and hear the capitalization. "I can smell the numbers, more acrid than the smoke."

"Yeah, but this time they didn't do the damage they were hoping to," replied Dom, deciding that even though they didn't know any names, he wasn't going to give them the benefit of a special capital letter.

He reached inside and picked up the wire, blowing fast and loud puffs of air on it in a futile attempt to keep it from burning his fingertips. Then he dropped it in his palm and flipped it back and forth from one hand to the next, trying to cool it without scorching his skin. Numbers drifted up from it, red hot and angry at first, but quickly cooling as they made their way to the ceiling. "Seems this time didn't work out for the bitch," said Dom. "I think this baby still has all of its mojo. Didn't hurt that it had already been in a fire." Finally it was cool enough, and he dropped it back on the table and with a couple of hard twists tore it in half. One half went into his pocket, while the other went on his left wrist, wrapped into a makeshift bracelet. With one frayed end he poked at his skin and drew blood, felt the rush of protection as the numbers entered his body. "Yow. Is that *ever* a relief."

"You sound like a junkie. May I ask what it is?" inquired Billy. Dom shut and locked the box again. "Wait until we're in the car and

Jenna has the other half of this." He patted his pocket. "She may as well hear it, too."

Billy nodded, and then Dom stood up and walked to the door. "Thank you, Sandra," he said as he walked to where Jenna was sitting. "I'll see you next time." The banker stood and waved and then headed for the room where the safe deposit box still sat, while Jenna stood and followed Dom out the door. "We'll get in the car and drive a little bit first," he said, throwing her the keys. "Any direction, as long as we get away before she starts to make a fuss about the smell, or the smoke that's soon gonna follow."

"Smoke?" Jenna climbed in and started the car, pulled out in a pause in the traffic.

"Our friend, still trying to make life difficult for me," said Dom. "Give me your hand." One hand still on the wheel, Jenna reached her right arm across. Dom took the second piece of wire from his pocket, wrapped it around her wrist, then poked her with its end. "Ow!" A tiny droplet of blood rose up, dark red bead intermingling with the wire. "That smarts," said Jenna, briefly looking down before returning her eyes to the road. "Oh! I can see the numbers that surround it. But why are they jumping away from me?"

"Son of a bitch! That's not supposed to happen." Dom reached over and stroked the wire, whispered to the numbers and convinced them to return. After a pause, they fell back to Jenna's arm, surrounded the wire and burrowed in under her skin, pushing their way—reluctantly, it looked to Dom—into the tiny wound, little bubbles of black and grey and orange moving aside minute pieces of skin. As they did so, he experienced another momentary flash—as if he was looking at the world, at the road they were driving on and down to the numbers burrowing into her skin—through Jenna's eyes. And then, just as suddenly, Dom was back in his own body. He shook his head to clear it, worried but not wanting Jenna to see it. Voice deliberately calm, he said, "That's better. It's okay. Just watch the road and let it happen."

"What is it?" Jenna's voice rose in panic, and Dom had to grab the wheel and steer the car over to the side of the road, where she at least had the presence of mind to put on the brakes.

Dom shifted the car into Park and shut it off, taking the keys out. "Sorry," he said, "I should've thought about this before I let you drive."

Now the numbers had entered Jenna's bloodstream, were flowing throughout her body, following the rhythm of her heart. It was like watching an X-ray movie of the human circulatory system, but with numbers instead of blood, and Dom knew Jenna could see it as well. And already they were finding their way into her nervous system, where they would do the most good. "It's mojo," he said. "Should go a long way to protecting us from disaster until we can get our hands on more."

"Where did it come from?" asked Billy.

"Well, until I tore it in half so that Jenna could use it as well, it was a necklace I'd made out of wires salvaged from Apollo 13. That's why the numbers have to find their way inside. The wires were the nervous system of the spacecraft, and connected to the craft's circulatory system, so this is mojo that works best from the inside-out."

Jenna was staring at her arms, face pale. "I saw that movie," she responded after a moment of trying to regain her composure. "They almost died."

"But they didn't, and that, combined with its wonderful series of synchronicities is what makes this little bit of metal—" he waved his wrist in the air "—so damned valuable to us." After saying this he finally noticed that Jenna wasn't looking any better. "Here," he said, opening his door and climbing out, "you scrunch on over and let me drive for awhile. I'll explain as we go."

Jenna climbed over the bucket seats and tried to settle in, but her knee bumped against the glove compartment, which noisily popped open. Inside was a manila envelope which slid down onto Jenna's lap, as if pulled along by an invisible wire. Numbers swarmed everywhere, but none of them appeared to be dangerous, and when

Jenna delicately picked up the envelope with her fingertips they all faded away.

"Jesus," said Dom. He'd opened the driver's side door but had stayed outside when the envelope appeared.

"Open it," suggested Billy. "The numbers that were here didn't seem dangerous." After a few seconds of dubious thought, Dom nodded in agreement.

Jenna slowly peeled open the envelope, then shook the contents out onto her lap. Two U.S. passports. Carefully, Jenna picked one up and opened it, closed it again and handed it over to Dom, eyes wide open.

Dom climbed into the car and leaned back before he opened the passport. He noted with some sort of distant interest that when he did look inside, he felt no surprise at what he saw. A picture of him, accompanied by the name Eric Wood; even his signature using that name. He turned to look at Jenna, saw the passport she was holding up, her own picture inside accompanied by the name Lisbeth Sorenson.

"Someone else is in on all this," said Dom finally.

"Someone who wants to help us, I think," replied Billy.

"But why passports?" asked Jenna. Her voice was tight and quiet, but Dom could hear the quiver of fear there.

Dom started the car. "First thing, we're off to Canada." He pulled out and headed for the highway.

"Canada? What do you mean? Why Canada?" Her voice was even more panicked now.

Billy put a hand on her shoulder. "Settle down, Jenna. Give Dom the time to explain things instead of getting so upset."

She closed her eyes, leaned her head back and took a series of deep breaths. "I'm sorry," she finally said, voice barely above a whisper. "The passports coming out of nowhere, that picture of me I *know* was never taken, and I have trouble with blood at the best of times, and seeing those numbers crawl *inside* me like that just made it worse. It was like something out of a horror movie, bugs climbing inside you and making your skin bubble and crawl and flow through your blood and you can see it like you're watching a Discovery Channel documentary and they're little and even though you say they're supposed to help, they—"

"Whoa!" yelled Dom. "Jenna, your freaking out is freaking *me* out. Shut the fuck up a minute and let me explain what's going on."

She turned to look at Dom, lip quivering but eyes set hard. "All right. Tell me, please." Her voice was deathly quiet now.

Dom took a deep breath, concentrating on the traffic for a minute. "Right," he finally said. "First, the passports. They're pretty obviously a gift from someone who knows what shape we're in. I doubt that crossing the border is going to help us get away, but there are things I have squirreled away in Canada, things that can help us deal with our situation here. And since they're closer than anything in the States, it makes sense to go that way. Although . . ." He scratched the bridge of his nose as he thought for a few seconds. "Don't know if I like the idea of someone out there knowing that about me already."

Billy shrugged. "Too late to do anything about it now."

"Not so," said Dom. "We could drive somewhere else, mess up their plans."

"We have the wire you just got us," replied Billy. "Will it last long enough if we have to go further?"

Dom pursed his lips. "Probably not. Shit. So Canada it is."

"What about the wire?" asked Jenna. "Why'd you have to poke me with it?"

"Well, synchronicity is what makes our world go round," said Dom. "Any time there's a sequence of numbers that hold some sort of coincidence, artefacts connected with that coincidence can be of great aid to numerates. Mojo."

She nodded, staring straight ahead.

"So Apollo 13 was loaded with mojo. The rocket blasted off on the 13th of the month, and it did so at 1313 hours. Coincidences like that create a rush of numbers that push their way in, forcing out the bland, everyday numbers that make up the fabric of life. When they do that, there's a dynamic that's created, one that numerates can use to their benefit."

"But I thought the number thirteen was supposed to be unlucky."

Dom shrugged. "I'm sure for some people it is. But how unlucky was it for Lovell, Swigert and Haise?"

"Who?"

"The astronauts on that ill-fated flight to the Moon," answered Billy.

"Oh."

"The three of them survived the disaster," continued Dom. "There was no way they should have made it back, but they did, and the sheer genius that they used to figure their way out of such a mess just added to the mojo. Numbers would have been flying in all directions during the time they were trying to fix things and map their corrections, burrowing into the wires and panels and diodes and everything else on board that capsule. So it stands to reason that artefacts from on board should be even stronger than normal, what with the synchronicity of the numbers on liftoff and the addition of all those numbers that saved their lives." They were finally leaving the city and heading north. Dom accelerated to a shade past the speed limit and then turned on the cruise control. "But all of the numbers were put to use to save the day, not to attack, not to take anything away from someone else, and not for personal gain, unless you count living to see another day as personal gain. And so the numbers in these wires," he waved his hand again, "are burrowing into us in order to protect us from trouble coming from the outside. They survived the onslaught of an explosion in the vacuum of space, they're going to help us survive the onslaught of this woman and her shadow who think they can get to us."

Jenna rubbed at her wrist. A quick glance over told Dom that the blood was gone and that the hole he had pricked in her skin couldn't be seen. She leaned back and closed her eyes, and Dom turned his attention to the road ahead.

The ride was long but peaceful, and after a few hours Dom began to relax again. They stopped twice for gas, once more for another toilet break, and any food they ate was takeout, greasy burgers or day-old sandwiches in the car, Dom washing them down with Coke, looking for the caffeine to help keep him sharp. He kept Coltrane playing in the background, and after an attempt to talk more about numbers was rebuffed by Jenna—"Right now I don't want to think about that stuff"—they made small talk, mostly about where they'd grown up, what school had been like, her job, and their favourite sports teams, hers being the Denver Broncos and Dom's the Boston Red Sox, while Billy professed to not liking sports very much at all.

It was summer, and the days were still long, so after about eight hours, when they finally pulled up to the border, the sun was still fairly high. Jenna had been driving since the last stop, and after she parked the car at the end of the fairly lengthy line of vehicles waiting to cross over, they got out and stretched for a few minutes, standing on the pavement and trying to enjoy the fresh air riding somewhere underneath the fumes from all the running engines. When the line moved again they traded places, Dom back in the driver's seat, and this time they stayed in the car, inching forward every couple of minutes, the only scenery a few weathered buildings that mostly belonged to small-time customs brokers, and beyond those miles and miles of empty farmland on both sides of the border.

After a little more than forty-five minutes, they were at the border station showing their new passports to the woman on duty. She entered information into her computer, asked a couple of perfunctory questions, then waved them through. As Dom pulled out he heard a distant, high-pitched squeal coming from behind, and he and Jenna turned their heads in time to see a sequence of numbers, rock-solid and built like a meteorite followed by a scorching-hot tail, plummet from the sky to the south and plough into the red Volvo three back from the truck now at the border station. The Volvo flipped violently into the air, its trunk buckled under the weight of the numbers' punch, and landed on its side, but already the numbers had bounced to the next car, a white Taurus, crashing through its back windshield and rebounding up through the roof, scribing a path with a smaller angle to the silver pickup at the head of the line and smashing this time through the hood, pinning it to the road, its box and rear wheels raised a foot or more off the pavement. People everywhere were scrambling from their cars, and border guards from both the Canadian and American sides were running to the scene. Sirens were screaming somewhere in the distance. Dom pushed the accelerator pedal to the floor and at the same time watched through the rearview mirror as the numbers, now a compact ball with no tail, leapt up high into the sky, leaving the truck to drop its rear with a crash to the road. An RCMP cruiser whipped by them on the way to the border, lights flashing and siren dopplering, numbers from the sound shift splattering up against the windshield like bugs, briefly occluding his vision before fading away.

"I thought you said we were protected!" yelled Jenna.

"We were!" He shook his head and corrected himself. "We are. Maybe these new passports were *too* new, maybe that's what signalled them. Looking for something never used before."

"More numbers," said Billy, pointing to the sky ahead of them.

"Oh, shit."

Two dark and ominous tornadoes were descending from a sunny, cloudless sky; as they watched, the twisters wound their way down and touched the ground, two fidgeting stains smearing across an otherwise perfect expanse, kicking up soil and garbage and rocks and all sorts of other detritus in their paths. Rather than wind and cloud, though, these tornadoes were comprised of immense quantities of numbers, patterns, strings and formulae. Both tornadoes danced and gyrated across a landscape of golden wheat, getting into position to catch Dom and Billy and Jenna as they drove through.

"What do we do?" asked Jenna.

"Here!" yelled Billy, taking the wheel from Dom's control and turning right onto a paved secondary highway. For a second Dom tried to wrestle back control of the wheel, and the car swung across the lane into the path of an oncoming combine, but they managed to get their act together and the car back into the right lane. A sheepish Dom watched the farmer in the combine as he leaned out the window to give them the finger.

"Give me more warning next time," said Dom. He wiped sweat off his forehead and glared at himself in the mirror.

"Sorry," replied Billy. "But you were so busy looking at the numbers I didn't think you'd seen the road."

Jenna leaned across the back seat and looked out the rear window. "They're still following us!" Her voice was panicked.

A sign flicked by, naming towns and distances. "I have an idea," said Dom. "We get there in time, I think we can shake this freak one last time." He gunned the engine and the car's speed climbed to 100.

"What if a cop catches you?" asked Jenna. "If we get stopped there's no way we'll beat those things."

Dom spit on his hand, leaned forward and smeared the saliva across the inside top of the windshield. "There's enough numbers in there from what the wire put into my body that it should mess up any radar gun," he replied. "If not . . ." He paused for a second, then shrugged. "Well, we'll deal with it when it comes, I suppose." He sounded calmer than he felt.

"There's another sign coming up," said Billy. Dom slowed down enough to make sure he could read it; there was a diner just a couple minutes ahead. He smiled.

"What?"

He glanced over at Jenna, who was watching him now instead of the number tornadoes, even though she was still hanging over the back of the seat. "A plan," he said. "Get out your driver's license, birth certificate, social security card, that new passport, and anything else that has a number on it."

The parking lot for the diner was dirt and gravel, and he spun up rocks and soil as he pulled into a parking spot between two large pickup trucks with roll bars and mud-caked sides. They dashed out of the car and ran for the doors, the tornadoes cutting swaths through wheat fields as they approached, their roar outside almost as overwhelming as the sound the search numbers had made down in Utah.

Inside was a young girl working as a waitress, blonde hair, tight jeans and a white t-shirt, and two older men sitting in a booth, one wearing a John Deere hat, the other with his faded-brown cowboy hat dangling from the coat hook on the post beside him; both wore faded jeans, one in a checked shirt, and one in a striped shirt and boots. All three stared at Dom and Jenna as they ran in, but before the waitress could ask if they needed any help—and Dom could see the prospect of helping either one of them didn't excite her too much, seeing how they both likely looked a little wild and freaky right then—Dom grabbed Jenna's hand and dragged her over to the booth nearest the other side of the door. "Give me your ID," he whispered, then ran and grabbed the salt containers from all the tables along that side of the door, twisted off the tops, and spilled their contents onto the striped plastic tablecloth.

"Hey!" shouted the waitress. "You can't do that!"

Dom heard the two men get up from their table, their boots clopping on the floor as they approached to back the girl up. He pulled out his wallet and peeled off ten American twenty dollar bills, thrust them toward the girl. "This'll pay for the mess and your time, okay?" Outside, the first number twister had just broken through the wheat field and was approaching the road. The sound of it was so deep Dom felt as if his heart was being squeezed by an angry, pulsating fist.

The waitress took the money, peered at a couple of the bills, then shrugged and nodded. Both men turned back to their table, shaking their heads and commenting on the couple of "fucked-up Americans." The waitress, though, just pocketed the money and kept watching. "Art project," said Dom. His voice sounded high-pitched and frantic to his own ears. He hurriedly wiped the salt across the table, making sure it was spread out as evenly as possible. Then, after closing his eyes for one frantic second to envision the pattern he was looking for, he began to draw a line in the salt with his finger, connecting the entry point from the corner of the table closest to the door with a hole he rubbed into being in the very centre of the table, using a maze very much like Pictish rings he'd studied up on just a year ago. The job was fast and sloppy, accompanied by lots of mutterings of "Hurry" from both Jenna and, somewhat more *sotto voce*, Billy; he looked up to see that the first twister was now in the parking lot and the second was just beginning to cross the road, both of them breaking up and settling into smaller patterns, no less deadly because of the change in size.

He did a couple of last-second corrections and grabbed all of Jenna's ID from her hand, quickly smeared the numbers away and shook them off the cards and into the hole in the middle of the salt maze, did the same for his own ID, then grabbed Jenna by the hand and pulled her back to the counter. The waitress stepped back with them, and let out a loud shriek when the door to the diner banged open and the first numbers rushed in, fluttering and spinning madly around the ceiling, the bass roar changing almost instantly into a high-pitched drone, this time a plague of numerate locusts. Jenna ducked and tucked her head into Dom's chest, and he put his arm around her, a natural reaction he was surprised to find he possessed—and it *was* him, not Billy—and the waitress walked quickly over to the booth where the two farmers still sat, obviously not sure why the doors had opened like that and why she was feeling so weirded out, but likely sure she wanted to be away from Dom and Jenna. Dom found himself briefly wondering if moments like this were what influenced stories about poltergeists and ghosts.

With a pulsating scream, numbers from the second twister

rushed into the diner, the interior now filled with a variety of black and wiry shapes and sizes, but so far the mojo Dom and Jenna were wearing on their wrists kept a safe bubble around them, and eventually the air began to clear and the numbers fell into Dom's makeshift maze, all of them starting at the corner entrance, all of them aware, or as aware as directed numbers could be, that the specific strings of numbers they were targeting were somewhere in the centre of the maze, but all of them also reduced to having to count every single last grain of salt as they went by.

"It's working," said Dom, and he hustled Jenna out the door and into the car. Within seconds, they were back on the road and speeding away from the diner.

Aside from the arrhythmic thumping of the tires driving over asphalt patches in the highway, everything was silent for awhile. Jenna leaned across the back of her seat again to watch for anything following them, and Dom and Billy scanned the sky ahead, but eventually they decided they could relax. Jenna turned around and leaned forward, her head in her hands. "What exactly did you do that time?"

"There are certain designs that attract numbers. The one I did was a kind of Pictish ring; when the numbers sense it, they have to get inside and follow it to the end. The salt is a little trick I picked up from one of my anonymous online pals. Until an absolute quantity of salt crystals has been settled on, it's an unstable group."

"Unstable?"

Dom shook his head. "I don't pretend to understand, but I know part of the reason it works is because of the mathematical properties inherent in a crystal. This guy—at least, I assume it was a guy—compared it to some sort of quantum effect, said that the numbers coming after you have this insatiable need to know exactly how many crystals there are, and that until they do it can go either way for them. If the numbers go to the centre of the ring without doing the counting, then the ring collapses in on them, just kinda eats them. As for our ID, scraping the numbers off and shaking them into the centre of the ring means that they can't track us that way anymore, because that's what the search numbers were smelling. They *had* to go to the ring, because our numbers were hiding inside it, and no matter how strong these fuckers are, they can't convince the numbers to avoid it and keep looking for us."

"Search numbers always have a little bit of autonomy," said Billy. "But they're pretty predictable, as well. If you have the time, there are several ways to set up little traps for them, devices that will lock them in place long enough for you to get away. But as we saw down in Utah, usually time isn't on your side."

"So where do we go now?"

"North, to Edmonton. Most folk in the States know about Calgary, so that's likely where she—they—will be watching, but there aren't many who pay attention to anything further north."

Jenna rolled the window down about an inch and leaned back, her head turned to the right. Dom couldn't tell if she had closed her eyes or was just watching the world go by, so he kept quiet, surveyed the surrounding landscape, the fields of wheat standing tall and still in the calm air. Off in the distance pump jacks worked oil or gas up from deep underground, swaying back and forth like slow-bucking broncs, and releasing ancient integers that hadn't been seen since the time of dinosaurs, the numbers briefly rustling back and forth in the air before dropping back to the ground and trying to dig their way back to their zone of fossilized comfort. Dom had tried to capture and use some of those numbers, once, but their forms had been so severely altered by time and pressure that they had been virtually unrecognizable to him, resulting in a minor backlash that had given him a square inch patch of rough, pebbly skin on his right thigh that had lasted for weeks and, despite copious amounts of ointment, had remained itchy as hell for weeks more after it had disappeared.

Sometimes, rarely, they would pass a car or truck, and a couple of times were overtaken by cars in a hurry to get to their destination, but the road was relatively peaceful. There were no more numbers threatening them, in the distance or up close, and Dom was used to this sort of lifestyle. He was constantly on the road, moving from one city or town to another, always on the hunt for more mojo, always looking for the one artefact that would put him over the top. Dom figured that he would eventually make his way across the pond to Europe, but there was so much still going on here in North America; many artefacts had come across with the earliest settlers and had continued to come, finding their way to lands where the history of numeracy had still been unwritten.

Ruth reeled off primes in her mind, trying to force herself back to the surface, but no matter what she did now, the numbers no longer wanted to work for her in any meaningful way. Above and around her, the shadow that had taken control seemed able to run her body without any special effort, and somehow she could tell that he was aware of her own struggle, aware but apparently not at all concerned.

She could still see out of her own eyes, was a part of every physical thing that her body took part in, but try as she might she could find no way to control any of it. Everything she did and saw felt distant, like wearing a thick set of gloves to turn the pages of a newspaper, or like looking through an antique window at the leading edge of twilight.

More immediate to her, after initially catching the edges of it, was the heavy sensation of anger that emanated from him. No, not anger; rage. His fury was so complete, and now that she was aware of, so overwhelming, that it took over everything else. *This*, she could touch and see and feel. There was no sense of distance anymore, and it scared her. Would she always be a party to his emotions? More frightening, would she eventually be pushed completely under by their strength, and eventually never find her way back to the surface?

She tried to close off her mind to the emotions and concentrated again on primes, this time not to fight her way back into control but just to keep herself afloat.

Perissos iskhuros teos esti, hos ēs emeos, said a voice inside her head.

She didn't recognize the voice or the language, and worried for a moment that he was playing games with her while she was locked inside her own body. But still, she decided to respond, perhaps with the faint hope that interaction would provide her with a clue for how to escape. *Who is that?* she thought, not sure if she was doing this right or, maybe, that she was buried so deep she'd already gone insane and was talking to herself in different languages and with a male voice.

Metagignoskō, nomizō . . . I'm so very sorry. It has been so long since I tried to communicate with anyone that I forget that I am not speaking in your language. It was a man's voice inside her head, thickly accented, although very oddly, like a melange of accents from many different times and places. *What I tried to tell you was that he is too strong for you, just as he was for me. Just as he'll be for anyone, I fear. Soon enough you'll do as he asks, speak your voice as his proxy.*

These words were not what she wanted to hear. *Who are you?* she asked again. *How is it that there's another shadow in here, not just the one?*

There was a long period of silence, a hesitation that she felt directly, as if she was standing there watching someone collect their thoughts before responding. *I'm told my name is Archimedes,* said the man, *but that is only from what I've been told, not from any memories of my own. All I recall is that I was wrenched out of antiquity when he was very young, and I have been tied to him all these centuries since, when he was both alive and dead.*

Ruth felt a charge of fear run through her then. If someone else could be stuck with her shadow for all this time and not be able to manage any change or escape, what chance did she have? Even worse, she realized that this might end up being her own fate, sitting lodged deep inside her own body, so far down that eventually she would lose whatever it was that defined her as a person, eventually to the point that she would forget her name, her essence, become nothing but an essentially voiceless shadow on display for nobody.

Why would he hold you so close that your shadow still stays with his, centuries after his death? How is he able to do this?

You do know who it is who took control of your body, I trust? asked the voice.

If Ruth could have frowned she would have. *At first I thought maybe this was someone who had been caught trying for the same thing I had been brought to*, she replied.

You would be wrong. How much do you know about John Napier the man?

It was like a body blow. She knew what the likelihood had been, but had fought to deny it until just now. Instead of trying to deny the reality of her situation any further, though, Ruth cast back into her memories, trying to find what she'd learned about him. If there'd ever been any mention about John Napier when she was in school, aside from the small possibility that they'd been taught his name in conjunction with the invention of logarithms, she couldn't remember. But in the years since, her wanderings in search of a numerate holy grail had brought her to many sources that had, even if only in passing, mentioned John Napier. *I know he was a mathematician, and inventor, too, in Scotland around the same time that Shakespeare was alive. Probably a pretty powerful numerate, too, I imagine.*

The shadow allowed itself a small chuckle. *Powerful is an understatement. An inventor, yes. But one thing I know, listening in on his thoughts when I get the rare chance, many of his inventions were exact duplicates of devices I had apparently thought up so many aiōnes before.*

He let that thought hang in the air while Ruth chewed on it for a few seconds. Finally, she asked, *You mean to say he* plagiarized *you?*

So it seems, was the reply. *From what I've been able to gather, reading and listening to Napier, and from the few memories I have of that time, he was looking for ways to curry favour with the leaders of his country in order to gain access to artefacts that would enable his numerate growth. It did not take long for him to become what is likely the most powerful numerate ever. A status he may still hold, hundreds of years after his*

*death and controlling the body of a hapless woman and the sorry, forgetful
shadow of a long-dead man with a knowledge of ancient Greek.*

The most powerful ever. Ruth didn't doubt it, right now didn't
doubt anything other than her ability to get out from under him.

Dom decided they would stop in the town of Drumheller for a late lunch, coasting along a dry, brown landscape into the town; once there, Jenna commented on all of the statues of dinosaurs that sat beside the road. In the middle of pointing one out she suddenly squealed with delight and told Dom to turn left. He did, and ahead of him he saw an enormous dinosaur, a T-rex, he imagined, standing beside a parking lot. Children and adults drifted by, not paying attention to him or to any other traffic, so he inched along until he finally found a parking spot.

"That thing is enormous," said Billy as they climbed out of the car, tilting back Dom's head so he could see to the top. From inside the mouth a hand waved, and Dom realized with a start that people could climb up the inside of the creature, like a toothsome predatory version of the Statue of Liberty.

"I want to go up," said Jenna. She was grinning madly from ear to ear; this was probably the first time she'd really felt happy since she'd fallen into this travelling disaster.

Dom grinned back, and after squinting his eyes at the dinosaur to check out the numbers and obviously deciding that it was safe, nodded. "But first, let's get some lunch. I need to refuel before I climb that much."

A restaurant down the road took American dollars, and after a restroom break they each had a burger and fries, and Dom ate a salad as well. Once they were done he told Jenna to pull some money from her pocket and taught her how to remove the serial numbers so they couldn't be tracked. "You don't actually physically remove them," said Dom. "It's not like you're using an eraser on paper. If you did, pretty soon a non-numerate would catch you out and accuse you of trying to pass some funny money."

"So what do you do?" She leaned across the table to get a better view, and Dom angled his body to help.

"There's something like a coating on the numbers, which is the little bit of mojo that the bills have that has combined with the numbers you have on your person, to say nothing of the mojo of every other person, numerate or non-numerate, who has ever handled the money."

Jenna looked up at him. "What, like all the stuff we carry?"

Dom shook his head. "Not quite. More like, we leak. All the time, no matter how much you protect yourself against it, your body is losing numbers, which then get replenished."

"It's a very large closed system," said Billy. "Think of it as a kind of ecology of numbers."

"Or like breathing," said Dom. "Some numbers out, some numbers in."

"Then what does this do?" asked Jenna, holding up her wrist and tapping the wire wrapped around it.

"Well, we leak, but without the protection of something, whether it's a temporary fix like a series of prime or random numbers, or else something a little more solid, like the wire, then to someone who is looking for us and knows our numerical scent, it's like we have a spotlight spilling from our bodies and lighting up the sky."

"A spotlight bright enough to overpower the sun," added Billy. "As long as you have the eyes to see it."

"Those numbers pour out of every orifice, large and small, even microscopic, every second of our lives. They're the symbols of our lives, the factors that create and re-create themselves every moment, reproducing in numerical form our lives right down to the cellular—hell, probably the molecular or atomic—level."

"And they're like fingerprints," said Billy, waggling the fingers on Dom's left hand, "so the numbers that your body produces can be compared to the numbers from Dom's body and the difference spotted by anyone with the numeracy and the knowledge to tell them apart."

"Someone like the person with the search numbers that keeps almost finding us."

Dom nodded, and said, "Right. So what we have to do is wipe away any scent of us in the numerical traces we leave behind. Yes, you can take the physical numbers right off as well. . . ." He smeared away the serial number on one bill, rubbing at it while concentrating on a sequence that helped reduce the numbers to nothing. "But if you watch how I work the numbers . . ." Here he concentrated and with a press of his thumb placed the physical numbers back on the bill, then worked them over so that the mojo numbers slid off and drifted up and through the ceiling.

"If they go up there, how do we know they won't be found and *we* won't be tracked down?" asked Jenna, watching them as they slid through stained panelling and out of sight.

"If the numbers stayed here in the restaurant, even if they fell to the floor, they'd leave a pretty solid path for someone to follow," answered Dom. "So what you have to make sure is that when you free the numbers from their constraints, like I just did, you have to give them a little push to make them ephemeral. Ghost-like," he said, seeing the question forming on her lips. "Once it gets freed from the item that has factored its existence, which in this case is the rather tenuous life of a twenty dollar bill, then it drifts up and breaks up somewhere high in the sky, with individual numbers usually falling to earth and rejoining the numerical ecology in all sorts of places, depending on the winds and the moods of the numbers they seek to join."

"You make them sound almost intelligent."

"Like we said before," responded Billy, "numbers do have some degree of autonomy. Ones that numerates create can have even more, like the search numbers. But all are still constricted by the natural order of the world. When Dom uses the word *mood*, he could just as easily be talking about which bonds work and which ones don't, if you remember back to high school chemistry."

Dom handed Jenna another bill. "You try."

She took it from him and concentrated on getting a response from the numbers, just like Dom had shown her. As she did, her focus seemed to waver for just a fraction of a second and all the numbers jumped crazily around, seeming to replicate themselves and even scatter like dominoes being knocked down after having been set up. She closed her eyes to shut out the strange, sickly sensation it gave her, and when she opened them again Dom was staring at her.

"Did you feel that?" he asked her.

"Feel what?"

Dom shook his head. "That's the third time it's felt like I've been inside your head, looking out through your eyes, like I'm an adjunct for a second."

Jenna frowned at him, pursing her lips. "I have no idea what you're talking about. What I *did* feel, and see, was the numbers behaving very strangely for me."

"I saw that," said Billy. "Did you not, Dom?"

Dom stared back at her for a second, and then just shrugged his shoulders. "I . . . did, but that's not what I was talking about." He shook his head. "Never mind."

Jenna turned her attention back to the money in her hand. At first the numbers kept slipping away from her, a very strange reaction, but after a few tries they were watching them float up through the ceiling as well. She smiled and looked over at Dom, who grinned and patted her on the back. "Good job."

Dom's palm slapped on the table. "Let's go climb a dinosaur, shall we?" said Billy. They got up, waved good-bye to the proprietor, and crossed the road to the giant T-rex.

Dom paid the entrance fee with coins from his pocket, which required less work to remove their traces. Then they climbed the metal stairs, the insides of the dinosaur lit with red lights and showing traceries of fake fossils along the walls on the way up. Adults on their own or in pairs and groups, families with noisy children, some being carried by sweating, overweight parents wearing knee-length shorts and canopy-sized t-shirts with various touristy slogans about Canada blazoned on the front; all were struggling up or down the stairs, sandals and shoes slapping and echoing on the steps, the sounds intermingling with the shrieks of excited and tired children.

"Remind me again why we're here?" asked Billy. Dom was breathing hard, which made it difficult for the shadow to get the words out.

"Something to do," answered Jenna, having trouble right now with her own breathing. "A chance to relax," Dom barked a short laugh, "not have to be on the road all the time, or running from those numbers."

"Plus," said Dom, still panting, "sometimes you just gotta do the weird shit. And what's weirder than climbing a giant dinosaur in the middle of a small town in the desert?"

Billy grinned in response, and Dom could feel by the stretch of his cheeks that the adjunct was feeling as relaxed as he was. It was a nice feeling, finally being able to take a little bit of time and just enjoy it for what it was, rather than worrying about what was around the next corner.

They came to the last flight of stairs, and once again squeezed up against the railing to let a large family tumble by, parents feebly calling for their kids to slow down and watch for the other people. By the time they got to the top, though, they had it to themselves.

The viewing platform was in the bottom of the dinosaur's mouth, small steps leading down to stand in its jaws, Plexiglas set up to keep people from tumbling or jumping over the edge, enormous fibreglass teeth sticking out as a jagged counterpoint to the lumpy but rounded landscape of the countryside around the town. Down below was a splash park, children running and screaming and getting blessedly soaked in the heat of the day. Not as hot here as it had been in Utah, but it was still warm.

Dom was enjoying watching the road that passed through town, noting the different numbers floating up from license plates, an intermingling of localities, numbers that were foreign to this place, but that were able to blend easily enough with the local numerical ecology. That didn't always happen with human-created numbers, although he supposed that plates from other states and provinces had been around long enough to negotiate their way in with the local ones.

In the middle of his reverie, Jenna said, "Oh my God." Dom looked over and saw her pointing down. Below them, in the splash park, water pouring from the fountains was being accompanied by a slow dribble of black sludge, foul-looking numbers, which were gradually fanning out across the concrete surface, emphatically not going down the drain with the water, a tide of tumbling dark figures, insect-like and scrambling to crawl over each other and strain against gravity.

Search numbers.

They were off and down the stairs, shoving by the family that was on the last flight, Dom grabbing the rail and pushing off the wall to avoid one kid who wobbled after taking each step. "Take random numbers of steps and then jump two or three," said Dom, demonstrating. Jenna followed suit. "Don't always start a set of stairs with just one foot, or the same foot." He was panting again, but kept up a steady flow of advice, so much that there was no way she'd be able to follow all of it. The look on Jenna's face told him she was almost ready to give up, and if he could keep her attention focused with more instructions to follow, he knew he could keep her with him, both mentally and physically.

There were more people to avoid, but it was easier on the way down, everyone hugging the railing and hanging on for dear life as they realized just how many steps they had to climb to get to their goal. They hit bottom and dashed through the gift shop, pounded the door open, ignoring the looks and comments from behind, and dashed across the parking lot, trying to get to the car while swinging wide around the splash park.

"They're . . . tired," gasped Billy.

"So're we," responded Dom.

"The numbers. They're not rising above the ground." Billy made Dom stop, and for a few seconds he just stood there, hands on his knees and trying to keep his head up to look. Beside Dom, Jenna was hunched over, coughing and crying at the same time.

Finally, enough of his breath back, Dom stood and peered over the rows of cars. "Sonofabitch, you're right. Fuckers can't even get up over the curb."

Billy nodded his head. "It's taking all their energy to keep from going down the drains."

"So how did they end up in the water, anyway?" asked Jenna.

Dom shrugged. "Dunno. Probably not worth sticking around to figure out right now, either. We could go and flush them down and they wouldn't be able to get word out to their boss, but other numbers might be coming over the horizon or bubbling up from underground, so I think we're better off just running again. Get some more mojo so I can take care of these bastards."

Jenna grabbed his arm. He looked down in surprise, and then she tugged. "So let's go, then."

They were back on the road, leaving Drumheller behind as they drove north. Jenna kept checking over her shoulder, but each look elicited a report that nothing had changed, and pretty soon all three of them began to relax again. "But not enough to take our guard down," said Billy, after Dom had commented on this.

It took a few more hours to get to Edmonton. They stopped once for gas, once more to use the restroom. During that second stop Dom bought some snacks and drinks, but the burgers had filled the gaps pretty nicely, and they only dipped in for the odd bite or sip.

It was almost time for supper by the time Edmonton's downtown came into view, a small cluster of steel and glass and concrete rising from never-ending farmland and, as they neared the city, out of and above endless swaths of near-identical housing and big box retailers. Dom looked over and noticed the face Jenna was making. "What?"

"Kind of ugly, don't you think?"

"The city?" She nodded, and he shrugged. "Actually, I'm kinda fond of the place," he answered. "You sure as hell don't see its best face, driving in like this. But the city has a lot going for it: great parks, which I like, and from what some friends have told me, some pretty liveable neighbourhoods." He changed lanes, took an exit off the road and found his way over to the far lane, turned once more onto another road, this one a strip of hotels, bars, and shops; there were hundreds of people walking and shopping, window or real, buskers playing guitars, beggars trying to put the tap on everyone who walked by. "Great pace here, too, considering the size, although even it is getting too big for its britches." He pulled into a parking spot and got out, stood with Jenna on the sidewalk. "It's too late to get to the bank today, so this is the best place to be. There are a lot of numbers happening in a place like this, and as long as we're careful about covering our tracks, we'll be safe."

"How can you be sure? You thought we were okay down in Drumheller, too."

Dom shrugged again. "Guess I can't be sure. But this is the best answer I've got right now, unless you or Billy have anything."

Jenna made a face. "Don't be an ass."

"I certainly don't," replied Billy. "I've never been here before, so I don't know what the city has that might be of help to us. We're in your hands, Dom."

"Right. Let's find us a couple of rooms for the night and then go get supper." He fished their packs out of the back of the car and they went into a hotel one block east. This time he gave Jenna some cash and had her pay for her own room, watching to make sure that she rubbed away the numbers, which she managed with only a little difficulty. When they got to their floor he told her to meet down in the lobby in a half hour, which Jenna negotiated up to forty-five minutes so that she could have a shower.

Once in the room Dom threw his bag on the floor and collapsed on the couch, immediately seeking out the remote control, scanning channels for sports. "You like athletic competition," commented Billy.

Dom nodded, settled on a Mariners-Blue Jays game. "The numbers appeal to me, and I've done well by the mojo that gets dug up. Especially in baseball." The two of them watched in silence for a few minutes, letting the easy rhythm of the play and the numbers drift over them. Dom was getting sick of long and difficult days, and he imagined that Billy and Jenna were as well. What he'd give to be able to attend a ball game in real life, and not have to worry about anything except not getting a sunburn or spilling beer on his legs when he jumped to catch a foul.

Finally, Billy interrupted the moment. "How are we going to avoid the search numbers this time?"

"Meaning what?"

"I suppose I mean that no matter where we've been or the steps we've taken, this person has managed to find us. And next time there is no guarantee that the numbers will be slow and weak, or that we'll be able to dash out of harm's way at the last possible second."

"Ah." Dom thumbed the remote and swung his feet over the edge of the bed. "Hang on a minute." He went into the bathroom and unzipped, pissed with his eyes closed—bodily functions with Bill inhabiting his body still kind of freaked him out—then splashed cold water over his face and let it air dry.

"Well?" The shadow sounded impatient.

"This is a different sort of city," said Dom, after a few seconds more. "Most places, all their streets have names. Main Street, Central Avenue, that sort of thing. They have a few named streets here, but most of the city is on a kind of grid, with the streets all numbered instead."

Billy grunted. "I see."

"Yeah. Hundreds of numbers, crossing each other all over the map. Every one of them sending out their own little waves of interference." Dom walked over to the window and opened the curtain. "Look closer at the sky."

Billy peered with Dom's eyes. "My goodness. If you don't look too close, that looks like smog."

Dom nodded. "Most people can't see it, of course. But those are numbers, constantly drifting up into the air from the interaction with each other, but not floating off too far because there's still the attraction from below. It's an amazing thing, and yet you don't find too many numerates coming to Edmonton."

"I wonder why?"

"Too damn cold in the winter." He opened the door and walked out to meet Jenna.

S he'd gotten up early and come down to the lobby about a half hour before and just stood there for the whole time, looking out the door at the people passing by, but Jenna heard Dom coming and turned to greet him, smiling. "This place feels safe," she said as they walked out onto the sidewalk. Dom pointed up at the sky and told her about the numbered streets and about how that affected the place in ways that rarely happened in other large cities, and she nodded a bit, trying to understand. Then they wandered off to find a pizza place that Dom said he remembered from the last time he'd been there.

"Tell me about yourself," said Jenna, after they'd been served their pizzas and drinks. She'd realized while walking here that they had not had the time to get to know each other, and for the first time since this had all started she felt like things were calm enough to spend some time getting to know Dom, instead of just learning about the numbers.

Dom looked up in surprise, but before he could say anything Billy chimed in: "Yes, I'm also curious. You're unlike any other numerate I've known, and I've known a few of them."

He took a big mouthful of pizza, chewing slowly as if to give him time to organize his thoughts. When he swallowed and washed it down with some beer, he asked, "Where do you want me to start?"

Jenna took a sip of her soda. "How old are you?"

"Thirty-one." Younger than she'd thought.

"Where were you born?" asked Billy.

"Nova Scotia. But I was raised a few hours north of here, in a little town called Peace River."

"When did you discover you were a numerate?" This was Billy again.

Dom leaned back in his chair, looked around the restaurant. There were two other tables in use right now, a couple sharing quiet and intimate talk, and a family of five making a lot more noise, but all of it happy, the youngest shrieking with joy from his high chair as an older sibling made open mouth faces while chewing on pizza. "These people all have it pretty good," he finally said. There was a slight choke in his voice, but Jenna chose to ignore it for the moment.

"What do you mean?" asked Billy.

Jenna held up her hand. "I think I know," she said. "You had what I didn't, right? A good family life."

His lips pursed, Dom paused for a moment before finally nodding his head. "Yeah. Loving parents, a little sister who looked up to me." He fiddled with his beer mug for a second, then took another drink. "But the numbers, they fuck you over something serious. I did the same thing your mother did, Jenna, except I did it a lot earlier. She waited until after she'd had you, but the numbers, they first spoke to me when I was twelve. I mean, I'd been seeing them all my life, I'm pretty sure, but I didn't know what they were until then, much less what I could do with them. And when they did crash down on me, I managed to hold them back for almost four whole years."

"And then?" Jenna closed her eyes, remembering her mother and anticipating what was coming next.

"I left." He drained his beer, waved at the waitress for a refill. "Walked out on my family and never looked back. Been more than eight years since I last saw them. It still took me a year or two to figure out what my numeracy meant; worked odd jobs for quite awhile until I got the hang of it."

"Have they looked for you?" asked Billy. "I have a sense that in my first life I did no such thing, but this is a story I've heard more and more over the decades." He stopped talking when the waitress arrived with another beer, who nonetheless had likely heard him talking with the accent and different voice, based on the look she cast back at him as she headed over to the noisy family's table.

"Yeah, they tried to find me. I know the cops were in it for awhile, but their numbers were easy to avoid, especially since there was nobody involved who knew they existed, much less how to control them, and every day away, I got better at handling them. I finally phoned one day, when I knew my parents would be out. Talked to my sister, told her that I was okay and that they should stop trying to find me."

"What was her answer?"

"She was pretty pissed off. Yelled at me, called me all sorts of names, then backed off, told me she loved me and they wanted me to come back home. Tough language from someone who was only eleven at the time." He grinned at the memory, took another swallow. "They were in a car accident a few months later. Dad's in a wheelchair now, and Mom and my sister were hurt pretty bad, but they got better. I still arrange for some money to mysteriously appear in their bank account whenever I can."

It had been hard for Jenna to lose her family the way she had, and must have been even more difficult for Dom, walking away like that and then not being there for them after the accident. It was appalling to think about, and for just a second she wondered if she should get up and walk away, get off this path to a life of hunting for numbers and secrets that Dom had buried himself in. Perversely, though, she caught the look of despair that had ever-so-briefly crept onto Dom's face, and thought of her mother and what she had left behind, chasing the numbers in the face of the same sort of loss, and realized that she was in this every bit as deep as they were now.

That realization didn't answer everything for her, though. "Then why are you still away?" she asked. "When all is said and done, how is it that you can't just let your family know that you're still around, maybe show up for Christmas once or twice." Her voice caught, and for a second she was sure she was going to start crying again, but she got a hold of herself and carried on. "The numbers spoke to me, too, but I didn't wander off and desert my father just because I could see funny things floating through the air."

Dom frowned. "Jenna, I'm not your mother." She felt herself flinch at this, but he pressed on before she could argue the point. "I can't speak for her, but I imagine that the lure of these numbers is more extreme for some of us than it is for others."

"My mom, she was pretty distant for a long time before she disappeared. I suppose when she did go it didn't come as much of a surprise, probably less to me even than to my dad." She bit her lower lip, thinking about those last days and remembering how she blamed herself, but she blinked rapidly for a few seconds and carried on. "I guess whatever numbers were speaking to her had her attention early on and just needed some time to convince her to leave us behind."

Dom took another bite of pizza, followed it with more beer. "Well, that's exactly it, and I can't stress it enough; the numbers, they call me. Whether I'm awake or asleep, it doesn't matter. Hell, once I even paid someone to put me into one of those sensory deprivation tanks. The numbers were fluttering around like moths, bumping against the ceiling of the tank, aggravating the crap outta me."

"I see them all the time, too."

He shook his head. "No you don't, Jenna, I can pretty much guarantee that. I've watched you, awake, even asleep when we've been in the car. The numbers do just the opposite with you. They're willing to be manipulated by you, but first they try to stay away from you. It's the damndest thing I've ever seen, but we've been so busy I really haven't had time to think much about it."

"What do you mean, stay away from me?" But even as she asked this she thought she knew the answer.

"I've seen numbers come close to you, but unless you are planning on using them or if it's something like the search numbers that were sent after us, then they leave you alone." This was Billy talking. "It's almost like there is a bubble around you, and none of them want or are able to pass through it."

Dom nodded. "Remember when I stuck you with the wire?" He pointed at the makeshift bracelet on her wrist. "The numbers didn't do what they were supposed to. Normally they would've crawled right in, but instead we had to convince them to do so, instead of them just melting off your skin."

Jenna stared back at him, worried that he was trying to tell her that he couldn't teach her what she needed to know. Dom frowned at her, then turned and with a gesture of his finger brought some numbers from the noisy family's credit card down from the ceiling. They coasted down, dropping momentarily near the floor before rising again, behaving like a flock of ducks thinking about landing on the water and searching for the best spot. They flew right at Jenna's head, then broke off in two directions while still several inches from her, some heading back up to the ceiling, others fluttering around Dom's head, some even slipping in through his skin, just folding up and squeezing their way through the pores, more random numbers to join in his blood.

"I've . . . I've never noticed that before." She was watching the numbers that were back up by the ceiling, eyes open wide.

Not saying anything, Dom pulled some more numbers from the air, but these ones he set in place so that they hung in front of her. "Take them in," he said.

"What?"

"Take them in. Bring these numbers into your body."

Jenna was confused. "How do I do that?"

"I dunno." Dom shook his head. "Remember, everyone has a different style. Maybe you have to grab them, maybe you have to lean over and swallow them. You have to experiment a little, see what way is best for you."

"Why do I need to learn how to bring numbers into my body?"

"Every once in awhile you'll come across some feral numbers that will be able to serve you to good purpose," replied Billy. Dom took another swig of beer, then let him continue. "Sometimes it's spillover from someone else's mojo, although that sort of thing doesn't happen too often, since people guard those numbers very carefully. Other times they might be numbers that you recognize as a part of a pattern you've been searching for."

"And," added Dom, "probably the most important one, or at least so I have been led to understand, would be numbers from artefacts."

"As I was going to say," said Billy. "When someone finds an artefact, it isn't just a matter of standing there and hoping it all works out. There are some rather devious numbers to ingest if you want to take advantage of what has been placed inside."

"Okay, I get the point." Jenna frowned, staring at the numbers as they spun about in a fidgety ball of Brownian motion. She reached forward and tried to grab them, but the ball broke apart, numbers spilling like black mercury from an invisible force field that surrounded her fingers. As soon as she removed her hand they re-congealed, picked up their orbits as if she had never been there to perturb them.

Feeling bewildered, Jenna pulled at the numbers again, and again they slid away. For more than a minute she worked on them, once even leaning forward and trying to gulp them down like a pelican sliding its lower beak through the water as it gathered up fish for its meal. Nothing worked, and the last move elicited some very strange looks from the waitress and the couple other patrons, as well as a stifled snort of laughter from Dom.

"Look for a way that works for you," said Billy, obviously trying to avoid laughing as well. "The numbers don't come to you, but you've proven to yourself and to us that you can interact with them."

"How?" She said this with frustration in her voice, and hoped the look she gave Dom told him that it was partly to do with his laughing at her.

"Good question," he responded. "How did you make that phone call happen, when we were still down in Utah? You can control the numbers, so just control them into your system. I think you had the right idea when you tried to get a mouthful there . . ." He paused to fend off another chuckle, and then carried on, carefully ignoring the glare she gave him. "You've controlled them doing other things for you, so now just ask them to enter your body."

She arched an eyebrow. "Ask them?"

"Sure. Why not? Invite them on in."

Jenna concentrated for a few seconds, staring hard at the spinning ball, and then, accepting the situation but irritated that she was having to do something so stupid, she said, "Numbers, please come in."

Across the table she saw Dom look blank for a brief second, and then shake his head as if he'd blacked out for a second and just come too. But then the ball shimmied back and forth a few times, and broke into a thin stream, soared across the tiny space separating her from them, and melted into her, a brief darkness of numeracy covering her like a robe and hood before dissolving away and into her body.

She jumped and shrieked, her chair tumbling back and slamming into the empty table behind them before falling to the floor. Dom, looking shaken, even frightened, turned and looked briefly to the waitress, already on her way over, and waved her away, then stood and walked around the table, put a shaking hand on Jenna's arm, and said, "Hold yourself together. Let me settle up, and we can discuss this more after we've left."

She nodded, breathing hard and staring wildly at the spot above the table where the numbers had floated. Dom pulled some bills from his pocket, tossed enough on the table to cover a good thirty percent, then picked up the chair and set it back in place. He had one last swallow of beer and then he led Jenna out and onto the street. Behind them she could feel the eyes of the waitress, the other diners, even the cook, on her back.

"Did you do that?" asked Jenna, after they had walked in silence for a block.

Dom shook his head. "Not me. You, Billy?"

Once again, his head shook, this time controlled by the shadow. "Certainly not. Jenna, that was just your way of controlling the numbers."

"But I've never done that before."

"Which is why you're with me. With us," said Dom, correcting himself. "Remember, everyone has a different way of handling the numbers, just like everyone perceives them in a different fashion." He rubbed his chin, obviously thinking. "Jenna, did you feel anything funny when you took in the numbers?"

She looked at him, right eyebrow raised. "Of course I did. That's why I freaked out."

Dom shook his head, and Billy asked, "Did it happen again, Dom?"

He nodded. "Just for a second or two."

"Did what happen?" asked Jenna.

Dom stopped walking and looked at her. "You really didn't feel anything?"

She gave him an exasperated look. "Of course, I felt something, I just told you. But the way you're sounding, maybe I didn't feel what you think I should have. So no, nothing beyond the weirdness of taking in the numbers like that. Tell me what you're talking about."

"A few times now, I've found myself looking at things from your eyes."

"What, like a shadow, like Billy?"

"I don't know, since I've never been one. All I know is I've been inside your body, and I don't know how it happened." He frowned, and they started walking again. "To be honest, at first I thought I was just hallucinating."

"Each time it happened, Jenna was using, or trying to use, numbers," said Billy. He spoke slowly, like he was thinking it out. But after a few seconds of silence he shrugged and said, "I see no answers. Not yet, anyhow." They walked on in silence, each lost in their own thoughts.

The sidewalks were more crowded now, people off work and out on the town for the night. Many looked like university kids, numbers of exhaustion from papers and exams and too many late nights spilling from them as they sought solace and short-term energy from an even later night boozing it up in one of the many bars here. But there were also families, older people and couples, more buskers, and a fair number of bums, staggering from person to person, Pachinko ball-like action taking each one further down the sidewalk as they looked for a jackpot, most people brushing them off with a curt "No" or, even more likely, just ignoring them.

Except one. Jenna looked like she was about to say something, but Dom held up his hand for silence, watched as this man ricocheted from person to person, and each one he approached reached into a pocket and pulled out money to drop into his open hand, although it looked to Dom like none of those people were even paying attention to the fact that they were giving him money.

"What are you thinking?" asked Billy.

"Shh. Keep watching for a sec."

By now the streetlights had flickered to life, doing nothing to add to the light already spilling onto the street from storefronts, but prepared nonetheless for when twilight finally faded enough to blacken the sky overhead.

The bum limped over to another person who was standing directly beneath one light, but instead of watching the interaction between the two of them Dom turned his gaze upwards, watched as the light flickered again, then went dark.

"Well, I'll be," said Billy.

"No shit," said Dom. "He's got something all right. Should we find out what it is?"

Billy nodded his head for him, and he turned to Jenna. "See that bum over there?" He pointed across the street. She nodded. "He's numerate, but probably doesn't know it. He's also really fucked up, so we'll have to be careful when we approach him."

"Approach him?" He heard Jenna running to catch up, since he'd already headed off to the corner. The street was too busy to jaywalk; he could use numbers to help, but there was no trusting that drunken frat boys might be out and a little slower to react to numeracy, and he also didn't think it was a good idea to advertise his presence to the person who was likely still on his tail, at least not until he knew he was prepared, and certainly not for something as minor as crossing the street.

The light changed and they crossed with the crowd, Dom keeping his chin up and watching for stray numbers from the bum. He could see by the guy's wake that he'd gone further up the street away from them; another light had flickered out. This was a huge leak, and if he didn't take advantage of it now, someone else would be there to try and beat him to it.

Jenna stepped in front and turned to face him, walking backwards but making him slow his pace. "What are we doing?" Dom put his hand on her shoulder and spun her around, pointed up to the light directly above them. "See that?"

She looked up and nodded. "It's burned out."

"Not necessarily. There are some people who will make streetlights go out whenever they get close to them. They have a pretty strong in-built numeracy, but usually they don't know it." He took her hand and kept them walking, watching the bum's progress; they were catching up, but slowly.

"That's happened to me before," said Jenna. "Maybe five, six times a year, I'll be driving by a light and watch it as it goes out. Always the same light, on the way to my apartment from work."

Dom nodded. "There's a lot to figure out about you, like how the numbers don't come into your body, but how you're still able to have spillage like that."

"Dom, you're leaving me dry here. What the heck is spillage?"

They were closer now. The bum seemed to have decided he wanted nothing else to do with crowds, and had headed down an alley. Dom picked up his pace, dragging Jenna along with him. "Spillage is just that, a big leak of numbers. If someone is numerate but doesn't know it, they lose their more powerful numbers, sometimes in a steady flow, sometimes in big splashes that happen in cycles. The big splashes will sometimes affect electrical things. Streetlights are prone to splashes, and usually it's the same light, like it's the one in the chain that is no longer immune, a sacrifice so that the others can continue to function."

"This fellow," said Billy, "seems to have shut down three lights just while we were watching him." He pointed to a third that had gone out just at the entrance to the alley. "That's an enormous spillage."

They reached the alley, and Dom stopped, looked for any numbers floating around that were waiting as traps, but there was nothing. He could get the sense of the big splashes that had come from the bum, but they'd raced up and away faster than he would have expected, and strangely enough he was left with almost no numerical residue from the bum himself. It was almost as if he could cover himself up and hold it all inside, but then would have to let go frequent bursts of numbers. "Jesus," he said. "Do you think it's something he's eaten? It's like he's farting, for God's sake!"

"Swallowed the mojo?" Billy sounded sceptical. "It's big enough to think it's something he's carrying, not just his latent ability, but I don't know."

Dom shrugged his shoulders. "Sounds stupid, yeah. But how the hell is he shutting down every light like that? No one leaks like that."

They entered the alleyway, the only light spillover coming from shops and traffic out on the street. There were no more street lights now that they were here, so they couldn't track his path that way, and there was still no numerical trail otherwise; Dom had never seen anything like this before.

Jenna clenched his arm now, pulled herself close to him. It was Billy who reached across and patted her hand, but neither of them said anything to her, or even looked in her direction. All of Dom's concentration was going outwards, trying to figure out where this guy and his mojo had gone, since he sure as hell didn't want a repeat of Utah.

"Hey!" The voice came from practically right beside Dom's ear, and at the same time cold air blew up Dom's pants legs. Jenna screeched and dug her nails into Dom's arm, and between his own fright and Billy's reaction, Dom was sure his heart was about to stop. He spun around, prepared to throw numbers in the guy's face and run like hell.

There was no one there.

Someone shoved his back, hard enough to snap his head back, and again he turned, slipping on what felt like ice instead of stumbling on what should have been pavement. Still nobody there, and where the hell was this ice coming from? "What the fuck is happening?" He yelled this, scared and exasperated in equal measure. Jenna still clung to his arm, and when he yelled she hissed and squeezed even tighter.

"You have a ghost following you," said the voice. Again he was hit from behind, this time dropping to his knees. "Hold still so I can check it away!" He was slammed again, his face pushed down and what really did feel like ice.

Right, though Dom. *No fucking mojo on me, but I'm not taking this shit anymore.* He stood back up, as quickly as possible reaching up into the sky with his mind, and pulled down an avalanche of numbers. It didn't matter what the numbers were, where they'd come from, or how much attention they brought to him. He just knew he had to stop this now.

Incomplete sets, broken-down theorems, strings and individual numbers, primes and wholes and even some imaginary numbers, all crashed into the alley with a clatter and banging loud enough to wake the numerate dead, although it wouldn't be more that a whisper of a breeze to the non-numerates out on the sidewalks and streets.

The numbers continued to pile up, some of them hitting with enough force to push him and Jenna around, others hopefully doing the same to his invisible attacker.

He wasn't being harassed anymore, so he waved a hand and stopped the flow, let the numbers begin their journey back up and into the numerical ecology. Some sprang into the air with great energy, others were more sluggish, skittering or even just crawling along the pavement of the alley before finally finding enough juice to push themselves back into the air. There was a small cloud developing overhead, about roof height, where the weaker numbers congealed together as they searched for strength from each other.

But some numbers remained on the ground, and many of these danced and bounced in a ball around a huddled figure that was scrunched up close to a rusted out Toyota pickup. Dom pulled Jenna over to a wall well clear of the guy—he could see through the numbers that this was the bum—then half-slid, half-walked across the ice and pushed the remaining numbers away.

The guy looked up into Dom's eyes, and he was shocked to note that the bum wasn't much older than him. "What the fuck was that all about?" yelled Dom.

The bum squinted up at Dom, then raised a shaking hand and pointed to him. "There's a ghost following you. I was trying to check it out of you."

"*Check* it out of me? What the hell does that mean?"

The bum reached into a pocket and slowly pulled out a greasy, slightly torn and heavily wrinkled paper bag. Dom's breath caught. Whatever was in the bag, as soon as it had come out of the bum's pocket he could see the strength of the numbers spilling out of as well as back into it. Around them the ice melted away, fading from a solid to a vapour without bothering to make its normal middle stop as water. This was some serious mojo.

Dom crouched down, held up both hands and smiled, hoping to show that he was friendly. "The ghost is a friend of mine," he said. "His name is Billy. Say hi, Billy."

"Hello," said Billy. Dom felt his smile stretch even wider. "What's your name?"

The bum's eyes were as big as saucers. "Martin," he said, voice barely a whisper.

"I'm a friend, Martin," said Billy. "I'm not the bad type of ghost that makes trouble for people. Dom here," Dom smiled and raised his eyebrows, "is my friend, and I try to help him."

"Who's that?" Martin gestured over to the wall across the alley.

"That's Jenna," replied Dom. He turned and waved her over. She crossed to them cautiously, looking up to the numbers that still circled overhead, most of them a little higher and flying a bit stronger now.

"Jenna, this is Martin," said Dom.

"Um. Hi, Martin." She gave Dom a funny look, then turned back to the bum. "Martin, can we buy you supper some place?"

Martin was on his feet in a second, right hand still clenched around the paper bag and whatever it held. "I'm sorry about trying to check you away, Billy," he said. "Where are we going to eat?"

Dom scratched his chin, smiling. "Well, we've already eaten, Martin, so we'll just follow along. Your choice."

"Big Mac, fries, large Coke." He headed down the alley, Dom and Billy and Jenna hurrying to keep up.

More lights shut down as they walked, but whenever he turned to look back Dom could see them all slowly flickering back to life. Now that he could watch more closely, he saw that the spillage was indeed coming from Martin, and that whatever was in the bag was somehow focusing it; numbers would leak from the bum's body, swirl around the paper bag like they were caught in a whirlpool, then get sucked into its folds. Then, every dozen paces or so, a congealed mass of them would streak up and out of the bag, ricochet off the light post overhead, enough scraping off from the impact to temporarily darken the light.

"You ever seen anything like that?" he whispered to Billy.

Billy shook Dom's head. "Never. One likes to imagine that one has heard of all the mojo that has been out there, even if only in rumours, but of course that would involve a splash of hubris, would it not?"

"Are you being a wiseass with me?" asked Dom.

Now his head shook. "If so, then it was also directed at me," said Billy. "I, too, have carried the belief that I knew everything I could possibly need to know, even if I didn't know how to find it."

They entered the McDonald's, and Jenna took a table while Dom and Martin went to the counter to order. When the food came they joined Jenna, and for several minutes they just let Martin eat, the mojo in the bag sitting on the bench beside him.

Finally, Dom said, "I want to ask you again, Martin, what you meant when you said you wanted to check Billy out of me."

Martin wiped some ketchup from his chin with his sleeve, then dipped another handful of fries in the ketchup and plunged it into his mouth. He chewed for a few seconds, swallowed, then said, "Push it out. Away."

"Where did the word come from? Why *check*?"

"The puck."

"The what?" This was Billy, his voice full of confusion.

"The puck," repeated Martin. He pulled the ratty bag up onto the table and slid its contents out onto the tray, where it sat beside his Coke.

Dom reached his hand half forward, caught himself, looked at Martin and asked, "May I look at it?"

Martin waved his permission, took a drink of his pop and then grabbed up another handful of fries.

Dom picked it up, turned it over in his hands, feeling the strength ooze from the hard rubber. It was a hockey puck, NHL for sure, but looked like it was quite a few years old. He was pretty sure he knew exactly what it was, but thought he'd ask anyway. "Where'd you get this, Martin?"

"From my dad." Martin ate the last bite of his burger, chewing open-mouthed as he leaned back on the bench. "I stoled it from him when I left home, back in high school. Bastard stoled it himself, so I figured it was okay. Besides, the thing was always talking to me anyways, every day trying to tell me stuff."

"Do you know where this puck originally came from?" Dom knew, was *sure*, but he needed at least a vocal provenance, if only for his own ease of mind.

"Dad told me it was from Bill Barylko's last goal."

Sonofabitch. He could see it now, could feel the conjunction of numbers and freak events that had led to the creation of this specific piece of mojo, could see the events in his mind, even though they had taken place before he had been born. This was one serious punch of mojo, this puck.

"Martin, do things drift in front of your eyes, always bugging you?"

Martin cocked an eyebrow at him. "No. Not always, anyways. Sometimes, I s'pose."

Dom hefted the puck. "This is the reason it happens," he said. "What if I told you I could help you get rid of those things?"

Now Martin leaned forward. "How?"

Dom leaned forward, too, trying to make it look like he was sharing Martin in something special. "I can take the puck and make it so it doesn't bother you again. When you get it back, it'll just be a regular puck. Still the one shot by Bill Barylko, but no longer one that makes all this stuff get under your skin and in your eyes all the time."

He felt a sharp stab of pain in his shin, looked over to see Jenna glaring at him. He kicked her back, smiled to see the look of surprise that accompanied the one of sudden pain.

"No," said Martin, who hadn't seemed to notice any of the under-the-table shenanigans.

"No?" Dom gritted his teeth. He had to have the puck.

"I said no," repeated the bum. "You can't fool me. You take the puck and then I never get it back. I think you should pay me for it instead."

"Pay . . ." Dom coughed, choking for a second even though he'd swallowed nothing.

"Yeah, pay me." Martin cocked an eye at Dom, giving him a look that showed that, despite the free meal, he definitely didn't trust him. "You figure you can get this from me with just a burger and fries and Coke, you're a fuckin' idiot."

"Um." Dom didn't know what to say. He'd expected to have to wrestle this damn thing from the bum, at best grab the puck and run like a son of a bitch, at worst put Martin down so he wouldn't get back up again. And here he was saying that all he wanted was some money.

Martin stood and re-pocketed the ratty paper bag with the puck. "Maybe I'll just go, then," he said. "Looks like you don't think it's all that valuable, so maybe someone else will want to buy it someday."

Dom reached out and grabbed Martin's forearm. "I *would* like it. What do you want in return?"

Martin gave Dom a look that showed how remarkably stupid he thought he was. "Jesus Christ," he said as he shook his head. "Money."

"You want money," said Jenna. "For that puck."

Martin nodded.

"Doesn't it mean anything to you? It was your father's, even if you don't care about the history of it."

Martin pulled the puck from his pocket and removed it from the bag, rolled it around in his hand while he stared down at the floor for a moment. Then he sat back down and looked up, first at Jenna, then at Dom. "These things I see, they're the reason I took this puck in the first place. I figured it would help me deal with the stuff, the little things that dance around the corners of my eyes." He paused at this, then as if in response to this statement slapped at some numbers that briefly hopped around his face as they bounced to avoid Jenna. It looked to Dom like the numbers were only marginally visible to Martin; he had a tiny vestige of numeracy, it seemed, but not enough to allow him control of the numbers around him, only enough to make him susceptible to their presence.

"And?" prompted Jenna.

"And the thing didn't help me with jack shit," replied Martin. "It was like it called to me, but when I took it I didn't get anything good out of it. I mean, it somehow let me do some things I wasn't able to do before, like when I was trying to check the ghost out of you, but it's only helped make my life crap ever since I took it." He sat back and folded his arms, puck still in his right hand.

"How much do you want for it?" asked Dom. It was all he could do to keep from licking his lips. Instead of fighting for mojo, or stealing it from someone, all he was being asked to do was pay. Nothing like this had ever happened to him before.

"Thousand bucks," said Martin. The look on his face now was defiant, daring Dom to offer less.

Dom pulled his wallet from his back pocket and flipped through the bills. "I've got seven hundred, but it's American." He dropped the money on the table between them. "That's not quite there, with today's exchange rates, but not too far off. Fair?"

Martin rolled the puck across the table with one hand as he scooped up the pile of bills with his other. "Fair."

He stood to leave, but Jenna put a hand out to stop him. "Martin, please be smart about how you spend the money."

He smiled at her, then at Dom. "Absofuckinglutely." And then he left, skipping a couple of times even before he had reached the door.

Dom hefted the puck, a smile on his face. "Couldn't have gone better," he said.

"I've never seen an easier time getting something that feels this powerful," answered Billy. "Knocked down in an alley a couple of times, then you buy the fellow supper and pay him money that isn't even your own."

"No sneaking around, no breaking in, no duels or brute force," continued Dom. "Remarkable."

Jenna stood. "Why do I get the feeling that the two of you have just ripped off poor Martin?"

Dom stood with her and they left, headed back towards the hotel. "You heard the man, Jenna," said Dom. "He didn't want the thing anymore, and even more important to me, he seemed to barely even use it. A good piece of mojo like this, it should be in hands that know how to care for it, how to use it the way the numbers intend it to be used."

"And how is that?"

Dom shrugged. "That'll take some time. I know the numbers are here. I'm sure you can see and feel them as well as I can. And I have an idea what the provenance of the puck is, just based on the memory of being a Canadian kid. I'd say that what Martin called 'checking' has a lot to do with it."

"Are you going to explain?" asked Billy.

Dom turned the puck in his hands. Solid black rubber, National Hockey League logo on one side, but otherwise nothing to distinguish it. "Bill Barylko scored his last ever goal with this puck." He frowned, trying to remember the story. "The goal was in the late fifties or early sixties, I think, and I do know that it won the Stanley Cup for the Leafs."

"Leafs?" Jenna shook her head. "That's a hockey team, I take it?"

Dom nodded, stepped sideways to avoid a pack of young teenage girls all carrying shopping bags. "The Toronto Maple Leafs. And then that summer he disappeared on a fishing trip. I think the next time the Leafs won the cup was the year that they found his body. I don't think they've won another since." He laughed. "Hell, there's even a famous Canadian rock song that refers to the story."

"So that would make this thing, this puck, a piece of mojo how?" asked Jenna. She looked sceptical.

"The numbers likely took on their power after all the events played out," said Dom. He opened the door to their hotel and let her walk in ahead of him. "The coincidence of the Leafs not winning again until the year his body was found means that the numbers built up a good amount of power. Already his scoring the winning goal would've given the puck a little extra something, but coupled with everything else it means that this thing carries loads of pent-up numbers, wanting nothing more than to amplify a numerate's abilities in their own special fashion." He pressed the button to call the elevator, and when they boarded let Jenna press the floor numbers.

"If this is such a famous puck, shouldn't it have been somewhere special?" Jenna leaned against the wall, hands in her pockets. "I mean, I don't know anything about ice hockey, but baseball and football have halls of fame where special things end up sitting in displays, don't they?" Dom nodded, smiling, which seemed to irritate her. "So if hockey has a hall of fame, why would this puck be out here, having just been bought from the hands of a street person, instead of in there, sitting under glass, on some sort of pedestal?"

The door opened onto Jenna's floor, but she let it close, rode up to Dom's floor, obviously not willing to leave without an explanation. Dom got off first, led her to his room, opened the door with his key card and leaned in to turn on a light.

Finally, sitting down on the lone chair in the room, he said, "I expect that if the hall of fame would hold onto Bill Barylko's puck, then it thinks that it does have it."

Jenna sat on the edge of the bed. "What does that mean?"

"What does it sound like it means?"

She made a face, for a moment looking like she wanted to smack him upside the head, but then a look of comprehension appeared in her eyes. "You replace them."

"If by 'you' you mean the person who goes in and removes the object, then yeah, you're right." Dom hefted the puck, then tossed it into the air, caught it with a downward sweep of his arm. "Obviously, I had nothing to do with this. Wherever the puck was, it was likely Martin's dad who scooped it."

"Provenance is usually important in finding numerate mojo," interrupted Billy. "Just like it is in antiques. Most often, if you know where the mojo came from you have a better idea of what it's capable of, to say nothing of knowing whether or not something isn't quite right."

"What wouldn't be right?"

Billy shrugged Dom's shoulders, but it was Dom who answered. "Don't really know. It depends on all sorts of things. But there are some pieces of mojo out there that came about because of something bad that happened, and usually the numbers that come from those things are hard to reign in. Angry. Enraged, even." Seeing the blank look on Jenna's face, he cast about in his mind for an example. "Like from the Holocaust, for example. I bet there's a whole pile of mojo that came out of those concentration camps, but I wouldn't want to be the one who messes with anything from them."

Jenna nodded, looking pensive, then stood and walked to the door. Dom didn't blame her for wanting to walk away from where this conversation was now headed. "What time do we meet downstairs?"

"About ten to nine. We'll go to the bank first, and then get breakfast."

She waved at him, a strange smile on her face. "G'night Dom. Night, Billy."

"Good night." The first word came from Dom, the second from Billy. Jenna raised her eyebrows at the combination of accents and voices, then left the room.

Dom sat for a moment, thinking about the look on her face as she had left, then shook his head, got his toiletries out and readied himself for bed. He'd lie under the covers and monkey with the puck until he was too tired to think, he knew, just to keep his mind off the fact that he'd just been flirted with.

The bedside alarm woke him at eight. The puck was sitting on the pillow beside his head. Dom slowly got himself together and then, everything packed and the puck in his pocket, took the elevator down. He was early and figured he'd have to wait awhile until Jenna came down, but she was already there, coffee in hand.

She smiled and stood when he crossed the lobby, handed him the cup and pointed to the sugar packets and creamers sitting on the little side table. "I thought this would help you wake up a bit before heading to the bank."

After stirring everything in Dom took a sip, felt the caffeine shaking the numbers awake in his veins. "Ahhh," was all he could say. He smiled and leaned back in his chair, eyes closed.

"Billy, I have a question," said Jenna. "I didn't sleep much last night, I was thinking about it so much."

"Go ahead," said the shadow.

Dom opened his eyes and looked at her, curious. She seemed a little flustered, but pressed ahead without much delay. "When you were with all your other hosts, how did it feel, doing . . . personal things?"

Billy raised Dom's right eyebrow. Dom thought he could feel the beginning of a smile as well. "Personal things?"

Jenna turned red, an immediate flush from neck to hairline. "Toilet stuff, sex . . ." Her voice trailed off, and she turned to face the far wall.

Dom felt himself getting an unwanted erection, fought hard to keep it down. He started reeling off multiplication tables in his head, but the numbers remained in the distant background. Billy smiled, whether as a way of placating Jenna or at Dom's predicament, he didn't know. Probably both.

"We had different ways of handling it," said Billy. "Some of my hosts didn't much care for sharing the space, even though it was usually their choice that I was present. Those ones usually tried to force me under whenever they were engaged in their toilette. Or, more rarely," he added after a brief pause, "in carnal relations."

"Why more rarely?"

"This is a lonely calling, the life of a numerate. Most of us, alive or dead, don't go out of our way to interact with other people, aside from those we need to." Here he lifted his hand and pointed to himself. "Or those we choose to, as when we end up getting involved in acquiring more mojo."

"Did any of your hosts sleep with someone who was aware of what they were?"

Billy sat quiet for a long moment. Dom was up to multiplying together two sets of five digit numbers now, trying to get the part of his mind that was not paying attention to the numbers to focus on drinking coffee and fiddling with the puck. "None I can recall," Billy finally answered. He smiled again. "Why?"

Dom stood, downed the rest of the coffee and marched over to toss it in the garbage can. "Time to go if we're going to make it to the bank," he announced over his shoulder and headed out the door without looking to see if Jenna followed.

"Time for a cold shower," said Billy in a whisper.

"You fucker," responded Dom, voice equally low. "She's a good looking girl, but—" He stopped talking as Jenna caught up. Maybe this would all be forgotten later and he wouldn't have to talk or think about it anymore.

Fat chance.

They got to the car and threw their bags in the back, then

climbed in, Dom behind the wheel. The bank was downtown, a short trip across the river, over a low-lying metal bridge that sat near a power plant and small but pleasant baseball park. He parked the car in front of the bank, plugged the meter, but before going in he led the way to another mailbox, performed the same routine he had in Bozeman, and soon had a new piece of ID.

The banker didn't immediately recognize him this time, but smiled and nodded when he saw his new driver's license. "Mr. Donovan. Of course. Business in Florida still good, sir?"

Dom nodded. "As good as can be expected," he said as they walked back to the room with the safe deposit boxes.

This bank didn't have a separate room for viewing what was in the box, so the manager unlocked Dom's, pulled it halfway out, and then excused himself. Dom waited until the door was shut and then he pulled it the rest of the way out.

"Big on sports, aren't you?" said Billy as Dom pulled out the baseball.

Dom shrugged. "You take it where you can get it." He was going to say more when another safe deposit box jumped out from its locked and secure location and bumped hard against his hip. Jenna squealed in surprise, and Dom almost dropped the ball to the floor. He stepped back and the box slid out further, until only the smallest possible edge kept it from falling to the floor.

"Something wants to be looked at," said Billy.

Dom nodded. Rubbing the ball to keep the mojo working for him, he stepped cautiously forward and opened the box, peered inside. A small box sat there, wrapped in aged brown paper covered with formulae written by at least a dozen different hands.

"What is it?" whispered Jenna.

Dom shook his head. "I don't know. The numbers on the paper seem to be set there to protect the box inside." He reached down to tear away the paper. "Maybe if I—ow!" He pulled back his hands and put his right index finger to his mouth. "Fuckin' thing shocked me!"

"Maybe it doesn't want to be opened right now," said Billy. He took control and reached down to try again, this time lifting the package out of the safe deposit box without any trouble. The drawer slid shut on its own, a gentle current of numbers flowing from the wrapper, almost invisible to them.

Looking around to make sure he wasn't being watched, Dom tucked the ball in one pocket and the wrapped box in another. Putting on his best innocent face, he opened the door and walked out, briefly thanking the banker on the way by.

"Where to now?" asked Jenna as they approached the car.

Dom didn't have time to answer. A sharp pain exploded in his skull, and everything was black.

PART TWO

. . . unskilfull and ſlothfull men have always purſued [Mathematickes] with moſt cruell hatred . . . you ſhall (even in this regard onely) encourage me that am now almoſt ſpent with ſickneſſe, ſhortly to attempt other mattters, perhaps greater than theſe, and more worthy ſo great a Prince.
                                                                —John Napier, 1616.

He awoke to the smell of tobacco, the somewhat less pungent aroma of Canadian cigarettes. "Dom?" It took a few seconds of painful searching to recognize the voice as Jenna's. He managed to squint his eyes open, saw her looking down at him, concern written on her face.

"What the fuck happened?" His voice was a croak, harsh and distant.

"My apologies, Dom," came another voice. "My helpers got a little carried away bringing you to meet with me."

"Take this," said Jenna, holding out a plastic cup of water and two Tylenols.

Dom grabbed and swallowed the pills and tossed back the water. Then he turned to see who had spoken.

The man was small, balding, with black-rimmed glasses and a greying moustache and goatee. He wore a brown leather jacket zipped up high to his throat, and faded jeans. A pack of Du Maurier cigarettes sat on the small wooden table beside him, as well as the mysterious package and Dom's puck and ball.

"Who the hell is this? Someone else after us that you didn't tell me about?" asked Dom.

Billy shook his head, which sent a sharp pain radiating out in all directions from the base of his skull. "No. Never seen him before," he croaked, sounding as bad as Dom felt, which was of course no surprise.

"You're talking about your adversary," said the little man, stubbing out his smoke and smiling. "I'm pleased to be able to tell you that I am not a confederate of that person. Big lump on the back of your head to the contrary, Dom, I'm actually a friend."

"Some way of showing it."

The man pursed his lips. "As I noted, my helpers got a bit carried away, but they were only trying to be careful. You were walking out of that bank with a rather big prize for the wrong sort of person, and we wanted to make sure you were chosen for the right reasons. And they didn't want you hauling off and throwing numbers at them, since neither one is numerate."

"Why didn't you just ask?"

Jenna sat down on the cot beside Dom and took his hand. "Because we're being chased, Dom, and because even if we weren't, you don't much trust other people." She looked over at the man. "Father Thomas has explained quite a bit to me while you were unconscious."

"*Father* Thomas? You a priest?"

"I was." He lit another cigarette, inhaled deeply and then blew several smoke rings. "Had a little trouble and ended up being defrocked. But the Church keeps me around, on call you might say, in case my special skills are needed."

"You're numerate."

Father Thomas nodded. "And still a believer, even after all the trouble. And so I get to have you here for a little chat."

"Chat?" Dom winced. The pain wasn't going away, which made him worry he'd had a concussion.

Numbers flew from Father Thomas and swarmed around Dom's head, piling into him without warning. Dom tried to react, but the sudden sense of well-being he felt held him back.

"That's right," said the former priest. "Stay still. It looks like my boys smacked you harder than I'd first thought."

"What are you doing?" asked Dom, feeling a goofy smile creep up on his face. "Drugging me?"

"Of course not. You don't learn about healing the soul without learning something about healing the body as well," replied Father

Thomas. "Since I can't have you wandering around in a haze from a possible concussion, I'm just putting your head right again."

The numbers dissipated, too quickly for Dom to get a hold of what forms and sequences they had taken. He rubbed the back of his head, felt the still tender lump there, but was certainly much better. "Quite the trick. Thanks."

"Just call it a laying of the hands. Well, except without the hands," said the former priest, taking another puff of his cigarette. He chuckled at his own joke.

"Now that we're all friends, perhaps you can say why you dragged us here in such an undignified fashion," said Billy, sounding a bit put out.

Father Thomas smiled and stood, walked over to Dom and knelt down in front of him. "Ah, the adjunct," he said, taking another drag of his cigarette. "What's your name?"

Billy grimaced. "Billy."

"Billy. Billy what?"

Dom's shoulders shrugged. "I don't remember."

The former priest stood again and paced around the room, stubbing out his smoke before sitting back down and facing them. "I thought as much." He leaned forward and peered at Dom. "The shadow is a little confused; I'd guess that some of your memory fractioned away at one time, Billy."

Father Thomas finished his latest smoke, stubbed it out in an overflowing ashtray on the table, then grinned and clapped his hands together once. "Well. Now that we all know each other, let's get down to work. What do you say?"

Dom felt at the receding lump on the back of his head. "What sort of work?"

"Let's start with who's chasing you," said Father Thomas. "Been causing you trouble, I imagine."

"How the hell do you know all this?"

He grinned again. The smile was beginning to make Dom feel like he was in the sights of a predator. "There isn't much I don't know," he replied, "especially when it comes to the two special adjuncts that are involved with the other side of this."

"You used a plural there," said Billy. "This woman is carrying more than one shadow?"

"Two. The two most famous that are out there, I suspect."

"Jesus." Dom blinked his eyes in shock. "Napier *and* Archimedes? Together? For real?"

"Together for real." Father Thomas lit yet another cigarette, took a deep drag and then coughed violently for a few seconds. He waved the cigarette at them. "Penitence," he said. "Smoke myself to death to make up for everything I've done. Or haven't done." He half smiled now, but Dom could see the haunted look in his eyes. "Can't really stand cigarettes, but suicide is not an option for a Catholic, even an excommunicated one. Luckily, the amount I smoke really cuts down on my appetite, which helps since I spend so much on these cancer sticks." He took another puff.

Appalled though he was, Dom shook the images of no longer innocent children that sprang unwanted to his mind and pushed forward with the conversation he imagined they were supposed to be having. "You said that Napier and Archimedes were adjuncts with this woman. How can you be so sure?"

"Because I had them taken away for safekeeping in the first place. Rather, it wasn't me, but it was someone I thought I trusted." He paused for another deep drag. "You'll understand me when I tell you that I couldn't place the artefact there myself."

Dom nodded, but Jenna shook her head. "I don't. Why couldn't you? You told me something about Napier before, but I still don't think I understand."

"You're still new at this, aren't you?" He grinned again, and this time Dom saw her shudder, but she nodded her head. "John Napier was probably the most powerful numerate who ever lived, and during his time many also considered him to be involved in black magic. He was a Scottish laird, a mathematician, an inventor, and more. The reason he and Archimedes are so closely connected is that many of his inventions originally came from the mind of Archimedes, and the fact that their shadows are together tells us that he lifted them *directly* from Archimedes' mind. He's also the man who invented logarithms, which possibly you'll remember back from your days in school." He stubbed out his latest cigarette and lit up another; Dom had never seen anyone smoke so much. "The man created more mojo than anyone else, ever, items that are still being discovered today, and he probably managed to place his shadow in, at the very least, a dozen artefacts."

"Most of which have vanished into myth," said Billy.

Father Thomas shook his head. "Most of which are in a safe facility on the other side of the Atlantic. But this one made it across the ocean, chasing after a very special artefact, and no matter what we tried, we couldn't get it back across the ocean, nor could we get the other artefact across."

"So why in the desert?"

"I wish I knew," he replied. He wasn't smiling now. "The artefact couldn't be destroyed, we knew that much, but the person I sent out to do the job was supposed to take it to a place where it would not be found." He looked at Jenna, shook his head again, then carried on. "Whatever happened, the artefact wasn't about to sit around quietly. It was able to send out discreet signals that Dom picked up."

"Three people," said Dom. "I picked up Billy as backlash from a duel between his original host and the new host for Napier and Archimedes."

Father Thomas raised his eyebrows. "Really. Well, that might explain the damage that resulted in the lost memory."

Billy shook Dom's head. "I'm pretty sure I didn't have that memory when I was with my last host."

"And yet if you did, perhaps you wouldn't remember. Correct?"

Reluctantly, Billy nodded. Dom could tell that the shadow didn't like the idea that maybe he had only just lost who he was in the past few days.

"But the signal still only went to two, not three. The numerate who took the artefact to the desert for me disappeared for a long time, fell right off my radar, and when she came back she had gone to the desert to retrieve the artefact."

Jenna fidgeted in her chair, looking impatient. "You were going to tell me why you couldn't take the artefact yourself."

Father Thomas raised his eyebrows. "Relax, young lady. As long as you're with me, the Napier adjunct is not going to track you down." He smiled one more time, then said, "Okay. I couldn't get involved because I'm Catholic."

Jenna leaned back in her chair, looking sceptical now. "Is this a moral thing? Because I have an idea as to why you were defrocked, and I have to say that besides creeping me out, it seems to me that morals or spiritual beliefs are not anything you should be able to fall back on as an excuse right now."

Father Thomas snorted with laughter, a laugh that quickly descended into more hacking and coughing. When he finally got it under control he had tears in his eyes, which he swiped away with a sleeve. "Alas, dear Jenna, it isn't any moral stance, which as you so aptly note, I am truly unqualified to take." He inhaled, held the smoke for a few seconds before releasing it as more rings. "No, it is well and truly just because I am a Catholic. The same would hold true for any person who is baptized into the Holy Roman Church, whether or not they still officially belong."

"To say that John Napier was rabidly anti-papist would be something of an understatement," said Billy.

"Indeed. His virulent hatred of everything Roman imbued everything he created, most especially those items of numerate nature. If I so much as touched an item of his design, it would, at the very least, severely physically injure me."

"At the least?" asked Jenna.

He nodded. "More than likely, though, it would do damage that would cut right to my very soul. And if I actually tried to use the artefact and its numerate latency, then I suspect that death would be quick."

A thought occurred to Dom, and he groaned inwardly at the idea that it hadn't come to mind before. "We're not here just because we're being chased, are we?"

Father Thomas didn't smile again. Instead, the look on his face was a sober one. He picked up the box in its paper wrapper and handed it over to Dom. "This item found you," he said. "I'd like to say it was me, but it wasn't. It was the numbers on the wrapping paper, which then called me."

Dom turned the box around in his hands, looking at it more closely than before. There were subtleties, the likes of which he'd never seen before, written there, a grasp of numeracy that almost made him feel like a rank amateur.

He made to hand it back, but Father Thomas shook his head. "You have to keep it. As I said, it chose you."

"Chose me?" asked Dom. "To do what?"

"It knew that Napier's shadow has been after you. I imagine it could smell it on you, could taste it in the numbers that try to follow you. There is a particular taint to those numbers, if you know what it is you're looking for." Once again he stubbed out a smoke, lit up another.

"That still doesn't answer the question, though. Why me?"

Father Thomas pointed at the wrapped box. "Inside that paper is an artefact that needs to be moved, now that Napier's adjunct is on the loose. The numbers written into the wrapping have always protected it, but those same numbers have apparently decided that you're the people to take it to safety."

"Where is this safe place?" asked Jenna.

"Scotland," replied Father Thomas, and he grinned again.

"Scotland? Why do we need to take this back to Napier's seat? And what the hell is in this, anyhow?" He tried to tear at the paper, and although it didn't shock him this time, the numbers written there congealed under his fingernails, rebuffed any attempt to rip it open. "Damn it, I've never seen numbers like these."

"You won't open it," said Father Thomas. "Not unless the numbers let you."

"You make it sound like the numbers are alive," said Jenna.

Before the former priest could answer, Dom said, "So we take this to Scotland because the Napier artefact from the desert can't cross the ocean."

Father Thomas shook his head. "No, I said that *we* couldn't take it across the ocean. I suspect now that there is a new host, they won't have any trouble crossing over."

"Then why should we be the ones?" asked Billy. "And you still haven't told us why it needs to go to Scotland."

"Because Napier is pissed off with you, and he is going to hunt you down no matter where you go. Because no matter how strong you are, and I can see that you are quite the talent, there's no way you'll be able to handle an already strong numerate coupled with the two of the strongest numerates in history." He chewed on his lower lip for a few seconds. "As to why Scotland, well, now that Napier is loose, there's no way that package you're carrying will be able to go anywhere else. The numbers won't allow it."

Billy turned and looked at Jenna. "There he goes again, talking like the numbers are intelligent."

Father Thomas shrugged, but didn't say anything.

But Dom pressed on with the other concern. "And so she and her adjuncts kill us there instead of here." He was feeling angry now, partly at what he was being told, partly at the fatalism he could feel sinking into his heart. "What's the difference?"

"The difference is that when you're in Scotland there's an artefact you can use to help yourself. And who knows, if you keep getting away at the last possible second like you've apparently been doing since this trio started to chase you, even they may start to believe that it wasn't meant to be." He glanced at Jenna as he said this, then looked back to Dom.

"So what do we need to do?"

"When you leave this room, I'll have two tickets to Glasgow. I've redone the numbers on your passports, removed your numerical smell to keep your pursuer off your tail for awhile. Rent a car when you get there."

"And then?"

"And then wait for the numbers to talk to you." He took another drag, blew his smoke to the side, and leaned forward, getting his face as close to Dom's as he could. He reeked of both stale and fresh tobacco, with a background tinge of alcohol.

"What the hell do you mean, wait for the numbers to talk to me?" asked Dom, breathing through his mouth to keep the smell down.

Father Thomas smiled. "You'll have to wait and see." He took another puff and waved his hand. "I don't mean to be stupidly mysterious."

"Where do we take this thing once we're there?"

"In a perfect world, you'd land at the airport and meet a priest I sometimes work with, and then he'd take you on to a place where it can be hidden away. If we were lucky, you could even get it all the way to the Vatican where we have a secure storage facility, although you would have to keep it on your person the entire time." He exhaled two thick streams of smoke out through his nostrils. "But here is where we have the Catch-22 of this operation: you can't do that because the Napier adjunct is on your tail, but you couldn't access the artefact before now *precisely because* Napier wasn't on the loose. And, with all of that in the mix, the artefact wants to be nowhere other than Scotland."

Dom leaned forward, head in hands. "Jesus. This is sounding like a nasty little maze."

"So will we ever get this thing to this priest?" asked Jenna.

"I doubt it. In fact, I probably won't even tell him you're coming. Not because of the whole death-to-papists thing, but because of what might happen to the secure facility he runs if word got out to some who don't know about or don't believe in numeracy. The last thing we would want is for these artefacts to be unleashed on the world, or for some sap with an undetected numerate capability trying to exorcize the so-called demons."

He opened the envelope, shook the contents out onto his lap. "Here are your airline tickets. The names match your passports. I've taken the liberty of reconstituting all of the numbers on your ID, although it's all been changed to help keep Napier off your tail."

"What if I don't want to go?"

He shrugged his shoulders. "I can't make you, but I hope that the chance to escape what looks like someone trying to kill you would give you pause about anything so foolish." He squinted, looking pained by some thought. "I suppose there is something else I should tell you, even though it may make you want to stay here."

Jenna sat forward in her chair. "What's that?"

"This woman chasing after the two of you—Jenna, she was your mother."

The room around Dom suddenly began to spin wildly, numbers unimaginable in their quantities and almost unrecognizable in their form piling up everywhere, bubbling up and pouring out of everywhere as well, and now, for a moment longer than any of the others, he once again found himself looking at the world through Jenna's eyes.

"*What?*" The sound that came out of Jenna's mouth was a shriek, an agony that Dom could feel as well as hear, still somehow inside her head as he was. She stood up, the chair tumbling over backwards and travel papers scattering across the floor. Dom watched as his body jumped up as well, as Billy put out an arm in an awkward attempt to comfort her.

And then he was back in his own body once again. He shook his head to clear it of the wrongness of everything he'd seen with the numbers, then looked sharply at the former priest, not prepared to say anything right now about what had just happened to him. "You said the woman *was* her mother. What the hell does that mean?"

Father Thomas looked grim, and shook his head, and Dom realized with a start that he hadn't seen anything of the strange numbers that had appeared when Jenna had been so shocked. "Whatever happened to her, she was subsumed by the Napier adjunct long before she actually laid hands on the artefact. I didn't know it when I first met her—she was able to shield herself remarkably well, a strength there that I had never seen before."

Jenna looked up, wiped tears and snot from her face and said, "I have to stay. I need to talk to her, tell her who I am. I can convince her to stop chasing us."

"She already knows who you are," said Billy.

Jenna turned and looked at him, angry now. "How can you say such a thing?"

Billy shrugged Dom's shoulders. "I'm sorry to tell you, Jenna, I truly am, but she must have picked up your scent down in Logan, the first time you found us."

"Yeah," said Dom, twigging on. "That explains how she was able to track back at the pay phone. You're family, Jenna, any numbers you leave lying around would be easy for her to sniff out." He turned and looked back to Father Thomas. "Maybe she only wants to kill me and Billy."

"As I said, anything left of Jenna's mother has been subsumed," repeated the former priest. "Much the same as it was for Archimedes, I imagine. If Napier was too strong for her to resist when he was just a shadow in a distant artefact, then there is no way that she is able to fend him off when he occupies her body. She's a puppet, a powerful numerate pulled into a close orbit around one who is even more powerful. She won't escape, and she won't ever be the mother you once knew."

Jenna sank down to the floor, body heaving with quiet sobs. Dom knelt down and cautiously put his arm back around her shoulders. "Hey," he said, leaning in close to her right ear. "Maybe we get this thing to wherever it belongs, and Napier realizes he has to give up, cuts loose and you get your mother back."

The look she gave him was a mixture of disgust and pity. Then she managed a small smile. "That's not at all likely and you know it." She sniffed and wiped some more tears from her face, then stood back up. Dom stood beside her, unsure where to go with this. "I'll go," said Jenna. Her hands were shaking. "If my mom is going to get to know her daughter, it's as someone who stayed strong and didn't give up."

Father Thomas nodded and smiled and lit yet another smoke.

"She was the best choice, I thought. Mormon, which is so far from Catholic that she would've been safe from any little booby traps that might have been laid into it." He gave her a gentle smile, which just looked moderately rather than extremely predatory.

"Did . . . did you send her away from me and my dad?"

He shook his head. "She was gone long before we met up, following the scent of the numbers for years before I became aware of her." He shook his head, staring at the wall on the far side of the room. "Whatever hold Napier got on her must have started with that trip, but she was able to fight it off for a good three years before she had to go answer the call."

Jenna scooped up the papers that had fallen to the floor, looked them over. "Right," she said, voice barely a whisper. She looked at Dom. "What do you say we get going?"

He felt pinned against the wall, by the painful look in her eyes, by the situation, and by his fear that he would end up as some sort of strange adjunct to Jenna again. But it felt more and more like a guaranteed loss for the home team if he stuck around, and he couldn't go and abandon her now. He reached over and squeezed her hand. The rational part of him sure as hell didn't trust the former priest, but the numbers he could sense coming out of this showed that they didn't have any other alternatives, and looking at Jenna he could tell that, shocked as she was by the news, what numbers she could see seemed to tell her the same thing. He sighed. "Okay."

The former priest smiled again; to Dom's eyes, this time he looked somewhat relieved. "Your flight leaves in ten hours. We have a well-shielded car, so you'll get a ride to the airport. As well, keeping that package on your person should keep prying eyes off of you long enough."

"I have my own mojo," said Dom.

"Why, yes you do," replied Father Thomas. "However, it all carries your scent. Anyone who knows what they're looking for can eventually crawl through the cover and find you. I'd hate for that to happen while you're thirty-five thousand feet over the Atlantic, not just for the two of you but for the hundreds of others who will be sharing your flight. The packaging on that box will smear away any approaching search numbers and, I think, will also send out some false numbers every once in awhile; think of those numbers as chaff. For the moment it's your best chance of keeping safe, at least until you're in Scotland and can start taking advantage of some of the things that are built into the memory of the land there." He walked over and opened the door. "Come with me. The two of you can have a nap, then freshen up before we get you to the airport. Your flight is a red-eye."

Somehow, Dom did manage to sleep, crashed on the cot where he'd been laid out after taking the knock to the head. Jenna slept on the other cot in the room, but when Dom woke up he could hear she was already in the shower in the attached restroom. He sat up. Father Thomas was gone. On an old and ratty green couch were suitcases, already packed for the two of them. Dom investigated his, laying things out in neat little piles on the scarred pine coffee table; everything he tried on was a perfect fit. Hell, there was even a paperback novel, a thriller that he hadn't read and that looked at least marginally interesting.

When Jenna was done, he took his turn, cleaned up thoroughly in view of the upcoming long day aboard a plane. As he shampooed his hair he felt for the bump on the back of his head, but it had completely receded.

Once out of the shower and dried off, he brushed his teeth in front of the dirty mirror, spit into the cracked china sink, then said to Billy, "You've been quiet. Same thing happen to you this time?"

"The same thing?" He watched in the mirror as his forehead wrinkled into a frown. "Do you mean you ended up looking out from Jenna's eyes again?"

Dom nodded, and explained the strange, alien numbers he'd seen. Billy shook his head in response. "Very strange. And nothing I've ever heard of before. But no, it was nothing like that."

"Then what?"

His teeth clenched together. After a few seconds, Billy finally said, "I suppose I'm just a little nervous about returning to anywhere close to my homeland. Will I find something that helps me remember who I am? Will I even live to have that chance?"

"We'll keep an eye out for those numbers," said Dom.

Billy shrugged Dom's shoulders. "I know. I also worry that he knows more than he's telling about Jenna's mother. Maybe he's even lying about it, and it's a perfect stranger who's hosting Napier, although don't ask me why I might think that. Although he'd have to be pretty damn good to get those numbers to slip by all three of us." He paused, making a face into the mirror.

Dom pulled a t-shirt over his head, then started combing his hair. "So maybe he's just so used to lying that it comes naturally, no matter what happens. If that's the case, then we have to go real careful here."

"We have to be careful no matter what, Dom," replied his adjunct. "But the other side of what I'm thinking is, why would he lie? He's a priest. Shouldn't it be in him to tell the truth?"

"He's an ex-priest, Billy. Which this day and age, probably means he was diddling young altar boys or something similar." He buckled his belt, then sat on the toilet to pull on his socks and shoes. "Fucker scares me."

"Napier and Archimedes and Jenna's mother scare me even more."

Dom picked up the package from the countertop and looked at it for a second, then pocketed it in his jacket. "Point taken."

There was a knock on the door, and then in walked Father Thomas. "Ready to go catch a plane?"

The ride was quiet, a big dark blue Crown Victoria that sealed itself from the outside world very nicely. Jenna and Dom sat in the back seat, Father Thomas and a driver up front. Jenna reached over and held Dom's hand on the way out, and the two of them turned and watched the city disappear behind them. The rooms they had used had been in the basement of a church, one of the nondescript Catholic churches of the sixties that inhabited the suburbs of so many North American cities. As soon as the car had turned its first corner, taking the church from his view, Dom had forgotten exactly what it had looked like. Which, he was willing to concede, might have been the point in his case. So instead he concentrated on watching houses and apartments and strip malls go by, followed by large quantities of big box retailers as they threaded their way along busy roads leading to the airport. The numbers of commerce were thick in the air here, enough that sometimes Dom had to fight the urge to jump out of the car and go track down some easy money.

"It occurs to me that you might have some questions remaining while we drive out to the airport," said Father Thomas, turning around and hanging his left arm over the back of the seat. He had rolled his window—on a warm night thankfully—but even so the cigarette smoke was ever present.

"How did Billy's host and Dom know to look in the desert?" asked Jenna. "How did they know where they were supposed to be going?"

"It called for them," was the reply. "The artefact that held Napier and Archimedes, or perhaps even their shadows, tucked inside but still able to affect things. Over time, numbers redesigned themselves or were redesigned and went out, placing hints in various locations that are known to be frequented by numerates: libraries, museums, on the web. Probably even movie theatres and ballparks. I'm sure both Dom and Billy could tell you about the subtle trail of clues they were able to follow, but likely a lot of them looked like they'd been in place for a long time. Decades, at least, maybe even more."

Dom nodded. "The trail I found made me think the artefact had gone to Utah with the Mormons when Brigham Young had taken them out there, back in the mid-1800s." He leaned his head back and closed his eyes. "The provenance sure felt right."

"My host—*our* host—" clarified Billy, "had found hints in documents about John Wesley Powell's journey through the Grand Canyon. There were three men who left his party, somehow scaled the walls of the canyon and then went missing, perhaps killed by Shivwit Indians." He turned Dom's head and looked at Jenna. "Or else by Mormons who were feeling a bit touchy about what they call Gentiles encroaching on their nation. The papers we found showed that the artefact had been carried by them when they left the canyon."

"These were *original* documents?" asked Jenna. "Not, like, photocopies or anything?"

Dom nodded, and Billy said, "Yes. We never thought that we were being led down the garden path. For our own research, it looked as if Powell's team had brought the artefact with them, but that the only numerate was one of the three who left." He stroked his chin. "Thinking about it now, it never occurred to us to question why the numerate might have disappeared like that."

"Why did the artefact have to fake a trail at all?" asked Jenna. "Why not just make a lot of noise and get itself found right away?"

"Because then any joker with a tiny whiff of numeracy would have been able to find it," replied Dom. "But anyone able to track down the clues it left lying around would be a skilled enough numerate to make the effort worthwhile. If your shadow becomes the adjunct of someone who knows what she's doing, you're much better off than if you slide into the body and mind of some punk who can't keep his formulae straight." Dom looked out the window now, watched the farmland and light industrial parks go by. He'd forgotten how far the airport was from the city here. "Jesus," he said. "That's quite the trick, numbers coming up from shadows buried for ages in an artefact. I knew they were strong, but . . ." He left the rest hanging, fingering the package inside his coat pocket. Suddenly, Scotland looked better than ever, provided this little piece of mysterious mojo got them over there and in one piece.

They pulled off the highway, drove down the long lane to the airport terminal. More farmland occupied either side of the road, yellow canola flowers marching off into the distance, and some distance to the south a farmer was out on an ATV, driving along the fence line, two big golden retrievers running along behind. Cars, trucks and vans were all lined up alongside the sidewalk on the departures level, so their driver double parked and popped the trunk. Father Thomas stubbed out his latest smoke and jumped out with the two of them, leaned back in and told the driver, "Circle. I'll be about thirty minutes." Then they pulled out their bags and the three of them walked into the terminal.

"No smoking allowed in here," said Father Thomas, pulling Jenna's big wheeled suitcase along by its handle, letting her deal with her own carry-on baggage. "It's surprising how easy it is to *not* smoke. I figure by now I've probably gone through fifty thousand cigarettes." He looked at Dom. "You'd think nicotine addiction would have taken hold something fierce by now, wouldn't you? Especially when the smoker has already proven to be an addictive personality."

"You're staying away from children now, I hope," said Dom.

Father Thomas laughed, short and sharp to Dom's ears. "Right ballpark, wrong batter. No, Dom, my crime was to help cover it up when one of my brethren diddled several children. He was my best friend, and I thought I could help him deal with it outside the law." He put one hand behind his head and looked down at the floor. "Instead, he got to four more children before adding another sin to his list, nice and quiet with a running car and a garage."

"Fuck," whispered Dom. "I'm sorry."

"Yeah, well, me too. I ended up being the fall guy in all this, drummed out of the church and addicted to a lot worse than just a few packs of smokes a day. But the numerates who also have the Calling, they've been good to me. I get a good room in the basement of the church where I can smoke myself to death without fear of sin by suicide, and I even get a part-time nurse," here he gestured back to their driver, following fifteen paces behind, "to give me a regular dose of methadone, to keep the pain from the cancer from bringing me down too fast."

"This would be where we're supposed to line up," said Jenna, a deep look of agony in her eyes.

Father Thomas pulled her suitcase into place beside her. "You're not rid of me so easy," he said. "Until you're up in the air, I'm kicking around, making sure nothing happens to you."

"Like not getting on the plane?" asked Dom.

He shrugged, then nodded. "Among other things. This is an

important job you're doing. I've screwed up enough in my life. God—and that's something I've had questions about for a few good years, now—has blessed me with the opportunity to make good. You came to the city where I was sent, to the artefact that I was sent to watch, and at this moment I choose to believe that maybe Fate does exist, the hand of God rather than the serendipity of numbers."

The line went down quite quickly, and soon Jenna and Dom had their baggage checked in and were standing in the security line. Here, Father Thomas shook both their hands and stepped back. "I wish the two of you God's blessings," he said, "but I won't perform the sign of the cross, in case that gets unwanted attention. What you'll find over there is as much an unknown to me as it is to you. I hope that you are successful, and that your actions make life easier for the both of you. For the three of you." He stepped back, and when Dom last looked back, having walked through the metal detector and collected his shoulder bag, Father Thomas was still standing there, head down, fingers twitching as if he did indeed crave a cigarette.

Dom turned and he and Jenna headed for their gate, hoping without any firm belief that all their troubles were now behind them. The flight departed on time, the takeoff a little more exciting than Dom would have expected because Jenna had never flown before and squeezed his hand so tightly that he lost all feeling in his fingers. Soon enough they were high above the prairie, watching the towns light up in answer to the night sky, and the stars overhead responding with their own lights.

After watching out the window for awhile, the two of them leaned their seats back. Jenna turned around, lifted the arm rest between them, and snuggled up against Dom. He put his arm around her shoulder and nuzzled the top of her head, enjoying the sensation of having her so close. She smelled soft and a little fruity, he imagined from the shampoo she'd used; he closed his eyes and inhaled more deeply.

They sat like that for almost half an hour, eyes closed, and Dom was sure by the feel of her steady breathing that Jenna was asleep. But then she spoke. "Dom?"

He opened his eyes, looked down. She hadn't moved. "Mm?"

"I've been thinking a lot about this the past day or two, and I figured I'd better tell you now."

He grinned. "Yeah?" A day or two ago he would've been unable to follow through with where he thought this conversation was going, unwilling to deal with having Billy in his head and listening in. But having held Jenna in his arms for this past little while, he suddenly found that any concern had evaporated. She extricated herself, sat up and looked him in the eye. "I really like you," she said. "Even though what you do and what you are seem to equate with being a thief, you seem to be a good guy. And you've been there for me. But . . ."

Dom felt his grin fall from his mouth. He didn't want to hear the rest of this, he was pretty sure.

"I'm pretty freaked out by Billy being inside you," she continued, after a brief pause, looking like she was collecting her thoughts. "I thought maybe I could get over it, but right now there are too many other things happening for me to even consider it."

Realization struck Dom like an ice cold hammer and he could feel his face turn into a mask of distant acceptance, whether his own or Billy's, he wasn't sure. "I see." Where the hell could he slink away and hide when he was stuck here on this goddamn flight with her?

She made a face. "I'm sorry. 'Just friends' is a lousy line to hear. But right now, friends is all I can do, all right? Even more now with the news about my mother."

Dom scared up a smile, but his heart was pounding. And yet all his extremities were numb, as was his brain. "All right. Better than just sensei and grasshopper after everything we've been through, I guess." She looked confused. "Teacher and student," he clarified.

Jenna nodded, then leaned into him again. "I'm glad that's taken care of," she said, snuggling in close. "Now I can sleep."

Dom stroked her hair, head leaned back, looking at the ceiling. On the screen on the seat rest in front of him a particularly bad movie played out in silence, punctuated by the occasional chuckles of those who were still awake and willing to be amused by such things. When her breathing turned to the steady rhythm of sleep, Billy said, "Not exactly what you were hoping for."

Dom grunted. He'd been feeling sleep coming on as well, but obviously his physical state did not necessarily equate with the adjunct's. "Does that mean you weren't hoping?"

His shoulders shrugged, a movement which caused Jenna to stir and mumble. They waited, but she remained asleep. "I guess the best answer is that you have to remember that I'm a shadow, not the real thing. Yes, I—we—exist, partaking of the things that your body does, but that's only because we are a part of you. Not a whole. An adjunct's single goal is to find the artefact that will enable it, me, us, to return to a physical state. Back to life, where we *can* enjoy the discomfort of an erection that must go unattended." Dom definitely heard a note of dry humour there.

"So you don't need to eat, or if I do eat, you don't get any satisfaction out of it?"

His head shook. "I know when you need to eat, sleep, piss, whatever. If I hadn't, I never would have got you through the blackout period down in Utah. But it doesn't affect me in any fashion. I can feel numbers, and the need to find a way to life. Sometimes that means that I have to leave a dying body and move on to a living one, and so I do."

Dom laughed quietly. "You make it sound like you're some kind of virus."

Billy was silent for a few seconds. "I never thought of it that way before, but you know, it makes a strange sort of sense."

"How so?"

"Well, think about how numerates go about discovering what's out there for them to use. Sometimes, obviously, numbers will speak to a numerate in a way that leads them down a path of curiosity."

"One that usually serves to fuck up any private lives they may have," added Dom. Jenna had slid all the way down, and her head was now in his lap. He absentmindedly stroked her hair as they talked.

"Point taken. But then the numbers can only take the innocent newcomer so far, right?"

Dom nodded, watched as a flight attendant walked by to answer a call from somewhere behind him. The crappy movie was still playing.

"So think about it, Dom. How do you find out about mojo and artefacts that are out there?"

Dom frowned. "Read about them. Find clues in places. Sometimes I just know they're going to be there, like the two McGwire home run balls."

"Two?"

"Yeah. Never told you, but that's the other one I grabbed in Edmonton. It's not as powerful as the first, but that one got fried in the backlash in Utah."

"Right. Well, back to artefacts. In lots of cases, you read about these things. Find them in libraries, antiquarian bookstores, places like that."

"I do," said Dom, nodding.

"So my question, then, is where do these clues come from? What causes them to show up in these books, in whatever sources they appear?"

Dom thought for a few seconds, but could only find the answer he'd always had. "People put them there. Numerates from the past, writing for future generations to see, proud of their discoveries, or maybe so that their own shadows can track them down decades or centuries later. Or non-numerates, just fascinated by a little piece of history that they don't realize has other significance."

Billy smiled, shook his head. "All answers that occurred to me, but every one of those is too simple an answer, Dom!" He sounded excited now, like a college professor lecturing on an especially salient point of logic that the class kept missing. "Think about it. When we were down in the desert, searching for an artefact that we knew was there, we had no idea what it looked like or exactly what it did. We were there because of numbers and shadows. If I understand correctly, the artefact we were seeking had numbers that were set to put out a call, do something to advertise its presence down there. And not only to let us know it was there, but to make up at least two different stories about how the artefact got there." He paused and scratched Dom's chin. "Or, to take it even a step further, the numbers that held the shadows of Napier and Archimedes somehow kept those shadows self-aware, even without a shell—a body—to carry them, and it was the shadows that sent out the call."

Dom shook his head. "Jesus, Billy. I'll accept that we're in the middle of numeracy like we've never experienced before, much less read about, but I can't buy where you're going with this. I mean, are the shadows in control? Hell, are the *numbers* in control? Don't even bother with a warm body now, just let a bunch of magic integers 'n' shit do the job." He paused to watch a flight attendant walk by. "I'll grant that what we saw was far beyond what we've come to expect from artefacts, but I still think any sufficiently strong numerate would be able to place the numbers to make it all happen."

Billy shrugged Dom's shoulders. "I don't know, Dom. I've been around a whole lot longer than you and never before witnessed a numerate that capable. I suppose if anyone could, though, it would have been Napier." He paused, and Dom let the silence hang, feeling that Billy was just searching for more words. "I'm willing to bet that in most cases adjuncts dropped clues while with a host, but I'm just as sure that there were times when they didn't, when they needed to place hints and were without corporeal assistance."

"Then I'll repeat my question: who's in control, the shadows or the numbers?"

"That, my friend and host, is a very good question. It's going to take a lot more thought, and we're going to have to find some way to empirically test this. Provided it's something we really want an answer for."

An idea occurred to Dom. "So if the numbers are in control, is that maybe an explanation why I keep finding myself looking at the world from Jenna's eyes?"

Billy shrugged Dom's shoulders. "I still have no idea why that's happening, assuming that it really is and you haven't imagined it."

"I haven't—" Dom stopped himself before he caught the attention of everyone around them and before he woke up Jenna. Voice quieter and more in control, he tried again. "I haven't imagined any of it, dammit."

"What I don't understand, then, is how this can happen without me being a part of the process, or at the very least without me seeing some telltale numbers that show what's happened. But there's been nothing of the sort."

Dom closed his eyes. "I don't have any answers. All I know is it's for real." He leaned back in his seat, felt sleep sneaking up on him. "Don't want to talk about it right now," he managed to mutter, and soon his surroundings faded away. His visions as he drifted off alternated between Jenna naked and numbers in books, beckoning to him, pages flipping so fast that they eventually turned into whirling vortices of numbers like the ones that had sought them out just the other day in southern Alberta.

The disadvantage of having been tucked away for so many years and centuries was that he had no idea how things in this world worked. Yes, with only a little effort and time he could convince the numbers to show him the mechanisms involved, but that didn't allow for the required cultural mores that might be needed; there were certain behaviours that numbers were likely incapable of demonstrating, were perhaps completely unaware of. And with all of his focus on the search, he couldn't spend the necessary time and resources deflecting unwanted attention, from ordinary people or from the gaze of some passing numerate.

The other problem was that he had no idea if he was complete. The shadow he had created was, to the best of his knowledge, the same now as it had been centuries before when he had hidden it away, and he knew who he was and had shown that he had all the power he remembered having, but that didn't preclude something having gone wrong with the transfer, with the source material, or just having faded away over time. There was less he could do about that, though. Instead, he resolved that once he was done he would track down all other adjunct formulae he had placed, take them all in and create the whole from the portions.

It took some effort to admit that help was needed, but eventually he dug down and allowed Ruth to come back up. As he expected, she immediately tried to wrest back control of her body and mind, but any move she attempted was easily parried, and after a few moments of bemusedly casting aside her efforts, he finally clamped down.

Ruth was still up front with him, but only enough of her to allow for the basic needs, including using her voice to speak for them, albeit with his words.

"We'll work together now, shall we?"

She was quiet for a moment before finally nodding her head. "All right."

He grinned. "Better. Stay on my good side and the rewards are many, once we've accomplished our goal."

He could sense her confusion at this. "Your goal? I would have thought that bringing your adjunct back was the goal. You have something else you plan to do?"

He nodded. "I do. Two things, as a matter of fact. The first step is to retrieve an artefact that is of special import to me, which, sensing what I do among the numbers today, means we will soon be taking a trip. The second goal arises from the first, and for the moment I shall leave it at that."

"A trip," Ruth said. "To where?"

He rubbed Ruth's jaw with her hand, searching for the beard he'd kept for most of his adult life. "Scotland, dear lady." He smiled. "After all these centuries buried in the deepest of slumbers, a return home is once again in the numbers for me."

They awoke on an announcement from the First Officer that food was about to be served. Dinner was mediocre chicken breast with limp green beans and a hard buttered bun, complete with plastic knife and fork, eaten in silence. And then Jenna opened the blind so they could watch the Atlantic Ocean drift by below. Dom wanted to reach out and stroke her hair again, or hold her hand. Once she turned to him with a smile, but before he could take that the wrong way she reminded him she'd never been on a plane before, and this was very exciting for her. He kept his hands at his sides.

Finally, after an excruciatingly long time, the announcement that they were soon to land in Glasgow came. Trays were collected and tables and seats put upright, the armrest between them went back down, and now Jenna did reach over and take his hand. "First landing," she said, looking at him for a second before turning to watch out the window again.

The landing was smooth, and the papers that Father Thomas had provided for them did their job as well on this end as they had on the other; both Dom and Jenna were waved through without any difficulty. More importantly, it meant that the Napier-Archimedes adjunct still had no idea where they were.

They collected their luggage and then went to rent a car. If it had been Dom's own money, he might have opted to hitchhike; he'd heard that things were expensive in the U.K., but what he was paying was robbery. Or, again, would have been robbery if it hadn't been someone else's money, in this case a Visa card that Father Thomas had supplied with his papers, to make sure that the names matched. As it was, he still decided to take the smallest vehicle, not wanting to blow his wad all in one shot.

"You've driven a standard before?" asked the girl at the desk, although it took him a second to interpret what she was saying, her accent was so thick.

He blinked. "Um. Yeah, I have. Not with my left hand, though. Or on the wrong side of the road."

She smiled and handed him the keys and his copy of the contract. "By the time you get to the motorway you'll be fine. Enjoy your stay."

His first roundabout was less than one minute after leaving the rental lot, and within seconds he, Jenna and Billy were all yelling at each other and the suddenly unfathomable street signs, Dom trying to navigate his way around the circle without hitting any other vehicles, twice remembering at the last possible second that he and every other car and truck and van out there were now driving on the left hand side of the road.

He got out of the roundabout, not quite sure he'd taken the right exit, and made his way to the first pullout he could find, parked the car, put it in neutral, pulled up the parking brake, and sat back, eyes closed. After a few seconds of silence, he whispered, "Holy crap."

Jenna snorted. He opened his left eye and looked over at her. She was trying to keep from laughing. He smiled and she completely lost it, laughing hysterically. A second later he was laughing with her, soon hard enough that tears were coming to his eyes.

When she was finally able to settle down, Jenna said, "We should have had a video camera going right then." She giggled again. "I picture all sorts of fast, frantic edits, sometimes the camera flipping on its side, even upside down, and the whole time the three of us yelling at each other, nothing but babble and lots of 'Omigods'!"

Dom wiped away some more tears. "It's like an insane movie comedy." He looked out to the road, watched the traffic go by, looking for flow, for numbers that would be able to help him handle this new way of driving. He imagined that if he hadn't just gotten off a seven-hour-plus transatlantic flight he might be more capable of handling this, but there was no getting around the exhaustion, and they had to get out on the road to wherever they were going, so he'd have to deal with it.

"Let me help," came a voice from the back seat.

"Jesus!" Dom jumped, opened his door, tried to climb out of the car, got tangled up in his still-buckled seatbelt, undid it and practically fell out onto the pavement. He stood, saw that Jenna had jumped out of her side and was looking at him and at the car with concern and fear.

Dom squinted through the back window, but at first couldn't make out anything other than the luggage that they had stored there. Then, very slowly, a figure formed, dark and indistinct. He could make out no features, but somehow Dom could tell that it was looking at him.

"We fear for your safety," said the voice, somewhat muffled from inside the car and competing against the traffic on the road at Dom's back. "Please go to the other side of your vehicle and we will come out and explain."

"We?" whispered Billy, but Dom just shut the door and walked to the passenger side of the car, stood beside a nervous-looking Jenna.

The back door didn't open, but instead gave way to a thin stream of numbers that behaved like nothing Dom had ever seen. They slid out of cracks and through the glass and fell to the ground, piled upon themselves and took on a dark visage, a swarm of gnats reinventing itself as a quasi-human shape. "Holy crap," said Dom, voice barely audible even to himself. "What the hell is this?"

Billy shook Dom's head. "I think it's a *who*, not a *what*." His voice was full of awe.

The numbers shifted, flowed together and apart, finally settled into a form that resembled the upper third of a mannequin. And then it seemed to nod. "*Who* is correct. And possibly in the plural sense." It floated around them, casting streams of numbers down to the ground, two or three flailing legs at a time sprouting from an amorphous chest to make contact with the road and curb and grass, then disappearing as others took their place.

"What do we call you?" asked Jenna.

"We have no name," replied the thing. It had become more solid, enough so that Dom figured if he kicked a rock it would bounce off rather than just sail through. "But to make everything easier, call us Arithmos."

"You're numbers," said Billy.

"That we are," said Arithmos, lurching momentarily close to Dom in order to avoid a puddle near the car.

"The package we brought over," said Dom. Now that he looked closely he could see that these were the same as the numbers that had kept him from opening the wrapping paper.

The sound of tires on gravel caught Dom's attention, and he turned to see that a police car had pulled up behind the rental. "How can I help you?" asked the officer after he got out of the car.

Jenna smiled, although Dom flinched as the cop walked right through the mass of numbers in front of them, but the man didn't notice them and the numbers just flowed around and reconstituted themselves. "No problems, officer, thank you. We were just a little messed up with our first time driving on the other side of the road."

The cop smiled in return. "Americans, are you?"

"She is," said Dom. "I'm Canadian." And then he almost winced, remembering that he right now carried a U.S. passport.

The cop's smile didn't disappear, but when he turned his attention to Dom it certainly didn't seem as bright. "Well, then, I'd suggest that you find a less busy road to practise on, and when you need to pull off you do so in a safer location."

Dom nodded. "We will, officer. Thank you."

The cop turned and started back to his car, but before he had taken four steps a sudden wind blew in, carrying with it a splash of almost horizontal rain as well as numbers that hit the ground at the cop's feet and then bounced into the air; they swirled around him for several seconds, and then settled down, an overlay of numbers on his body like he'd been dipped in honey and then rolled in an anthill, the numbers seething and boiling and jumping but not leaving him.

Dom looked for other numbers, something to grab a hold of to protect himself, but the only other ones he could see were the agglomeration that called itself Arithmos. Before he could even think of how to utilize them, though, the cop turned and spoke again, jerkily, like a puppet.

"Napier will soon set foot on the island," he said, only now his voice was thick, slurred, and almost too quiet to hear over the highway traffic. "The celebration has already started in anticipation, and will soon be here."

"Celebration?" Jenna's voice was tight and quiet. "What's happening?"

The cop, still covered by the sheen of numbers, stumbled back to his car, unwilling or unable to answer. Arithmos moved to their own car, throwing up something like an arm to beckon them. "We need to go now," said the numbers. "If you're found and not ready for it here, in Napier's homeland, you won't get away again."

Dom didn't need to be told twice. He ran around and climbed in at the same time Jenna got in the other side. Arithmos was already in the back seat, and with a quick glance back at the cop—who was now leaning against the hood of his car, gazing blankly at his windshield—Dom pulled back onto the road with only a minimal shudder and grinding of gears. "Where to?"

"Left," said Arithmos after a pause. "We go north, out of the city."

"And what was that about a celebration?" asked Billy.

"Concentrate on getting out of the city, first," answered the numbers. "We're safe for now."

As much as that statement lacked any ability to reassure Dom, he soon fell into the rhythm of driving, something that was easier to do with Arithmos riding shotgun. It was morning rush hour in Glasgow, so there was a lot of stopping and brief starting again, several lanes of vehicles kicking out exhaust, other drivers showing looks of moderate frustration, the sort of attitude taken with traffic they might live with every day, that they disliked but would have become accustomed to. Twice they passed accidents on the side of the road, once just a fender bender, the second time serious enough to require an ambulance, one of three emergency vehicles that had squeezed past them along the shoulder a half hour or so before.

But then, finally, they were free of the city, coasting north on a highway surrounded by trees. There were still lots of automobiles, but it was no longer bumper to bumper, and Dom's hand, sore from gripping the stick shift, could finally relax, as could his shoulder; he hadn't realized how tense he'd been while he'd been tied up back in Glasgow. The surrounding countryside wouldn't have looked out of place in British Columbia or Washington: lots of conifers and, now that the traffic was thinning out, the sky had clouded over and rain was beginning to fall. Dom turned on the wipers.

"Wherever we're going, will we make it there today?" asked Billy.

Dom looked at the number creature in his rearview mirror, knew that its attention was focused on him even though he could see no eyes. "We could, if we wanted to. And we still might. But the lot of you will be slapped around by jet lag pretty soon, I think. We have one stop to make first, and then when we get to Oban, if we're safe to stop there, we will, and give you a chance to sleep on a real bed."

"How long a drive do we have?"

"Less than two hours." Jenna turned on the radio and fiddled with the tuning until she found a pop station. Madonna, almost as far from numerate as a singer could get, was playing, and when she was done a thickly accented Scottish announcer came on and babbled incomprehensibly—at least to Dom's ear—for several seconds before turning them over to commercials for local businesses, unfamiliar names all. The country had been looking so familiar, and already Dom was getting used to seeing other cars driving with him on the left-hand side of the road, and then hearing Madonna had just added to the sensation of nothing having changed, but to hear the DJ and the ads, to look at the mass of numbers huddled in the back seat, he felt an even stronger sense of disconnect than he had when he'd woken up in Utah, riding a bus he'd been brought to by a previously unknown adjunct.

The rain was suddenly heavier now, a dense sheet of wet that wasn't so much falling as it was skidding from somewhere over the horizon, scribing a line that was almost exactly parallel with the ground. Alongside the road, trees whipped and flapped in the furious wind, and Dom needed two hands to keep the car from bucking its way over to the ditch or into the path of another vehicle. He flipped the wipers to high speed, but they barely made a dent in the rippling waves that smeared across the windshield. Outside, other cars on his side of the road were marked only by wavering orange or red dots that seemed to be floating freely in a newly formed ocean.

"Jesus," said Dom. "This is fucking ridiculous. The wipers aren't doing jack shit." Keeping one hand tight on the wheel, he leaned forward to smear some numbers across the inside of the windshield, intending them to help keep the rain off, keep his vision clear.

Before he could call up even one number, though, there was a shimmer of darkness in the back and then Arithmos rose up on the armrest beside him, shouting "No!" Its voice now was deep and grating, rock being dragged across iron, and loud enough to send stabbing pains shooting through Dom's ears. He winced, managed to keep the one hand on the wheel while the other pulled back to cover one ear.

The numbers looked like a shadow cocking its head. "He's here."

Dom blinked. "Oh, shit. Here? Now?"

Arithmos shook its head. "No, he hasn't found us yet. But this is the celebration you had asked about. This weather we're seeing is a welcome for Napier. Certain elements of the numerate ecology of Scotland are, to put it bluntly, allies of John Napier. But right now, in this car, you're safe from detection, as long as you don't perform any numeracy on or in the car."

Dom glanced over, saw that Jenna was watching the road ahead of them, a bleak look on her face. "How do we stand a chance if even the weather is on his side—*her* side?" she asked. Outside, he saw that vicious-looking numbers now slapped up against the car, blown there by the wind or caught as they sped along the highway, but any that touched the windshield or the side windows slid right off, unable to find purchase. Arithmos seemed to be right about them staying safe.

"For every friend, Napier had an enemy," said the numbers. "For all his power some four hundred years ago, there was much that John Napier couldn't do, because of all the forces that were aligned against him."

"So what's different now?" asked Dom.

Arithmos disappeared, rose up again in the back seat. "Many of those enemies are no longer alive, and the vast majority of those don't exist even as adjuncts. The numbers that took his side, meanwhile, have had all the ensuing centuries to build and multiply, to push aside the numbers that had fought his existence." Their strange passenger leaned back and seemed to look out the window.

"The numbers really are intelligent," whispered Billy.

The sound that came from Arithmos was hoarse and scratchy; Dom chose to interpret it as a chuckle. "Facts sometimes take a long time to sink in with humans."

"Wait a minute," said Jenna. "Did you have anything to do with the help we got when we were in the States?"

"If by 'you' you mean numbers, then the answer is yes," replied Arithmos. "When it became apparent you would need passports to take you across the border, we created them."

"How did you know we would end up in Edmonton, where the package was?"

"We didn't. The package followed you."

Dom shook his head. "Jesus. If I'm that easy to track, no wonder Napier hasn't had any trouble keeping on my tail."

"That's not strictly the case, Dom," said Arithmos. "Any time you use numbers you're involving us. We're with you every step of the way. Therefore, it's no problem to move things into place so that you find them." The car was buffeted by one more blast of wind and then things calmed down. "Ah," said the numbers. "It's breaking up. The cheering is over, and now the hunt truly begins anew."

Sure enough, the rain was less heavy, and off towards the horizon Dom could see that blue sky was peeking through in several places. The numbers that had been slapping up against the invisible shield that surrounded the car had all but disappeared, a few straggling formulae flapping like tattered flags from the antenna and the windshield wipers, but that was it, and less than a minute after the change in weather they had snapped loose and been flung away into the distance.

The first numbers from his homeland found their way to him two hours out. Many miles above the Atlantic, flying at immense speed, Napier had spent the first hour or two of this new style of voyage shut away from the outside, allowing the woman to put on the front, giving her enough autonomy to keep her body and his mind from dissolving into a weeping, helpless ball at the very thought of where he was and what he was doing.

But eventually he was able to shake off the paralyzing fear. Before climbing into the airplane, Ruth, his host, had reassured him that this mode of travel was very common these days, and much safer statistically than many other modes. Talk of statistics had intrigued him, of course, and a thorough examination of the numbers involved in the operation of this airplane had offered some reassurance, but all of that had lasted only as long as they had been on the ground. As soon as the thunder had started and Ruth's body had been shoved back in their seat Napier had cut himself off and hid, too terrified to experience what was happening, too terrified to admit it out loud, even though both his hostess and the other shadow he carried with him would have no doubt.

But now, smoothly sailing through the upper reaches of the atmosphere, surely higher than the Greeks had ever imagined Icarus to have flown (*True*, came the thought from the other shadow, himself also terrified at the thought of where they were and the speed at which they travelled), Napier had come out of the shell where he had hid himself, and quietly had begun to seek out any numbers he might recognize. At first there was nothing, and he knew he shouldn't be surprised. This high up must be something of a desert for the numbers, he guessed, with only cast-offs from these flights through the sky and the odd lost number unable to find its way home being the only fragments of a population.

But eventually, a small set of integers had slapped against the window where Napier sat and had hung on, parts of it flapping uncontrollably in the freezing hurricane from which he was separated by only a thin layer of metal and glass. He put his hand against the window and, after a moment or two in which the numbers seemed unsure about what to do, they jumped the barrier and became a part of him.

Almost instantaneously they jumped from him again and raced up and down the aisle, two times each from back to front, and then disappeared from his view, storming back towards Scotland at a pace that made the airplane seem no faster and no more powerful than a simple horse and carriage. A piece of Napier went with those numbers, and very shortly he and they had made contact with other numbers, and almost before he knew it there was a firestorm of activity and celebration in the ecology. Everywhere around him in and outside the airplane there were suddenly numbers of all types, sounding the trumpets as it were, almost gleeful that he, John Napier of Merchistoun and rightful heir to all that the numbers could give him, was soon to be back on his rightful soil.

The seat of his power, the place where he could not fail in his search.

Slow down," said Arithmos. "Coming up soon there should be a sign for Seil Island. Take that turn and follow the road."

About two minutes later Dom passed the sign. He flicked on his left-turn signal and turned in, then followed a small road that was surrounded by trees and farms. Soon they were at a bridge, a stone structure that crossed a small body of water no wider than eighty feet, the bridge a single high arch. Underneath the bridge was a small green patchy-looking motorboat, heading south, one person on board using one hand to steer the motor and the other to bail out the boat, regular sweeping motions casting a fair amount of water over the edge, enough to make Dom wonder how the craft stayed afloat.

"The Bridge Over the Atlantic, the locals call it," said the numbers in the back seat. "It's been a problem ever since it was built, back at the end of the eighteenth century."

"Problem?"

"Made it too easy to come across," answered Arithmos. "Things stay hidden easier when fewer people can stumble across them. Cross the bridge and follow the road south. We're almost there."

"Right." Dom put the car back in gear, waited for another car to come his way across the single track lane on the bridge, then did as he was told. More trees, more farms, a few other buildings.

Parked in a small lot on the island side of the bridge were two large tour buses, several dozen soggy seniors milling about in a parking lot, checking out two small buildings that were likely tourist traps of some sort. As the rain began to let up, others spilled from their buses and walked as quickly as they could to the bridge, looking anxious to cross it on foot before the rain returned.

A couple more terse directions from Arithmos, and then he had Dom park the car on the side of the road, directly below an old grey stone church that was perched high on a bluff. They climbed out, the numbers sliding through the rear window and standing beside Dom. "Right," said Arithmos. "Follow the road below, leading to that farm in the distance."

"We're going to a farm?" asked Jenna.

"Deeper. The road to the farm is only to lead you in, and to fend off the mildly curious."

Dom and Jenna followed the road down, passed one driveway into one farm, kept going until they were near to another. "We turn right here," said Arithmos.

Dom looked. To their right was a barbed wire fence, several cows standing on the other side, watching them with the usual mild disinterest of domestic farm animals.

He turned around and looked to their approach. The car sat below the bluff, the three stained glass windows of the church sparkling, the sun finally having broken through completely. Sheep sat further up the hill, behind a fence towards the car, most of them calmly grazing, but one big ram, with immense curled horns and testicles hanging down practically to the ground, stood on a rock and watched them, keen eyes seeming to study every move Dom made. "I don't like the way he's watching me," said Dom, staring back.

"It's not you," said Arithmos. "It's me. That old fellow isn't like what most folk expect of domestic sheep; he can sense my presence, and wants to protect his harem. Let's move on before he gets so anxious he keels over from a heart attack."

Dom and Jenna walked over to the fence. There were small wooden steps built into a fence post to make passage over the wire easier. "Aren't we trespassing?"

As soon as they'd crossed into the pasture the cows had spooked and run to the most distant point they could find. "Private property is a little different here than you might be used to, Dom. And we have had an agreement with the landholders for centuries, now. I also understand that this place has become something like a park, although the amount of visitors is kept down, numbers that stay and help make it a little less visible. Even if you have a map, those that are laid out here mean it's an easy place to get lost in."

"Numbers have an agreement with the people who live here?" asked Jenna.

The mass of numbers shifted, a shrug. "We work through others when needed."

They crossed the pasture, then climbed over another fence to a path, the road still in view to the right. It wasn't too hardscrabble, but there were a few rocks and holes to avoid. By now the clouds had been banished from horizon to horizon, and Dom paused for a moment, took off his jacket and tied it around his waist. Jenna did the same.

"No traffic," said Jenna, as she pulled the knot tight. She was right; the road had been without a single car since they had gotten past the bridge.

"There are other reasons tourists come here besides the bridge," said Arithmos. "But that's the main one. Perhaps today the storm and the numbers that accompanied it convinced many to do other things. Here," it said, thrusting an appendage to the left. "Follow the path into these trees."

The change was almost immediate. Where they had been in a farmer's field that could have passed for one almost anywhere in North America, now they were in a wood that looked like every magical forest from a fairy tale. It was old, so very old, and it seemed to breathe on its own. The numbers here were flat and low to the ground, dwellers of the forest floor that somehow couldn't reach up and escape from the branches of the trees that bent over to look down on them.

"Welcome to the Ballachuan Hazelwood," said Arithmos, voice barely a whisper.

The trees were low, stunted, and gnarled, branches spreading out like slender fingers of an arthritic, many-handed giant. Branches and trunks alike were covered by mosses and lichens, and it seemed to Dom's eye to be a different species not only for each tree but even for each branch. Like elderly spinsters at a society ball, each tree wore its jacket of lichen proudly, unashamed of the tattered look of their coats, each fiercely proud of the latest fashion it could muster and acutely aware that its glory days had long since passed.

Billy gently cleared Dom's throat, then spoke:

"Hear the voice of the Bard!

"Who Present, Past, & Future sees;

"Whose ears have heard

"The Holy Word

"That walk'd among the ancient trees!"

"That's a poem," whispered Dom, feeling the meter as Billy spoke it. "What's it from?"

His shoulders shrugged. "I don't know. A distant memory, one that somehow felt right for the moment."

"Well, if we get a chance, when we're all done we'll try and find it. Maybe it's a clue as to who you really are." Jenna grabbed Dom's arm and pointed. A small animal was walking through the undergrowth, but at best Dom could only see a dim shadow as it moved, more aware of its progress by how the trees seemed to defer to it than by its actual presence. The last two trees seemed to bow down, blocking their view of whatever was approaching them.

Then Dom and Jenna slowly stepped forward, swept the weathered branches out of the way. "Jesus," whispered Dom.

In front of them stood a badger, staring calmly into Dom's eyes. Leaves on the trees trembled for a moment, even without a breeze, and then settled.

"This animal is a familiar for this part of your journey while in the land of Napier," said Arithmos. "The numbers that live here are old, senile, and therefore ill-equipped to carry the memory of what has been placed here. And before we were placed in the package that went to America, we were given only enough information to take you to your first stop."

"So this badger is to help us?" asked Billy.

"The numbers here may be ancient and tired," replied Arithmos. "But they are more than enough to hide something if needed, completely unable to be enticed or forced to reveal that same item, or to work in any way with a numerate."

"Ancient and tired?" Jenna knelt down and touched some numbers poking out from beneath the undergrowth. They made a feeble effort to slide away from her, but unlike other numbers couldn't get away, and were all bent and warped in odd fashions.

As she did this, Dom again found himself looking through her eyes. Just as quickly, he was back in his own body, but before he could say anything, Arithmos spoke again.

"You might say they're senile. A good numerate can still call upon them, but we doubt even Napier would be able to compel them to do what he wanted for more than a few seconds."

"So how does the badger fit in?" asked Dom.

As if in answer, the animal walked past them and, with one glance over its shoulder to make sure they followed, picked a path through the raggedy ancient forest. Dom and Jenna both had to duck low many times, dodging limbs and lichens and pale numbers all.

After only two or three minutes they arrived at a copse of trees that, if anything, looked older than all the others. The badger nosed at the base of one tree, then sat back on its haunches.

"Your turn now, Dom," said Arithmos.

Dom raised an eyebrow. "What? I'm supposed to sniff the tree?"

"Just touch it." Arithmos said this with a hint of impatience. "That's the tree the badger has picked out, so the next move is yours."

Dom stepped around the unmoving badger and reached down, touched the same spot where the animal's nose had touched. The trees all around shifted at the contact, and now as Dom looked up he saw the last shred of blue sky covered by green. The trees were no longer shrunken and low, instead stretched as high as they possibly could, creating a green vault with reaching, arthritic limbs. He could hear their groans as they did so, could see numbers the likes of which he'd never seen drifting from the branches and falling to the ground like a gentle shower of leaves in an autumn breeze.

The ground spoke then, a chorus from the roots of every tree around them, a cacophony of voices climbing into the air, most of them speaking languages or dialects unrecognizable to Dom. He jumped back and looked at Jenna, but she shrugged and shook her head, and in response Billy shook his head as well. Even the scraps of words he could make out as English did nothing to tell him what was happening, what was being said.

After no more than a minute, the voices quieted. Everything was still and silent for another few seconds, and then the tree Dom and the badger had both touched creaked and groaned, and with a grinding and popping noise, its trunk split in two, from the ground or below, reaching up almost four feet high. The bark peeled back first, followed by the rest of the tree, and Dom instantly jumped back with a yelp, landing on his butt with Jenna's hand suddenly and painfully clutching his shoulder. Inside the darkness of the tree several pairs of eyes peered back out at him, curious, insistent and unblinking, reflecting green from the surrounding light, with just a hint of yellow flashing through for the briefest of moments. The weight of their gaze was heavy, but he couldn't turn his eyes away, scared as he was right now.

The badger stepped forward then, burrowed its way into the open tree and came out with something in its jaws. The trunk stood open for a moment more, and then the attention of the eyes turned from Dom and was cast downward, and with more noise, rustling of leaves and snapping and clacking of wood, the tree sealed itself whole again. Dom felt himself relax, tense shoulders finally easing down, and sensed the entire forest do the same. Sunlight returned to dapple the leaves and ground, and the branches of the trees no longer seemed bent into unnatural positions.

The badger shuffled across fallen leaves and dropped the item from its jaws to the ground in front of Dom, and with one last glance back, turned and disappeared into the forest. With a look up at Jenna and Arithmos, Dom reached down and, thumb and one finger only, delicately picked up the item.

Whatever it was, it was covered in dirt and the detritus of generations' worth of forest floor, even though it had quite plainly been stored inside the tree. Inside, something long and thin rattled. Dom went to wipe away the gunk as best he could, but Arithmos stopped him with the soft but firm touch of a numerical limb.

"It stays safe from Napier's eye as long as it remains covered, so don't clean or open it yet," said the numbers. "Pocket it safely and keep it until we gather the other two parts."

Dom tucked the cloth away as he stood up, and then he wiped off the seat of his pants. Jenna reached out and stopped him, then proceeded to slap the dirt off his rear. He smiled at her and said, "We have to do this two more times?"

"One is close by, one a little further. We'll leave the wood now."

Dom and Jenna stood still for a moment longer, just listening to the quiet of the wood. Finally, Billy said, "I suppose we should go."

Jenna nodded her head, reached over and took Dom's hand, and they walked back the way they'd come. Back on the road, Arithmos pointed up above their car. "Your next stop is the kirk."

"Kirk?"

"Church," said Billy. "Is that where the next package is?"

The numbers nodded. "We can't go in; it's consecrated territory, and we would dissipate before we set foot in the door, completely unable to retain this form. But there will be another familiar waiting for you inside."

"Consecrated?" asked Dom.

"Not like you'd imagine. It's a rite that uses numbers in order to keep certain other types of numbers out. Numbers that once upon a time were considered demons."

"Like yourself?"

"Like myself." With that, Arithmos faded from sight.

Dom looked at Jenna, and then with a shrug he walked along the road to the edge of the long driveway up to the church on the hill.

Jenna kept pace beside him without saying anything. The doors to the church were locked, but as a symbol of everything that could possibly be different between this place and home, the key was in the lock and a small sign was on the door, welcoming visitors to the church and to view the stained glass windows, and asking that they lock the door again on their way out. Feeling bemused, Dom turned the key and in they walked.

It was an old stone church, with three beautiful stained glass windows behind the pulpit, facing the road down below, and more stained glass windows on the two side walls. Unsure if he was looking for another badger or some other animal, Dom looked about the place, but there was no sign of any life.

"What do you suppose we're looking for?" asked Billy.

Dom got down on hands and knees and looked underneath the pews. Nothing, not even a bug.

He stood up, hands on hips, wondering what to do next. From behind him came a soft wheezing sound, and he turned to see Jenna asleep already on one of the pews, head back and slumped to one side.

"Hell," he whispered. "Now what?"

Billy shrugged Dom's shoulders. "Have a seat, I guess. Arithmos told us the familiar would be here and present itself to us, so we wait. And I can feel it, you're every bit as tired as Jenna."

Dom nodded and eased himself into the pew in front of her and stared at the stained glass windows until they blurred and darkened.

The sound of a door slamming shut startled him awake. Lights came on overhead, and from around the corner came a small man wearing John Lennon glasses, grey hair in a U around the back of his head, mostly bald everywhere else. He wore casual beige slacks and shirt with a blue sport coat over top, and carried a green cloth bag over one shoulder. Even through the haze of interrupted sleep, Dom could see the man wasn't surprised to find them here.

"It's after midnight," he said. "I imagine the cricks in your necks must be fierce painful by now."

Dom leaned forward, rubbed at the back of his head and his neck, silently agreeing with the little man. He stretched and twisted, trying to pop out the kinks. "We shouldn't have fallen asleep," said Jenna. She sounded worried.

"Ah, but you did," said the man. He set the bag down on the pew in front of her, pulled out a thermos and three scratched and pitted old plastic cups, poured coffee into one and handed it to her. "Cream and sugar are inside the bag," he said, then poured another cup for Dom, who took it with a grateful nod. He shuffled out of the pew and got himself some cream and sugar, took a sip and felt the heat and caffeine work its way into his system. From the corner of his eye, Dom saw that Jenna pretended to sip from the cup, a gracious gesture, but then she let it rest on the pew beside her.

"My name's Ewan Ivey," the man said as he poured himself some coffee.

"Dom. And this is Jenna."

"You've been to the Ballachuan Hazelwood."

Dom spat the sip of coffee he'd just taken back into the cup, surprised. He sank down into his seat, and Jenna came over and sat beside him. "How do you know?"

Ewan looked around him. "The kirk told me," he said. "Caught me way far away and on foot, it did, which is why it took me almost five hours to get here, as first I had to find an automobile."

"The church told you," said Dom, at the same time that Jenna asked, "We've been in here for five hours?"

Ewan nodded and took another sip. "I no longer live on the island," he said, "nor do I pay much attention to the word of God anymore. But the land around the kirk and I keep a close bond, and things that happen in the Hazelwood have always been worth noting."

"And so you came all the way back here, just because we'd been to the wood?" Something about all this didn't seem right to Dom, but so far Ewan hadn't made any overt moves against them, so he didn't know just yet how far he should let this conversation go.

Ewan smiled. "Aye."

"But why?" asked Jenna.

Ewan sat in a pew opposite them and watched Dom use his sleeve to wipe away a ring his coffee had made. "Most who are here or who have been here know nothing about what goes on in the wood below their kirk, and that has been for the best, I think most would agree."

He leaned back in the pew, took another sip of coffee. After a moment to savour the taste, he said, "You've walked out of that wood with a package. The numbers that surround this building are no friend to Napier, but they are to me."

Dom pushed the coffee cup away from him, regretting having taken a sip. "They made us sleepy," said Billy.

Ewan grinned. "They just knew what you needed most that would keep you in place until I arrived. You needed to sleep, so you slept."

Jenna looked to the door, then stood. "We have to go."

Ewan shook his head. "First you have to give me what was given to you in the Hazelwood, and then you have to show me what you were to collect in here." New numbers began to float up from Ewan, irrational numbers spinning themselves into a small, tight ball. Dom jumped, spilled his coffee over the pew in front of him, tried to squeeze by Jenna, at the same time reaching down to grasp the hockey puck and hoping to hell it would be enough to stop this guy. He felt himself rush across the floor, almost skating, and slammed into the little man, sending the ball spinning wildly out of control into a corner.

Ewan stood back up and looked around, then, not seeing Dom, turned his attention on Jenna. More numbers bubbled out of him, and a swarm of them rained down on her, pushing her back into her seat and pinning her there, even though Dom could see that most of them were missing their target. Once again Dom swung around and hit Ewan, wishing he had more knowledge of how to go on the offensive. He'd spent all his time learning how to be a sneak and how to defend himself, and until this puck had never had any mojo that took the fight to someone else. He hit Ewan again, watched the man look around in confusion, blood running from his nose. But again he stood, and this time he managed to spin up a new group of numbers and fling them in Dom's general direction.

In panicked response, Dom threw up a wall of Euclidean space between the two of them. The numbers from Ewan quickly found themselves halving the distance between the two men with each second, but the number of halves had stretched out to infinity. As long as Dom could keep that wall up between them, any numbers thrown his way would find themselves lost in forever, even as they came close enough that he could feel their metaphoric breath on his face. But the longer Dom fought to keep Euclidean space open, the longer he would go without being able to pull down any other numbers; it was likely to be an exhausting stalemate. Just then the front doors banged open, and with a couple of flickers most of the lights shut off. A shaded blur rushed across the church and slammed into Ewan, who managed one explosive whoosh of breath before he crashed into the opposite wall and dropped to the floor, blood already pooling from the back of his head.

Dom let the numbers he'd been using dissipate, stood beneath the pulpit, breathing hard from the effort. The ram they'd seen down at the farm stood in front of him, and after one loud bleat, it turned and ran from the church.

Dom turned, saw the numbers still spinning in the corner, somehow still not vanishing now that their creator was dead or unconscious. He ran over, coaxed patterns out of the chaos, cast them away to dissolve as he managed to pull out each new set of numbers, watched as they flattened themselves, reintegrated, once again became commensurate, before finally rejoining the ecology, no longer a threat.

Done there, he walked back to Jenna, careful to step around the body on the floor—Ewan did indeed appear to be dead. She was sitting up, head turned to avoid looking at Ewan's body. Her face and hands were covered with dozens of very fine cuts, each one still slowly seeping blood.

"How are you?" asked Dom.

Jenna didn't answer, although she turned to look at him. The look in her eyes was vacant, lost. She opened her mouth and blood leaked out, a giant bubble of it, bursting and dribbling down her chin.

"Jesus!" Dom sprang back, then caught himself and jumped towards her, but she seemed to come back into herself and waved him off.

"Animal," she managed to say, more blood spilling from her mouth.

"What, the ram?"

Jenna shook her head and pointed with a wavering finger at the ceiling.

Dom looked up, but in the ill-lit space of the church he could see nothing. But with everything silent, he could hear it. A rustling, followed by a couple of echoing chirps.

"A bird," said Billy. "It must be the familiar Arithmos told us about."

Dom held out his hand, and with a lazy loop through the air a small bird, about the size of a sparrow but with a reddish breast and cheeks and blue-grey crown, fluttered down and landed on Dom's finger. It pecked at his hand, two gentle taps at the web of skin between his thumb and forefinger, and then flew across the church, coming to rest on the floor in the corner behind the altar.

"I don't suppose the stone is going to part as easily as the tree did," said Dom, but when he got there he was surprised to see that indeed it had, one piece of stone bending inwards on itself and revealing another package, similar in size and shape to the other in his pocket. He picked it up and pocketed it beside the other, and the small bird immediately launched itself into the air to disappear into the shadows high above them.

"Let's get out of here." He went back to the pew and took Jenna's hand, helped her stand. She still looked stunned, but followed him out of the church with no problem, stepping around the body on the floor without looking down. There was a second car on the road below, probably Ewan's, and the cows and sheep at the farm across the road were kicking up a fuss, and lights had come on at both farms down the road.

Arithmos was waiting outside, about fifteen feet away from the door. "Get to the car as quickly as you can. We'll soon have more company."

Halfway down, Jenna stopped and leaned over, vomit and blood spilling out in the moonlight, splattering on the gravel and some splashing back onto their shoes and pants, taking heaving breaths that for a moment turned into sobs when she was done. Dom rubbed her on the back, and when she was done he helped her straighten back up and kept walking. "You okay?"

Jenna turned her head to look at him, tears in her eyes. He rubbed gently at her chin with his sleeve, managed to get the puke off, but the blood just smeared. "Fine," she mumbled. "Not too much pain." She turned her attention back to walking, and a few seconds later they were at the car.

Arithmos was already in the back seat. "Let's move," hissed the numbers as Dom helped Jenna into her seat. "We need to get off this island now."

Dom yawned as he raced down the road. He was exhausted, and not even the coffee and the recent fracas had managed to shake the cobwebs from his head. He looked over to Jenna, saw that she had leaned her head back and had closed her eyes. The bleeding seemed to have slowed, maybe even stopped.

"Who the hell was Ewan?" asked Dom.

"Nobody but a pathetic little treasure hunter," replied Arithmos. "He'd sell his grandmother for a good artefact, and apparently he knew that one was there." Here Jenna opened her eyes and looked over at Dom, but he did his best to ignore her. "We think he knew that Napier's shadow is back on native soil, and wanted in on the action. What we hadn't expected was that he would lay a trap for anyone coming into the kirk looking for the artefact."

"Why didn't you stop him?" asked Billy.

"He's a numerate. He controls numbers."

Dom nodded and turned his attention back to the road. Ahead were a set of headlights, seemingly coming straight towards him. "Lights," he said. "Looks like someone doesn't want us to get off the island."

Jenna opened her eyes and said, very quietly, "You're driving on the wrong side of the road."

"Jesus!" Dom swung the car back to the left and needlessly waved his hand as the oncoming car flashed its lights and rushed past. He lifted one hand from the wheel and rubbed at his eyes. "Wake up wake up wake up wake up," he muttered. His heart was pounding, a loud and rolling rhythm that threatened to jump out of his chest.

"I'm sure you're not the first tourist to forget what side of the road he was driving on," said Jenna. Her eyes were closed again.

"Tourist or not," said Arithmos from the back seat, "I think it would be best if you don't die in something as common as a car accident while carrying those artefacts in your pocket."

"Right," answered Dom. "Sorry. It won't happen again." They rode in silence for awhile, crossing the bridge without having to stop for any oncoming traffic, and soon enough Dom brought the car to a stop by the highway. "Which way again?"

"North," replied Arithmos. "Left."

He waited for two cars to go by and then followed them, quickly gearing up to the speed limit. Wouldn't do to be caught by the cops breaking the speed limit, not with blood all over Jenna like it was.

"Speaking of cops . . ." he whispered. Three sets of flashing lights were approaching from ahead. Two police cars and an ambulance whipped by, sirens wailing. "On their way to the island?"

Arithmos grunted. "Yes. Someone's found the body by now. We can only hope that nobody identified your car while it was parked there."

Dom frowned. "What are the chances of that?"

The numbers were silent for a moment. "Twenty-seven vehicles drove past while you were in the kirk. Chances are good at least one paid attention to your presence."

Dom signalled, then carefully drove into a pullout set beside the road, stopped and yanked up the emergency brake, but left the car running. "I know your mom has been able to follow us by zeroing in on any numbers we use, but there was no sign of her or Napier after the numbers I used back in the church."

"What are you going to do?" asked Jenna, eyes still closed.

Dom looked over at her, worried about just how badly this had all hit her. She sounded almost like a zombie right now, voice flat and barren. "I'm going to change the numbers on the plates, just enough to keep us safe."

There was silence for a moment, and then Arithmos said, "We don't disagree." He climbed out and stepped around to the front, crouched down and traced his index finger along the edges of the numbers on the plate. Above him was nothing but the night sky and overhanging trees; before he started, though, he sent up a few tentative numbers, quiet sequences that could passively search for active numbers that carried the smell of the Napier-Archimedes adjunct. After a few minutes they all fell back to earth and crawled to him to tell him the same thing, that there was nothing untoward to be found.

There were only two numbers on the front plate, along with five letters, which meant he couldn't make as big a change as he had hoped. Still, he had to do something. But when he tried to smear the 53 into a 63, the 5 resisted. 58 wouldn't work, either, so after some messing around he finally settled on 52, which looked a whole lot more amateurish, but seemed to be the only number that would take. To help it along he ran some other numbers over top, intended to redirect attention of anyone looking their way. Then he walked to the back and did the same thing with the plate there.

"Wouldn't let me change the numbers the way I would've liked," he said as he climbed back into the car.

"The plates are issued based on when they were issued," replied Arithmos. "There are few options for the numbers, so they tend to hold fast."

Dom signalled and pulled back out onto the road. Traffic was increasing, but it still didn't amount to much, and so far there were no flashing lights in his rearview mirror. "If that's all, then that's a relief. I was worried that maybe I'd lost my skills, or worse, that Napier and friends were close by and taking a hand in it again."

"You can believe that we would have given you notice if such a visit were imminent."

The rest of the drive was uneventful. Jenna kept her eyes closed, and was still enough that several times Dom got worried and reached over to touch her shoulder. Each time she just reached up with her hand to brush him off without looking at him. The cuts on her face and arms looked more like scratches now, and only once did he see blood leaking from the corner of her mouth, but she reached up and wiped it away before he could say anything, smeared it on her pants and otherwise didn't move.

Just before they reached Oban, Arithmos said, "It's a big town. Very busy, popular with the tourists. There are at least two numerates we know of who live there, and of course it is also very possible that one or more are visiting right now."

Billy turned Dom around and looked into the back seat. "So what are you saying?"

"We have ways of keeping our presence a secret, but close proximity can nullify that. So we'll leave you here, and find you again on the other side of town. Stay cautious." And with that, the numbers vanished.

Oban *was* a busy town. There were tour buses everywhere, and signs advertising ferry trips to a variety of islands showed one of the reasons why the town was so central for tourists. There also seemed to be plenty of shopping, and all of it looked like it was along the main drag through town, so progress was very slow, on a road only two lanes wide, with plenty of pedestrians dashing across in front of vehicles to see a store or a friend on the other side of the road, or else a car up ahead stopping and waiting for a perceived parking opportunity. Dom did his best to stay patient, drumming a quiet tattoo on the steering wheel with his fingers and watching numbers float by, looking for anything special. And there was; yes, he could see the usual numerical ecology one saw in busy towns everywhere, but there were some signs to be seen that this place was different than most he'd visited before.

The numbers took on a different layering here, the way rational and irrational numbers behaved with each other and with the formulae that they sometimes created before his eyes, little bits of evolution that sometimes took, sometimes didn't, numbers finding themselves in an untenable situation and fraying and untwisting almost immediately after combining, drifting off to find other numbers that matched better, or perhaps to just remain lone integers, destined for who knew what part of the world.

Dom imagined that the differences he saw were due to the age of the town itself. He had been in some small old towns in New England in the States and the Maritimes in Canada, and it had indeed seemed that the houses there carried a different sense of numerical history than the more recent communities that he was used to. Here, the buildings were older than anything he normally saw, and not just one, but pretty much all of them, marching along the street, squeezed tight against each other, stone and brick and wood, every one of them covered in a sheen of numbers that looked to have been there since the day they'd been built, content to stay in place, it seemed, rather than venturing off and joining the rest of their kind in the world at large.

Dom smiled to himself, and from beside him, Jenna said, "What?"

He turned and looked at her in surprise. Her eyes were open, and she was sitting up again. There was still a hint of blood on her chin, but it looked to have dried, so Dom fought the urge to wipe it away; it was something she could take care of later. "You're awake," he said.

"Why were you smiling?"

Dom shook his head, looked back to the traffic in time to tap his brakes and keep from denting the bumper in front. "Just realizing once again that the numbers around us really do seem to be living things."

"You'd think that the presence of Arithmos would have settled that for you some time ago," responded Billy. "But I have to say we've certainly seen numbers behave in ways I've never seen before. Centuries around them, and until I tied myself to you, Dom, I'd never seen numbers act with a semblance of free will." Dom raised an eyebrow and looked at himself in the rearview mirror. "Never?"

Billy shook Dom's head in response. "Never. At best, any autonomy given to numbers was laid in by the numerate who had given them their goal, their marching orders. The better the numerate, the more the numbers could bend to the situation and continue their work."

"Like the numbers back in America and Canada, the ones that kept chasing us," said Jenna.

Billy nodded. "Exactly. Most numerates keep the numbers close at hand, do their little magic tricks with something that is right there. These ones, though, Napier was able to create sequences and formulae that jumped through a whole series of difficult hoops from a very long distance away."

"But even then, they didn't seem to operate as intelligent beings," replied Dom. "Maybe as smart as hounds on the trail of an escaped convict, but nothing like we've seen with Arithmos." The conversation petered off as each of them retreated into their own thoughts. They finally drove past the last part of downtown, and although they were still in Oban, the traffic opened up now, and within minutes they were on the other side of town and moving along at a reasonable pace once again. Dom felt himself relax, happy that no cops had gotten to them while they were stuck in a position that would have been impossible to wriggle out of.

"I'm back," said Arithmos.

Jenna turned around and faced the numerical being. "I've been wondering, where did your name come from?" she asked. "What does it mean?"

"It's Greek," answered Billy. "Same root as arithmetic."

"The built-in properties of numbers and their ratios, and how they relate to the universe around us. But it means more than that. It's the word that your kind once used when referring to the life that numbers had taken on."

"Alive like you're alive?" asked Dom. "Sentient?"

"More so the ecology of numbers, the idea that the surrounding world of numbers was alive in a way very similar to the biodiversity of this world. Although we know that there are humans who have entertained the idea that numbers have become alive *because* of how we've been used by numerates."

"So we've helped you evolve?" asked Jenna.

"Perhaps," said Arithmos. "If so, though, it seems to be very restricted in time and place. We show some autonomy in other lands, but the properties of the British Isles, as well as a few other select locations on the planet, allow us to come together and think on our own, such as you see me now." The numerical creature paused for a moment, as if to roll around some thoughts, then carried on. "Think about search numbers. There was a time when numerates would send out such things, but they were always brute force, simple. Somewhere along the way, though, the number patterns became not only more sophisticated, but able to make adjustments in midstream. Not the way we were originally designed, but this elegance allowed us to show at least a modicum of intelligence and adaptability."

"Intelligence and adaptability are not the same," said Billy. "Animals adapt, right down to insects and lower. That doesn't mean they're smart."

"In the end, you'll have to take our presence as the best argument available. But think about what you just said. We are *numbers*, things that should, by all rights in your logical world, be figments, metaphors. And yet not only are people like you able to make us perform for you, we numbers show traits that, at the very least—the *very* least, let us stress—equate us with living things. Numbers who know when to congregate, when to separate, can make decisions based on contingencies that our creator likely could not foresee."

Dom thought about the search numbers in Utah, behaving like a flock of crows, finding new places to circle, and about the numbers in Drumheller, climbing out from the drain, losing whatever had helped them stay coherent, and yet still struggling to find their way up and out. And these numbers in a place that Arithmos argued was *not* conducive to numbers behaving independently and intelligently. He'd not ever seen numbers so adaptable before.

"It's quite the moral quandary," said Billy, interrupting the silence.

"How so?" asked Dom, but before Billy could reply, the numbers in the back seat said, "Ah, someone is beginning to understand."

"Jesus." Dom drummed his fingers on the steering wheel, feeling impatient. "Understand what, exactly?"

"I think I get it," said Jenna, nodding her head.

But before Dom could explode with the frustration of being the only one left out of the loop, what was being said crystallized in his head. "Oh. Wait. If the numbers are self-aware, and we're controlling them, then . . ." He let the thought fall away, unwilling to vocalize it.

"It's just another form of slavery, maybe," said Jenna. She didn't look happy.

"*Not* the word I was going to use." Dom signalled, pulled out into the opposing lane to pass a small, slow RV from Belgium. He gunned the motor to swing back into the proper lane before a car coming at speed around the bend did them all in, then tried to find the words to finish his thought. "Look. We don't, or at least most of us don't, talk about chickens and cows and pigs and other farm animals as slaves, do we? So even if I grant that the numbers I use are sentient, that doesn't mean that I'm enslaving them, especially since I cut them loose after I finish using them."

"Chickens and cows and pigs aren't self-aware like humans, Dom," replied Jenna. "They're alive, but their concept of self is very different from our own, if they have one at all. And numbers trying to crawl out of a sewer in the Alberta Badlands says nothing to me about self-awareness. Arithmos here seems the exception, not the rule. There have been numbers all over the landscape here, and none but this conglomeration sitting behind me and lecturing me have shown any hint of self-awareness."

"I would suggest to you that there is no way anyone, no matter how powerful, could predict that the numbers would need to attempt to do such a thing to continue the task that was put to them," said Billy. "What a person of such power *might* be able to do, though, is cajole, maybe even frighten, those numbers into continuing their task well after it would have been a reasonable decision to back off."

"As much as we appreciate being compared to livestock," said Arithmos, "it seems obvious that this small controversy will not be solved any time soon, at least by the people who are in this vehicle."

Dom grunted and looked in the mirror, but didn't answer, and Jenna just turned her attention to the landscape going by. "How much longer?" asked Billy, after a few moments of silence.

"We'll have another few towns to pass through before we get to Ullapool. Another town where I will have to step away, even though it is nowhere near as busy as Oban."

"I would have thought, judging by the amount of automobiles that Dom has had to deal with over the past however many miles of road, that worrying about someone seeing anything is not much of a concern," said Billy. "How can such a dead road lead to a busy town?"

"We'll take no chances," responded Arithmos.

It was true. The further north they travelled, the thinner the traffic became. They were still on a highway, and there were still some cars and trucks to deal with, as well as the odd RV, most of those last seeming to come from continental Europe, but it was by no stretch of the imagination a busy road, and there were now long sections where they and the paved road were the only indication that civilization still existed.

The sky was the colour of slate now, an unbroken layer of cloud that showed no differentiation anywhere that Dom looked. Gusts of wind pushed at the car at regular intervals, trying hard to lift it off the road, but no unnatural numbers were involved; it was just nature doing what nature did.

And then overhead a roar pounded across the sky from left to right. Dom pulled over to the side of the road, but could see nothing through the clouds, no numbers, nothing to tell him what it had been. He opened the door and climbed out, as did Jenna. The wind fought her for possession of the door for a second, and she struggled to close it, her hair blowing across her face. Just as she shut the door another screaming roar rushed out of the sky towards them. Dom and Jenna both flinched, then watched overhead as a British fighter jet broke out of the clouds, dark green streaking in and out of the wisps overhead like a reflection of an especially slick and speedy rock skipping across the surface of an enormous, unsettled pond. It was very quickly out of sight and earshot, and everything was quiet again for a moment. Then Arithmos was standing beside Dom. "This will do," said the numbers. "You'll find yourself safely to town from here." They looked to Dom. "You want to go to the Point of Stoer, north of Ullapool. It's late enough that you should spend the night in Ullapool, though. When you come out on the other side of town tomorrow we will be there again."

A car came down the road, and Arithmos faded from view as it drove past. The driver of the other car waved and Dom waved back, watched as he drove on and around the distant bend. Wind tried to toss him out onto the road, and he held onto the roof of his rental for balance. "This place easy to find?"

There was no answer; the numbers were gone, not just hiding. "Well, let's see what this Ullapool looks like, shall we?" Billy opened the door when Dom didn't respond, and climbed in and closed the door before Dom retook control. Jenna climbed back in and wrestled her own door shut, and then with a quick shoulder check—no cars, no surprises—Dom pulled back out and followed the road.

Ullapool was a very pleasant little town, with a ferry terminal that took people and cars to the Outer Hebrides, and enough amenities to show that it must have been something of the go-to destination for people in even smaller towns for many miles about, as well as plenty of tourists: a decent sized grocery store, a library, lots of hotels and bed and breakfasts, more restaurants than just the usual fast food blight that every similar small town in North America suffered from, and plenty of small specialty shops.

They found a couple of hotel rooms without any trouble, and after showers and changes of clothes, Jenna and Dom met up and headed down to a fish-and-chip shop they'd seen near the ferry terminal. The wind was still fierce, the air damp and cool, but the town itself acted as something of a windbreak from this angle, so they kept themselves bundled up in their jackets and found a place to sit near the water where they ate in silence, watching the gulls gather nearby as they awaited potential scraps, surfing the wind and occasionally dropping down low to check out any speck that looked a likely prospect.

Finally full, Dom scattered his last handful of chips across the rocks on the beach, and the gulls dove down in a white and grey and yellow mass, full-throated as each let the others know that this was his or her prize, and the rest of them should just bugger off right now. A few of the unlucky ones walked up closer and stalked around Dom and Jenna for a time, watching them with one eye , but Jenna finished all of hers and pocketed the garbage from the both of them, and then stuck her tongue out at the birds. Dom laughed, as did Billy at the very same moment, a dissonant sound that affected even Dom's ear, and the look that Jenna gave him cut the laughter off almost immediately. The birds that were within range to hear all launched themselves into the air immediately, and after one quick circle to make sure that they hadn't missed any precious morsels, rode the violent currents of air towards another prospective meal, one that would presumably be less disturbing.

"It would have been nice to come here just for a vacation," said Jenna after a minute.

Dom raised an eyebrow. "Vacation to me means sunny resorts an' shit. Not that I ever took a vacation."

Jenna shook her head. "I grew up in Utah. I figure I've had enough sunshine to last me the rest of my life." She hugged herself. "I mean, I'm cold, and the weather is miserable, and we haven't even seen much in the way of rain yet, but if it weren't for the numbers and for Napier and friends coming after us, this would be a really neat place to visit."

Dom looked out over the harbour. Not far out a seal reared up out of the water, stared back at him for a moment before diving back down; numbers unlike anything he'd ever seen trailed in the animal's wake, but even from here he could tell they were nothing to worry about. Far away, a ferry was coming in from one of the distant islands, fighting its way through the choppy water. Across the water a hole opened up in the sky, and for a few moments the sun shone through like a spotlight. Dom smiled. "It is pretty country, isn't it?"

"A harsh land," said Billy. "Harsher than the seaside I once . . ." A pause, and then, "Another memory! I once lived near the ocean." Dom felt Billy frown. "Or I did for awhile, at least."

Jenna grinned. "Can you remember anything else?"

Billy shook Dom's head. "Not yet. But that's something. Maybe just being back here is shaking some things loose, first the poem and now this small thing, like a slightly faded transparency laid over what's in front of my—our—eyes right now."

Jenna stood, put her hand on Dom's shoulder. "I want us to get an early start tomorrow." She held out a hand and helped Dom stand as well, held his hand for a fraction of a second too long, then gave him a quiet smile before letting go. "It's going to be a big day, I think. Get this part done, only one leg left."

Dom nodded, but it was Billy who answered. "Spoken like a true optimist."

On that note, they walked back to the hotel in silence. Outside their rooms, Jenna gave Dom a peck on the cheek and said goodnight.

He didn't sleep well that night; thoughts of Jenna wouldn't stay out of his head, and he tossed and turned for much of the evening. Twice he tried to talk with Billy, but both times received the briefest of answers; his shadow was off somewhere or sometime else, trying to dig up more memories and unwilling to concentrate on anything like conversation. But eventually sleep did claim him, a slumber accompanied by the gentle whisper of local numbers regularly scraping over the roof and brushing against the window as they were blown in from the sea.

Oddly enough, the best chance that Ruth had to escape from Napier, to dump him from her body for good and for real, came when he was likely at his strongest.

The flight landed in Glasgow, and even the captain of the plane sounded surprised at how easily everything went. She could see numbers through the window and sense others further afield, all scrambling to ease John Napier's path back on his own soil, their plane being bumped ahead of others in the queue, time and again getting preferential treatment.

And when they exited the plane—naturally the first off, even ahead of those in business class—the explosion of joyous celebration had caught even Napier off guard, the sensation of rapture only equalled, or perhaps even surpassed, by an absolute raging hatred, a blinding and seething anger towards their prey that Napier had obviously passed on to the numbers in the short time they'd been in contact with each other; she could practically smell the origins of that animosity on the numbers, having lived these past days embedded in it every moment. It was in the midst of this celebration that Ruth sensed an opening.

They were both overwhelmed by all the numbers and by the astonishing variety of those numbers that had come to greet Napier, but Ruth was able to slip away from attention soon enough, seeing how she was emphatically not the reason the numbers were there to celebrate. She steeled herself to push back, surprised still that Napier hadn't noticed anything amiss, but just as she had found some background numbers she felt she could manipulate, the other shadow spoke to her, hopefully softly enough that Napier wouldn't detect the internal voice: *Mā. I mean, please don't. He'll know, the very second you call to them. And then he'll push you so far down you'll never find your way back out again.*

The words were not enough to stop her, but just as she reached out towards the numbers Ruth felt her right hand—her real right hand, which at the moment was still controlled by Napier—twitch, and then she watched as the numbers she'd been so focused on do a little dance through the air before flying off, tearing up into the sky as if they'd been launched on a rocket. No words were spoken, but at that moment Ruth could feel one small portion of Napier's attention turned inward, glaring down at her as if she were at the bottom of a deep, dark well.

She was certain then that she would never get out.

They'd woken up to rain, torrential sheets of it that now sometimes fell straight down, sometimes shifted position and came at the car from one side or the other. Breakfast in their laps as they drove north, the landscape on this side of Ullapool lacked in trees, but certainly not in water. The wipers were working overtime, and Dom drove much slower than he wanted, unsure not only where the turnoff was that he needed, but right now not even sure sometimes where the road was.

Through momentary gaps in the rain he could see some hills reaching up to be swallowed by the clouds; back home, the mountains reached up to meet the clouds, but here it seemed more accurate to say that the clouds came down to settle in with the mountains, everywhere on them green foliage accompanied by purple heather. Stone walls traced their way across the countryside, on rare occasions accompanied by a farmhouse, on even rarer moments another vehicle on the road, invariably driving far more recklessly than Dom would have liked. They saw sheep as well, but he imagined that the majority of farm animals were smarter than he was and today made sure they stayed somewhere less affected by the weather.

"Hungry," he said. They had found that Dom could watch the road with one hand on the wheel, while Billy used the other hand to bring the sandwich up from his lap or his coffee up from the cup holder to his mouth, and somehow this allowed him more concentration for the road than if he were doing it all himself. He took a bite, chewed loudly for a moment, swallowed and grunted for another bite. Then

Billy put the sandwich back down and he grabbed the wheel with both hands again.

There was still no sign of Arithmos, but after fuelling up that morning Jenna had grabbed a map. Roads were scarce in this part of Scotland, so it wasn't too difficult to find their own way. Arithmos had said their next stop was the Point of Stoer, and so rather than sit on the side of the road and wait for the numbers to come around, they had pushed on.

Driving slowly, his attention focused hard on the road, Dom still drove right past the turnoff and had to stop and back up about a hundred feet. There weren't too many people stupid enough to be out on a day like today, though, so he had little concern that he would be rear-ended by a speeding metal surprise.

The road to their destination was a single track, barely wide enough to handle the little car he was driving. They passed pullouts at fairly frequent intervals, just like when he'd been on Seil Island the other day; surprisingly, within the first ten minutes he had to use three of them, waving to drivers as they went past on their way from one place to another, barely able to see their upturned palms behind cascading sheets of water, but knowing they were waving, since it seemed all drivers here were friendly and polite.

The land was desolate, a few tiny faded white farmhouses sitting back among rolling green hills, very little vegetation aside from grass and rare low shrubs. Some sheep were cropping at the grass while they stood at the bottom of a hill or hid behind some scraggly bush or a low stone wall, trying to keep their rears to the wind, and once, at the top of a hill just before he rounded a bend, Dom saw something standing and watching them from the top of a hill, possibly a very large dog.

After the first three cars and one tractor about ten minutes later, there were no more vehicles. The wind picked up even more, rocking the car back and forth a few times, but without any sign of accompanying numbers that could be seen as a potential threat. The rain, which had let up for a few minutes, began to fall again, slicing through the air in waves, rattling against the windshield, a sound like someone hurling random handfuls of gravel as they inched along in the suddenly low visibility.

"Should you pull over?" asked Billy.

Dom grinned. "Jesus, Billy, you don't usually sound worried." He squinted ahead and saw a turnoff, pulled in and slipped the car into neutral and pulled up the parking brake. "What the hell." He flexed his fingers, heard and felt the knuckles crack. "Getting pretty tense with this."

The wind and rain were even louder without the wheels running against the road. They sat and listened to it for awhile, watching the whole time for any sign that the sky might be clearing up, and waiting for Arithmos to appear. "Not going to happen," Jenna said finally, leaning forward to look up at the grey through the windshield.

Dom felt Billy arch his eyebrow. If anything, that was an understatement. No longer were the blasts of rain feeling random, but instead it was a constant roar, slapping against the car in a perpetual horizontal waterfall. The wind now rarely took the time to slow down enough to allow the car to settle back down, and outside the windows was a running drab watercolour, green and grey smeared together seemingly forever.

There was a thump against the back of the car, and Jenna let out a small squeak as Dom spun in his seat, trying to see out the back window what had made the noise. Nothing was there that he could see, which of course meant nothing right now.

The noise came again, and the car shook a little.

"Probably a sheep, found itself a nice place to hide from the wind and rain," said Dom, hoping his voice sounded more certain to Jenna than it did to him.

Both back doors flew open and just as quickly closed again, but not before the inside of the car was turned into a cold shower. As soon as the doors were closed Arithmos was sitting there. "Drive again," said the numbers.

"Why the hell did you need to open the doors?" Dom got the car back in gear and pulled out onto the road, hoping to hell he could tell where the road ended and the sky began.

"They just opened in response to us," replied Arithmos. "It wasn't on purpose."

Dom leaned forward and tried to force his eyes to see through the weather. "Can I use some numbers to clear the way?"

"No," said Arithmos. While Jenna reached into the back and found a t-shirt that was still dry enough to wipe things down, the numbers continued: "The Napier adjunct is close. We sent up the weather to try and slow them down, but it will only hold for so long. But we should have a safe haven soon enough, as long as you can get there in time." Dom picked up the speed a bit. "Don't worry about traffic," said Arithmos. "There will be no one else on the road here."

The feeling of the road soon changed, the sound of pavement giving over to the pops and bumps of gravel. "Drive forward another fifteen seconds at this speed and then stop," said the numbers, leaning over Dom's shoulder.

Dom counted down from fifteen and then stopped the car, skidding briefly through loose gravel. The wind promptly stopped, and although the rain continued to fall, it came from above rather than the side, and no longer sounded so angry and powerful.

With the car shut off, the only sounds were the rain drumming on the roof of the car, the wind gusting enough to frequently rock the car back and forth, and the breathing of Dom and Jenna. Outside, Dom thought he heard something other than the weather, and after a few seconds he could see some hints of shape and movement in the grey atmospheric blur that surrounded them. He gripped the steering wheel, looking for numbers he could call down if this went all wrong.

Then, out of the mist of the low lying cloud, stepped a small herd of sheep. Dom chuckled at his nervousness. "Is this the spot?" he asked.

"Yes." They opened the doors and climbed out, and before they had their doors closed again their hair was plastered to their heads and water was running down their faces in tiny persistent rivers.

The sheep slowly ambled away up the hill, stopping now and again to crop at the wet grass. In the distance stood an old lighthouse, and nearby was a trail leading along near the edge of tall cliffs. "The lighthouse was designed by numerates," said Arithmos, almost shouting to be heard over the wind and rain. "The father and uncle of Robert Louis Stevenson, who, they were unhappy to discover, had no numerate ability himself. The structure itself serves as a sentinel, keeping watch much as the trees of the hazelwood and the kirk of the island did."

"So the next package is nearby?" asked Jenna. She was leaning into Dom to keep the wind away from her face.

"Up the hill, yes," said the numbers, and they proceeded to move in that direction. The sheep scattered as Dom and Jenna followed.

"You still have the original package, we know," said Arithmos. "You are carrying the others that you have retrieved since arriving in Scotland?"

Dom tapped his pocket and nodded.

"Excellent. Then listen carefully. This will be the last bundle. When you get it you will likely have but moments before Napier is able to find you."

"What the fuck?" Dom turned on Arithmos, but the numerical creature was still heading up the hill, and he had to step lively to catch up.

"What you will have will help you avoid Napier and his host, but it will also serve as something of a beacon. Jenna will be unaffected, and will be able to move on to a safe place near the Old Man of Stoer once you're gone."

"Gone?" Jenna reached out and took Dom's hand. "Do you mean he's going to leave me?"

"It's the only way Napier—or rather, the numbers Napier sends—won't stay around. We would explain more thoroughly, but the moment approaches, and we would rather you both be safe, rather than just one of you."

"As opposed to dead," muttered Billy. Dom ignored him, and the wind made it likely that Jenna hadn't heard.

The hill was steep, and dangerously slippery in the rain. Twice Jenna almost fell, but both times Dom managed to steady her, which she did once for him as well. They walked, heads down, Dom shivering as his thin jacket soaked right through, for a good twenty minutes before they came to something that relieved the visual monotony of green grass punctuated by the odd occurrence of sopping-wet sheep droppings. It was a concrete pad, about the size of a large trailer, with three abandoned and rusty chair frames somewhat artfully arranged on it. On the other side of the pad there was a gravel track wide enough for a car, and further up the hill sat more pads, along with more detritus that showed that people had once lived here.

"Why don't we walk on the path?" asked Jenna as she slipped on the grass again.

"The fields and forests are where you are safest," replied Arithmos. "Not the roads. You're further from prying eyes as long as you're amongst the green."

Dom waved an arm at the concrete. "What happened here? It looks like a giant came down and plucked away all the houses."

"People used to live here, yes, but they were convinced to move on. When this hiding spot was chosen it was a quiet hill, and already the tourists have been enough to cause difficulties once or twice. Locals who actually lived here were even more trouble; none could be bargained with as those down on Seil Island." They were near the top of the hill now, and Dom looked up ahead to see that several trees stood along a ridge. There was something funny about them, but for the life of him he wasn't able to figure it out.

Jenna noticed as well. "They're flagging," she said. "But in different directions."

"What's flagging?" asked Billy. Dom wiped rain from his eyes, trying to see what she meant.

She pointed. "See how the branches all tend to lean in one direction? Trees that grow where there is pretty much constant wind will do that. I learned about it in high school, when we took a nature walk up a mountain for science class once. But these ones are all wrong."

Dom saw it now. Every tree leaned over, stunted by the bad weather and probably pretty poor soil, its branches reaching out in supplication in the same direction, one side of each tree bare aside from the hunched shoulders of the branches as they turned towards the other side. But some trees pointed in one direction, some in another, which made no sense since it seemed that the wind would come quite steadily from the ocean, in which case all of the trees should be leaning inland, away from the water.

The rain let up as they got to the trees, and he was finally able to see that they were spilling small, secret numbers, all in binary.

And there was his answer. Binary. The trees were flagging in binary. But try as he might, Dom couldn't make out the pattern or message they were giving off, aside from the hints of the numbers which only barely whispered at him before fading up into the grey above.

He reached out and touched one of the trees as they walked past it, and immediately found himself somewhere else, standing on a low rise, no trees, concrete pads or Jenna around. But his hand was still out, and he could still feel the now-unseen branch, gnarled and old beneath his fingers.

An invisible hand lifted his off the branch, and he was back where he'd been. "No time," said Arithmos. "Please keep walking with us."

Dom quickstepped to catch up. "What is this place?"

"It's where we hid the last package in safety. After today it won't be much use, though."

"And what do the trees do?" asked Billy. Obviously he couldn't tell what the hard-to-see patterns were for either.

"They were the protection. The binary codes the flagging produces disguise this area, make it impossible for ordinary people to not only see, but to visit. Flagging in the direction of the wind is Open, flagging the other way is Closed, and that sets up a numerical interference pattern that keeps this place invisible. Anyone who comes to the border will end up on the other side without knowing they were ever even close."

"What about people who fly overhead?" asked Jenna. "Don't they see it?"

"Numbers are numbers no matter how they show themselves," said Arithmos. "Even with aerial photography, the film or digital file just shows what is expected, not what's really here."

Past the line of trees, Dom could see that they were the front edge of an enclosure, a circle of binary patterns that camouflaged an oval about forty by sixty metres in size. They walked along the top of the hill almost to the far edge of the oval. Looking down the other side of the hill was more pasture, and further down, more trees and water. The rain had finally stopped, it seemed, and from up close Dom could see how deep and rich purple the clumps of heather were, a pleasant counterpoint to the persistent green of the ground and the drabness of the sky.

Arithmos stopped them at a large stack of rocks, giant slabs sticking out from the ground at several different angles, accompanied by three man-sized boulders. "The last of the set is here," said the numbers.

Dom stuck his hands in his pocket and frowned. "So does it come out to me, or do I have to toss all these big frickin' rocks to the side so I can get at it?"

"Be patient," muttered Billy.

Dom shook his head. "Patient ain't the word for it. If Napier's gonna show up I'd rather we just turned and walked away, but I know damn well that'll only put it off for a little while." He stuck his hands in his pants pockets and looked around; the rain had stopped, but the hard wind still blew in from the ocean. "So let's do it."

Arithmos leaned forward and the numbers that made up its body swarmed around the rocks, a thick black layer of tiny figures and formulae performing functions too numerous and too quick for Dom to follow. The three large boulders rolled towards them, fast enough that Dom and Jenna had to jump out of the way for fear of having their feet flattened. Once they had stopped, the slabs of rock parted, reminding Dom of a set of bad teeth, all gaps and jagged edges pointed in varying directions.

Embedded in a little hollow was another package. "Pick it up," said Arithmos, now reconstituted in human-like form.

Dom reached down and grabbed it. "Do I open them now?"

"You do."

Jenna grabbed her shoulders and shivered. "Hurry, Dom. I'm not comfortable just standing here."

"We're safe while we're in the circle of these trees, Jenna," replied Billy.

"I'll still hurry," said Dom. "I'm not too comfortable, either."

He pulled everything from his pockets and placed them on the slab that was closest to the ground. The first package, the one that he'd received in Canada and that had supplied the numbers that made Arithmos, he set directly in front of him. As soon as the last package hit the stone, the first one opened itself, paper unravelling in a strange simulation of aging in a stop-motion film.

Inside was a small wooden box, about nine inches long, five wide, and three deep. It was very plain, no paint or stain or carvings, just a simple light brown wood, with a burnished brass latch and tiny iron padlock holding it closed, sanded smooth.

Arithmos reached forward and touched the padlock, which clicked open and fell away. The box opened. Hand-written numbers were laid out on the underside of the lid, but the body of the box was empty. "Open the others."

Dom opened the other packages and shook out their contents. Ten cylindrical rods fell to the rock, and Dom quickly put down a hand to keep them from rolling off. Each rod had numbers on it, each numbered at one end from 0 to 9. Other numbers were etched into the rods, all around their circumference along with diagonal lines to divide them, from top to bottom. All were a faded off-white, none of it uniform, some portions stained darker, some closer to true white.

"You put them in—" began Arithmos, but Dom waved off the creature. He could easily see the pattern. The front of the box unlatched and tilted down, and then each cylinder clicked into place before the front was closed again; the cylinders were now in place, a little loose so they could spin freely, but not about to fall out now. His hands shook from both nerves and excitement, but he managed to put it all together in less than thirty seconds.

Jenna sat down on the flat rock opposite Dom. "This is what the big deal is? What exactly is it?"

Arithmos turned its attention to her. "Have you heard of Napier's Bones before?"

She shook her head. "Well, aside from the little bits I've caught since this whole mess started the other day."

"They were a tool invented by Laird John Napier to make multiplication and division easier. Think of them as a precursor to the slide rule. The original sets would have been made from wood, or metal, perhaps even ivory. The user would line them up to get a quick answer to a math problem."

"So that's what this is? A quick answer to math problems?"

"Yes, although fashioned from different materials than any others might have been. Before Napier died, he made a deal with one of his friends who also practised what people then thought of as the black arts. Upon his death his bones were stripped of their flesh and from them there were to be carved several sets of these mathematical tools."

"The cylinders," said Billy. "They're carved from the skeleton of our persecutor."

Jenna shuddered.

"You said several sets." Dom pulled a hand from his pocket and slicked back his wet hair, getting it away from his eyes. "What happened to the others?"

"They weren't made, at least as far as the numerical ecology can tell. Either Napier's family got word of the plan and put a stop to it before he could do more than the one, or if the so-called craftsman who did the one set died or lost interest or went out of business, we don't know."

"So now that I have it, is there any way I can get it to the Vatican, like Father Thomas talked about? Maybe we can find this priest friend of his." Dom gave the box a slight shake, listened to the distant rattle that sounded from inside.

Before Arithmos could answer, though, a loud series of cracks sounded, and they all turned to watch as the trees that protected them violently surrendered their branches, one after the other breaking off and flinging high into the air, carried by the wind and then dropped to the ground further up the hill. Seconds after this finished there was a sound from the sky out over the ocean, a whisper that quickly rose to a roar. Dom turned, saw numbers, whole sets whose purpose he didn't recognize, streaming in and out of one small portion of the clouds, a mile or so off shore.

"Jesus." He didn't know if that came from him or from Billy, he was so caught up in the sight.

The numbers pushed the clouds aside, shuffled them out of the way like curtains at a window. Or, he saw more clearly, like curtains on a stage. Light streaked down from the hole in the clouds, a spotlight from the sun, focused on one small section of swells and whitecaps.

"This is not good," said Billy.

In answer to that comment, the numbers in the clouds began to swirl in a new fashion, hustling the hole in the clouds closer to shore. The shaft of light moved with them, like a searchlight from a police helicopter, tracking an escaped prisoner.

Dom was that fugitive.

"Shit!" He looked around, hoping to find a new way out, but nothing came immediately to the eye. "Hey!" he shouted at Arithmos. "What the fuck do I do?"

"You leave now, before Napier is close enough to change our balance." It pointed at the box in Dom's hands. "Open it. The cylinders are like axles," said Arithmos. "When they're spun they reveal new numbers. If you spin them all at the same time, thus," here it mimed running a hand along the lot of them, like it was playing a game that required random numbers, "then the Bones will take you elsewhere."

"Wait a minute. What do you mean, elsewhere?"

The numbers shrugged and looked down the hill, already breaking up. The shaft of light was now shining on Dom's rental car, which reflected the light back up the hill along the path they had followed.

"Places. Here on the Isles. Away from that."

"What about Jenna?"

"You have the Bones, and Napier's focus will allow him or his host to see nothing else right now. As soon as you spin them that will become even more evident." The light was halfway up the hill now, picking up speed as it came closer. "Once you and Napier have left, we will lead her to her next stop."

"How will I know she's safe?"

"You'll have to trust us."

Dom looked into Jenna's eyes. She was scared, as was he. "He wants the Bones, Dom. And you. I'm an afterthought, even if my mom is able to stick her head up from the deep. I'll be okay." She stepped forward and kissed him on the lips, hard. "Do it. Find a way. And I'll definitely see you when this is done."

Below, the light had reached the trees, but the flagging camouflage had been completely destroyed; the light still headed on an unswerving path towards Dom, probably less than a minute away now. He looked down to the Bones, trying not to think about what new trouble this would get him into. Instead he concentrated on the trouble that was coming, that was just about in his face.

Numbers swooped out of the clouds, bounced along the ground as they accompanied the spotlight, all of them looking malicious and hungry. The light itself raked across the grass and heather, tearing furrows in the ground and burning intermittent lines as it cast itself in a multitude of directions, making sure that it didn't leave out any clues in its hunt. Steam rose as the outside edges of the light touched the sopping ground, and Dom could hear a hiss rising up as well.

Seconds before the first numbers and the first hint of light touched his foot, Dom spun the Bones.

PART THREE

. . . Discovered thinges he shall looſe and remit, Of Magick art, well ſhall he knowe and wit The myſteries and ſecreet ſorceries The mightie God he makes a babe to be . . .

—John Napier

All was black around Dom, but he sensed someone else with him, outside of his body, which seemed to rule out Billy. Beyond the presence, though, Dom could sense nothing else. He could feel nothing, not even himself. It was like he had no weight, no existence. Perhaps he was dead.

I don't think so, came Billy's voice, not through his ears, but in his head.

Hey, I can hear you, replied Dom. *And my lips aren't even moving.*

So who else is here? What am I feeling?

I dunno. I don't even know where the hell here *is.*

Weight slowly settled down on him then, and one by one Dom's senses drifted back into place. "Open your eyes," said a voice. Arithmos, he thought at first, but the voice sounded different somehow.

Small waves gently slapped against rocks, and somewhere in the distance a dog barked, a strained and desperate-sounding yap. Dom stood on a strip of grass overlooking a small beach covered with stones, and behind him was a row of small, pleasant old houses, all of their windows boarded up with storm shutters. They were beside a harbour; land surrounded all of the water except for a small opening to the right, an egress to the ocean that eased between two hulking and ominous hills.

"Walk towards the Soutar," said the voice, and he was given a soft shove to his back. "It will try to keep you safe, as it keeps danger away from the people here."

Dom spun around, but there was only a wisp of numbers flitting about like gnats on a summer day, nothing else. "Who's talking?" He clutched the box with Napier's Bones tight under his arm, and with his free hand fished for the puck in his coat pocket, looking for protection.

"Just walk," said the voice again, quiet and in his ear. "Turn back, walk towards the Soutar."

Dom spun again. Still nobody. "Is that Arithmos? I don't even know what a Soutar is."

Numbers came out of the air, folded in on themselves and formed into a new figure, squat and boxy. "Arithmos? You're not looking like yourself."

"You may call me Arithmos, but I am different numbers this time, different forms from different places and times. But there is no time for all of this now; please do what's best for you and for the good folk of this village and come with me. We walk to the Soutar."

Dom followed, box of Bones still clutched in his hands.

Within moments they had left the tiny village and were walking up a small paved road, trees on one side and farmland on the other. The weather here was lovely, completely unlike what he'd been in just moments before, just a few puffy clouds in the sky, which was slowly shifting to a deep blue as the sun felt its way to the horizon behind them. There were no signs of people being out and about.

"Where is everybody?" asked Dom.

Arithmos turned towards him, stumbled and turned back to catch itself. "Sorry," it said. "Walking is a rather different sensation. I don't know how you do it, really."

"You speak of yourself in the singular," said Billy.

"I do," said Arithmos. It seemed to shrug. "As I said, different numbers."

"Jesus," said Dom as he shook his head in frustration at the redirection of the conversation. "Answer the bloody questions, will you?"

"Right." The numbers stumbled again, caught themselves, and then slid into a smaller circular shape, lower to the ground, with six legs. "I hope you won't mind my new form," it said, scuttling along the edge of the road. "But if I have to concentrate so hard on getting from one place to another, I'll never be able to answer you."

Dom kicked a loose rock, watched it skitter across the gravel and through the cloud of numbers, kicking up dust that intermingled with the form. He didn't say anything, though, just waited for the thing to reply to his questions.

"First off, everyone in the village is either inside or else they have taken their vehicles and left. Before we arrived they could sense something that hasn't been felt on the Black Isle for at least two hundred years, and while they may not have the words to put to it, it's in their bones and their blood. So right now they hide."

"What happened to Jenna?"

"I don't know," said Arithmos. "It's safe to assume that your departure left her free from harm, though. Your spinning of the Bones loosed more forces than you know, and the repercussions are going to travel wide and deep."

"Repercussions?"

"Think of it like a signal. The Bones are back where they were meant to be and they've been spun, generating very loud, very random numbers. They are a locus, the source of all numerical attention throughout Britain."

The thought of it made him dizzy. If he was carrying the source of "all numerical attention," as Arithmos called it, then not only was Napier after him, but almost every number in the land. Numbers that he often used for personal gain, as well as protection. What could he do against numbers if they decided they'd had enough?

"You've been quiet," said Arithmos. They were on a steeper section of road now, and it had adjusted its legs again, still looking for the ideal configuration. "I believe that I can anticipate your concerns. May I try?"

"Go ahead," said Dom.

"I know some of what you discussed before. Individual numbers are not sentient. Numbers that group together can be, although not always. But even numbers such as those that comprise me, while sentient and in control of my situation, are prone to control by numerates."

"So I could use you now? Call up your numbers to help me?"

Arithmos paused, one leg halfway up into the air, twitching and shimmering. Finally, it said, "You're strong enough, yes. But I've decided to throw my lot in with you as best as I may. That decision came because of choices I—we—have seen you make during this journey, and because of who you face." The leg came down, but it still didn't walk. "Was I wrong in this decision?"

Dom absentmindedly waved his fingers about for a second, and then shook his head. "No. No, you weren't wrong."

They started walking again. "This leads to another troubling question," said Billy. "One that came to me just as Dom spun the Bones back at the Point of Stoer. What happens if Napier tries to control you?"

"Then his shadow takes control," replied the number creature. "I have set up as many protections as possible so that he doesn't detect me and call me to his aid, but if the call comes, I'll have to answer."

"Sonofabitch." Dom gritted his teeth together. "So what the hell do I do then?"

There were no eyes, but as Arithmos paused it seemed to turn and look him in the eyes. "Spin the Bones again, and go where they take you."

They walked in silence after that, no sound from boats or cars to accompany them. Eventually they came out above most of the trees, high on the hill. The view showed them a similar hill across the gateway to the harbour, open ocean to the right. No ships were in sight, although several oil drilling platforms rested in the harbour, waiting their turns to journey out to the North Sea.

"We're here," said Dom. "But why are we here?"

"This is one of the Soutars," said Arithmos.

"You used that word before," replied Billy. "What's a Soutar?"

"The village we left behind is called Cromarty. In ancient times, the Black Isle—which isn't really an island—and the villages along it, which now includes Cromarty, were protected from pirates by the two Soutars." It gestured down with one leg, and then across the water towards the other hill.

"What, these hills protected them?"

"The Soutars were giant cobblers, shoemakers of immense proportions. There were days when the villagers would stand in the distance and watch as the Soutars tossed their tools across the entrance to the firth, sharing them with each other, or sometimes just doing so as a game."

Dom looked around him. The hill he was on seemed like any normal hill, with farmland and trees, a fence, and even a bench for visitors to sit on. The hill across the water was, if anything, even more bare of features, an easy slope from the far side of it, more steep leading down to the water. "These shoemakers—Soutars—just how did they protect the villages from pirates? Their tools?"

Arithmos scraped at a piece of road with one leg. "You mock. Someone who has jumped from one side of Scotland to another and who is right this moment speaking with a cloud of numbers, you somehow can't bring yourself to accept giants in these hills."

Dom stuck his hands in his pockets and looked out to sea. But as he prepared an answer he saw a shape out on the water, distant, not yet anything definable. Even from there he could sense the numbers that lay within the shape.

And then beneath his feet there was a rumble. The ground shifted, started to tear itself apart, and he was thrown to his back. One hand went for the puck, while the other gripped the box of Bones even harder.

Above him, at the very crest of the hill, a figure pushed itself up out of the soil, trees and rocks and fence shedding from its back, a mad vision of a man arising after having been buried in sand at the beach. The very hill gave way, seemed to shrink in size as the figure rose higher.

It was enormous, judging by the trees around it, at least seventy feet tall, broad of shoulder and with a huge pot belly. While its skin seemed to be made of soil and stone, it wore a huge tanned leather apron, covered in dark stains, in which rested a variety of equally outsized tools.

It turned its huge square grey and brown head, looked briefly down at Dom and Arithmos with cold stone eyes, then turned its attention back across the water, where its mirror image had risen from the soil of the other hill.

"Brother!" it called, a deep cough of a voice, the shock of which caused the waves in the entrance to the harbour to jump high and white. "Shall we share our tools while we await the intruder?" It didn't speak English, somehow Dom knew that, and yet he could still understand it.

The far Soutar, hundreds of yards away, spread its arms wide and grinned, its teeth white and flat, an albino slate embedded and somehow polished to perfection. "A fine plan, brother," came the distant rumble.

The Soutar on his side of the water turned and smiled down at Dom. "A show for you and your friends," it said, and it took a hammer—bigger than the car Dom had been driving—from its apron and spun it in the air, two quick flips, then with an overhand pitch flung it across the water. The other Soutar caught the hammer, hefted it, and then with an even wider grin fired it back across the water, faster, each throw back and forth speeding up, until Dom was sure that the silver blur of the tool was going to break the sound barrier. The air around the hammer's path was heating, the hammer itself beginning to glow red hot, and with a joyous whoop the closer Soutar pulled a set of tongs from its apron and tossed that as well, quickly joined by two tools thrown by its brother. All four were whipping across the water, both Soutars' arms steady windmilling blurs catching and throwing faster than Dom could track. The air around them was filled with a constant roar now.

Unsure if even Billy could hear him inside his own head, Dom shouted, "Should I spin the Bones now?"

Two clanks, one loud on his side of the water, one delayed and a little more distant, from the far side, as both Soutars caught their tools in one hand. The closer Soutar turned and bent over Dom, who was still sitting on the ground. "The Bones are a last resort," it announced, its grating voice clapping against his body and threatening to crush his heart and guts. Rocks on the road around him bounced like pebbles on a bass drum. "If you choose to use them in our presence, and we are as yet unprepared, then we will be unable to protect the good people of this firth from the coming threat." Its voice was out of sync with its mouth, which, Dom imagined, didn't even move in conjunction with whatever its natural language was.

"I'd listen to it, Dom," said Billy, his voice quieter now that the tools had stopped flying.

Dom stood up, rubbed his ass as he looked up at the giant cobbler. He could feel his heart pounding a severe tattoo in his chest, and even though the Soutar seemed to be grinning down at him now, he didn't feel any better about things. Still, though, he kept the lid to the box of Bones shut tight.

But as a natural reaction, he felt his fingers attempt to count off primes, anything to stave off the weight of the creature's attention, but Billy stayed his hand. "No numbers," whispered his shadow. "Remember Arithmos."

Dom nodded, kept his fingers still. The Soutar smiled again, then stood tall and looked out to the water. "A pirate of a different sort today," it called to its brother.

It was a cloud of numbers, racing low and sleek over the waves, a dark shimmering smear briefly occluding the water as it rushed on, a vast shadow with nothing to cast it. Every few seconds a small spout of integers would throw up into the air, fall behind the pack very briefly, then with a frantic burst of speed catch up to the rear.

Without a word, the Soutar on Dom's side of the water heaved his silver hammer high into the air, and Dom watched as it cut a steep arc through the sky. But it fell well short of its mark, sending up an enormous wave several hundred yards away from the numbers, which continued at their speed, apparently unfazed by the idea of two giants throwing tools at them from the shore. The other Soutar had also thrown his hammer high into the air, and it landed with a splash later than the first, and at an angle to it. The wave it sent up was as large as the initial one, but speeding along at an angle to its twin.

Holy shit, thought Dom. He could see what was coming. The two waves were going to meet exactly where the numbers would be, unless the numbers were bright enough to slow down or change course. But he had an idea that they had their senses only on the prize, the Bones he carried in the box, and anything else was of no consequence to them.

The waves crashed together as the numbers tried to slide over them, and the interference patterns set off by the meeting of the waves threw everything into immediate chaos. Irrational numbers exploded into the air, enormous geysers sent integers and patterns and binding formulae flailing away from the pack of numbers, which had halted as if it had hit a brick wall. The waves, instead of moving on, had circled back, came in from different angles, and new numbers arose from the interference they created, spun the remaining numbers under Napier's control into a black vortex, and with an undignified series of bubbles like farts in a bathtub, swallowed them all.

Both Soutars leaned over then, plunged their hands into the earth and focused their gazes out on the water. All was deathly quiet for a few seconds, not even the sounds of the waves against the shore reaching Dom's ears, and then there were two drumbeats, loud, resonating thumps, the sound coming from somewhere deep in the water. A few seconds later there were two more, echoing all through the harbour, and then the hammers leapt from the water as if they'd been thrown, each one flying fast and true into its owner's hand.

The Soutar was breathing hard, and with its free hand it reached up to wipe moisture and loose soil from its forehead. "Not the same as pirates, no," its voice boomed. It lowered itself back to sit on what remained of the hillside, as did its brother across the water. "Tiring, that, after so many seasons asleep."

"Aye," answered the other, as it toyed with the hammer still in its hand, flipping it into the air and catching it by the handle, but not looking at it, but rather casting its gaze out to sea. "Almost sad, not being able to see the blood of pirates spilling into the salt water as they begged for their lives."

"Ho!" The nearest Soutar stood again, smile on its face, but as it tried to take a step, the ground at its leg reached up and grabbed hold, froze it in place. Before it could call to its brother for help, or take its hammer to the treacherous rock and earth, more of the ground flowed up its body, twisting and grinding its way around the giant's body, reconnecting it to the hill, frozen in place. Numbers followed, spilling out of the hole the Soutar had left like bats from a cave as twilight hit, millions of them scattering into the air and swooping about in tight circles, searching. The same was happening to the Soutar across the water as well, its hammer frozen in mid-air, spin halted as it hung well above its hand. There, the numbers had jumped high into the air and were crossing the water to join their fellows on Dom's side.

The Soutar managed to turn its head and look down at Dom. "Spin the Bones," it rumbled, its voice comparatively soft, and without any doubt, horrified. "Go!"

Dom opened the box, and as Arithmos beside him degenerated into its component numbers and began to skitter across the ground towards him, he spun the Bones.

Where are you taking me?" For the first ten minutes after Jenna had left Dom behind, she had been alone, running as fast as she could along the side of the hill and casting back glances as often she dared. She had seen the spotlight of horrible numbers burning down on the dewy heather, racing up the hill and almost to Dom's feet, and she had seen Dom spin the Bones and the flash of new and brilliant numbers explode from nothing all around him in a swirling, sparkling tornado that completely engulfed him for a moment, and then dropped away to reveal that he was no longer there. At that moment the spotlight of numbers had hesitated for just a fraction, and then had turned her way, and she had turned and ran again.

But only moments later she had sensed something else, and had turned to look in time to witness the numbers hesitate, and then fraction away before they dissolved into nothingness, and shortly after that she had been rejoined by Arithmos, the mass of numbers dropping from the sky to form beside her and almost giving her a heart attack in the process. But it only took a second or two for her to realize who it was, that the control Napier had over the local numerical ecology had expired for the moment, and that Arithmos was the numerical being she knew and felt she could trust.

"There is a large rock on the far side, after a bit of a climb," said Arithmos. "When we get there, underneath it you'll find an artefact that we are told you will be able to use."

Jenna rolled her eyes, feeling strands of frustration with the numbers rising up above the still-present panic. "I can see numbers, and sometimes I can even convince them to do what I want, but even Dom has trouble making his mojo work with me." She held up her wrist and showed the strands of copper wire still twisted there. "If he can barely do it, how do you expect me to be able to handle any numbers?"

"You'll have to wait and see," said the numbers. "In the meantime, we carry on."

A thought occurred to her then. "Wait a minute," she said. "What do you mean, an artefact you've been *told* I can use? Who told you? Why aren't you able to figure that much out for yourself?"

Arithmos shrugged. "You'll find out soon enough. In the meantime, we do need to hurry."

They walked for a little less than an hour, for the first while Jenna stumbling along the wet side of the hill before finally finding her way to a trail, something that she was sure was normally visited by tourists, but desolate and abandoned on this wet and miserable day. The wind was still blowing, and in those rare moments when it wasn't raining, the water from the surrounding hillside was blown up and into her face.

"The Old Man of Stoer," said Arithmos.

Jenna, her head down and feeling miserable, wet hair matted over her eyes, looked up at this. "Excuse me?"

The numerical creature pointed straight ahead, and her gaze followed along. She stood near the edge of a point of land that dropped off to the ocean, and thrusting high out of the crashing waves stood a tall finger of rock. "That tall rock," said Arithmos, "is known as the Old Man of Stoer. From here, it isn't far to our goal. It is, however, somewhat slippery on a day like today. Treacherous, even."

Jenna bit her lip, trying to hold back both frustration and fear. "What do you mean by treacherous?"

"You'll have to climb down to where the ocean meets with the headland. You'll be up higher than the waves can reach on a normal day." There was a pause. "It may be more than a little difficult for you."

Jenna sat down on the path, not concerned that her bottom could get any wetter. "And what if I say no?"

The numbers seemed to settle down onto the path beside her. She watched them for a second, then looked out to the ocean, watched the birds wheel around the giant rock, gliding easily on the buffeting, vicious winds. "We can't control what you do or do not do," they said. "However, we know for a fact that without the artefact we have set aside, Dom will not make it through the next twenty-four hours alive. Indeed, we suspect that twelve hours might be too optimistic. Which means that Napier will get his hands on his Bones, an event that will likely result in the extinction of the numerical ecology as we know it, to say nothing of major changes to the non-numerate world."

"How so? What exactly is it that Napier will do?"

"Even as an adjunct, Napier is too powerful. With the Bones at hand, his plan is to reconstitute his body. When he does this, we anticipate the reaction of the entire numerical ecology will be to allow itself to be absorbed into Napier, and become a part of his essence. It's not that numbers will once again do his bidding. It's that numbers will be the integral part of his existence. With one move he will sweep us all into his being. Not only does that reduce us all to slavery for what will likely be next door to eternity— because numbers are a key element in the forward motion of time— but it changes the properties of how the world works, which means that everything in your world that relies on mathematics suddenly becomes suspect, perhaps even unworkable. At least without Napier's permission."

Jenna closed her eyes and shook her head, then put a hand down to help push her back up to a standing position. "What if I fall?"

"We'll be there to aid you," replied Arithmos. "You won't fall, we guarantee."

She shook her head. "Some guarantee. Every time I've tried to do something with numbers, you all have scattered away from me. What are you going to do, hold me up with good wishes?"

"Good wishes and some decent climbing gear," replied the numbers as they set off for the edge of the hill.

"Climbing gear?" Jenna didn't know whether to be appalled or amused.

Arithmos nodded. "We can't carry you, we can't grant you wings, and we certainly wouldn't wish for you to fall to your death climbing down amongst the rocks, since even if you did have experience in these sorts of things the weather would not be terribly conducive to a safe endeavour. Therefore, we have enough climbing gear to be able to help you down safely."

The climbing gear turned out to be a simple harness, carabiners to clip into place, and a rope long enough to descend from where it was already tied around one large rock. It was cold and wet and Jenna wished that she had gloves and a warmer coat, but at least she was wearing decent enough shoes for making her way down towards the water. With Arithmos leading the way, she cautiously set off, hoping that she would make it in time to be able to help Dom and Billy, hoping just as much that she would just be able to make it in one piece.

I mages crashed into Dom's mind:

In a museum, it looked like, jars of all sizes, yellowish fluid inside them the final resting place of plants and animals from all around the world. Somehow, Dom was watching from the side and above as a man leaned down, looked through curved glass of an extra-large jar at the visage of a fox, long dead, eyes shut tight against the light and its mouth pulled back in a final leer. Close now, the man fell back to the floor with a terrified scream when the fox opened its right eye and slammed its head, once, against the jar. Bubbles rose from its mouth, bursting one after the other as they reached the lid.

We are in London, said Arithmos. *The Bones, they won't stop spinning.* The numbers were nowhere in sight, but he could still hear them.

Dom blinked away the vision, looked down at the box in his hands. Sure enough, the Bones hadn't stopped, if anything seemed to be going faster.

As long as they keep spinning, there is much they awaken here, continued Arithmos. *I am showing you some of it.*

"Why?" asked Billy.

They create chaos. Some for you, most against you. The ripples travel widely, wake everything in their path. It's best you see what's coming.

There was more to see: high on the side of an old building, statuary scraped to life, relief carvings of saints leaned out over the streets, stretching to escape from their stone captivity, succeeding only in dropping shards of rock onto pedestrians below. One finally pulled itself completely free, wrestled with freedom for the briefest of moments, and then plummeted to the sidewalk, narrowly missing several people with its initial bulk, but hitting many in the explosion of hundreds, thousands of tiny fragments. Numbers glistened in the blood of every wound, fell to the sidewalk to mingle with the stone and dust, struggled to escape and join the search for Dom and the Bones.

"I don't understand," mumbled Dom. He'd finally been able to take stock of where he stood, knew he was on a sidewalk alongside a river. *The Thames*, whispered a voice in his head, many thousands of people jostling for position, not one of them concerned that he might have popped up seemingly out of nowhere.

Closer now, the ripples were visible, easy to see now that Dom knew what he was looking for. They stroked and prodded a great metal lion nearby, and with an immense creaking and grinding that stopped everyone in their tracks, it stood and turned its head to look at Dom.

And he suddenly realized he wasn't seeing this somewhere in his mind's eye.

There were screams from all around, and a mad rush of people running in all directions, some out into the street where a couple were hit by vehicles unable to stop in time. Dom opened the box, tried to put his hands to the Bones to make them stop, but no matter how hard he pushed he couldn't touch them, his hand shoved away, like a magnet against the same pole.

The lion stepped out onto the sidewalk, staring down at him with blank eyes. It opened its mouth to roar, but the sound that came out was far more hideous and frightening, metal against metal, a high pitched scrape that drove right down through his bones. "What the hell is happening?" he asked, voice a hoarse whisper.

Help is coming, said Arithmos. *Just stay alive until it does.*

"Just stay *alive*?" Dom's voice cracked as he yelled this. "What the fuck sort of advice is that?" His voice seemed to break the spell, and the lion jumped forward and swiped with one immense paw. Dom reached into his pocket, made contact with the puck, and skated away over fresh ice around and behind the lion, bounced off a nearby lamp post and fell to the pavement. The metal beast turned its head, sensed him again, and with a grinding crash lunged forward, teeth clamping down on air only because Dom was able to find the puck again. This time it led him out over the stone wall and down a madcap slide of ice onto the river, the water below and ahead of him freezing over, a spreading fan of translucent white stopping the surface flow of the river. He pushed it as hard as he could, skating away from the shore, but the lion leapt over the stone wall and down onto the ice he'd left behind, and even though Dom concentrated everything he could on his escape, Arithmos showed him his pursuer, more images like a movie running through his mind. The lion crashed to the ice, which buckled and cracked under the impact, but it held, thick and strong and not yet ready to melt. The beast's metal feet quickly gained purchase and then it was rushing after him, cheered on by dozens of green copper lion heads embedded in the walls along the river's embankment, their chorus of approving, frightening voices muffled by the rings lodged in their mouths.

The ice reached far ahead of Dom, and a distant part of him thought to be amazed by the incredible power of the puck in his pocket. The river buckled and froze around a tour boat off to his right, and pieces of the vessel broke away from the sudden stop; several people standing outside at the front of the boat were pitched over the edge, and Dom caught a glimpse of red staining the ice where they lay.

Ah, came the voice of Arithmos. *The ripples have reached help.*

Dom looked around but couldn't see anything, and then Billy said, "Up!" From above came two creatures, both something like small dragons.

The closer one dropped onto the lion, a crash of metal on metal, while the other fell into place, still flying, beside Dom. "Keep moving," it said, voice scraped from a place dry and deep.

Dom glanced over, saw that it wasn't a dragon, but rather a gryphon, and that it was made of stone. Numbers from the spinning

Bones rolled over it in fast waves; these were what kept it animated and flying, the numbers shifting and bending like muscles overlaying its body in a flickering grid pattern. "Where am I going?" he asked. A look back now showed that the lion had batted away the other dragon or gryphon, which was lying in pieces scattered across the ice, and it had resumed its pursuit.

"Swing left, back to the shore you were on," it said, leading the way. Dom turned hard and pushed even harder for the shore, and the lion, seeing he was scribing an arc, moved to cut him off.

"Now let go of your artefact!" yelled the gryphon, and it swung around and grabbed Dom by the shoulders. He felt a tearing pain in both arms as he was lifted into the air, but as soon as he let go of the puck in his pocket the ice stopped forming in front and began to melt in behind.

On the sidewalk above the river, hundreds of people scattered when the gryphon let him down, but many more stayed closer to take pictures. Dom turned and looked, saw the lion drop through suddenly thin ice, plunging to the bottom of the river with no sound and only the feeblest of motions.

Dom could hear sirens now, from all directions. The gryphon that had pulled him off the river stood motionless for a few seconds, then said, voice growling but quiet, "You'll be safest at Westminster Abbey. Consecrated ground offers some protection against my kind rising at times like this."

"You saved me. Don't I want your kind to be around?"

Life from stone and metal, said Arithmos.

More images in Dom's head:

Soldiers, stepping down from the pedestals that celebrate their contributions in wartime, waving metal rifles and swords as they read the numbers in the air, looking for the path towards Dom. Around them people scattered, fear as thick as the numbers right now.

In a distant green park, monsters that looked like a child's primitive idea of dinosaurs come to life, stretching long petrified legs as they began their march to the Bones. A child at the park, too slow to respond, was knocked to the ground by a swinging tail, bleeding and shattered in his mother's arms, as still now as the statues once were.

"The dragons and gryphons will work with us," said Billy. Dom could feel his sudden understanding wash over both of them. "The rest won't, or can't. Napier can work those numbers in his favour."

"Correct." The stone gryphon nodded its head. "No matter how we were created, stone and metal know their ancestry and allies, and while all of the others may bend to Napier's will, our kin—dragon and gryphon both—have always given freely of their essence when we've been created, been there to help defend the land and the city that was once, millennia ago, our home." It flapped its wings, rose into the air. "Now. Use your artefact and follow me to the Abbey. It's your only chance, at least until the Bones finally stop their spinning."

Dom pulled the puck from his pocket and held it tight in his hand, skated after the gryphon, dodged traffic and pedestrians and raced between buildings, trying to keep it in sight. Twice in the distance he saw large stone or metal figures walking towards him, but both times they were too far away to worry about, at least for the moment.

He rounded a corner and found himself in a narrow lane, this one miraculously free of people. The gryphon hovered just above the pavement, facing him. "Follow this road," it said, gesturing with its head. "There's a back entrance to the Abbey; it will be open for you. Once you're in you'll be safe, at least from marauding stone and metal." It flew straight up then, launching itself high above the buildings.

Dom again put the puck back into his pocket and ran, hoping he wouldn't come across any more creatures, and hoping almost as much that any witnesses down by the river wouldn't have been able to keep up with him. More sirens were sounding, and the police were another worry, but he made it to the Abbey after only a moment of panic, when from around a corner a walking statue had stepped and caught him in its dead stone glare, a sight that caused him to run even harder. And then he was there, and sure enough, a small door was open, and he dashed across the open space and into the old church. Numbers seemed to jump out of a distant nook as the door shut itself behind him, but they were far gone before he could do much more than blink. He ran down some hallways, made a couple of wrong turns that he had to double back on, and then he had joined the crowds of tourists that regularly filled the Abbey, thankfully none of them likely even aware of what had happened down by the Thames. Across the open space of the Abbey, past the crowds, something flashed in the corner of his eye, but when Dom turned to look it was no longer there, no matter how long he stared.

"I've . . . been here," said Billy, interrupting Dom's searching.

"Can't come as much of a surprise," replied Dom, trying to keep his voice low. "You're British and this place is pretty damned famous. But were you here as yourself or as an adjunct? That's the question."

Dom could see no place to sit and rest, so he walked over to a corner and leaned against the stone wall, watched the people walk by. He opened the lid to the box, saw that the Bones were finally slowing down. Numbers still sloughed off of them and spilled to the floor, but the seismic waves that had emanated from the box earlier were no longer so apparent.

"Consecrated ground," said Billy, as he watched the numbers drop to the floor.

"Good thing," responded Dom. Everywhere he looked there were statues decorating crypts, representing the dead kings and queens and knights of old. Tourists shuffled past them, some pausing long enough to read badly worn memorial inscriptions, but most just taking the time to try and read the dates, those numbers so old and worn that they could barely rise above the metal or stone where they had been written.

Dom felt a grinding sensation from the stone he leaned against, something distant and huge moving either outside the old church, or somewhere deep inside. Numbers poked at his back, and he stepped away from the wall and moved on, casting a glance over his shoulder, hoping like hell something new wasn't going to burst through the stone and come at him.

He fell in with the flow of people, but only passively paid attention to the sights as a tourist might see them. Instead, he watched the statues for signs of movement, watched the numbers coming from them for anything new or different. One tableau was a remarkable sculpture of a grinning skeleton Death, rising up from below and threatening a man and a woman with a sword. He stood and watched that one for long enough that eventually the numbers from the spinning Bones had built up enough to seep into the floor and travel the distance to the skeleton. Its toes wiggled slightly, and Dom quickly stepped away.

"Consecrated doesn't mean impossible, I guess," he said, once he was far enough away to be sure the skeleton was no longer moving.

Billy nodded, but before he could say anything a hand had taken Dom by the elbow and pulled him into a quiet corner. Dom spun around, hand going to the puck and ready to throw some numbers at whatever or whoever this was. But he quickly backed down—even though it was just a shadow flat against the wall with nobody to cast it, and with a different shape since the last time, he knew that it was Arithmos.

"I thought you couldn't exist on consecrated ground," said Billy.

"It's painful, almost incapacitating, and leaves me with little ability to do much besides appear to you," answered Arithmos. "But it's important enough for me to be here to put up with it."

Dom set aside the thought of numbers being able to feel pain and asked, "What's happening now?"

"Word has gotten around," said the numbers. "You won't remain safe in here for too much longer. Remember, if I can come in, so can others. The protections here can only hold so long"

"We also won't be safe if we leave," replied Dom. He looked at the numbers. "And I thought Napier had turned you."

The shadow on the wall tilted its head in agreement. "Fair

enough. So we have to find a safe way to get you out of here. And it was a different set of numbers turned by Napier, even though the ecology shares its memories."

Dom held up the box. "Doesn't help that the damn Bones are still spinning."

"Agreed. They're slowing down, as I'm sure you've seen, but they still haven't stopped. It's a feedback loop that keeps them going. It is the nearest thing to a perpetual motion machine you'll ever see, I would imagine. Numbers all across Britain are worked up about the pending event, and their reaction helped spin the Bones into a frenzy."

"'Event'? Jesus, what the hell sort of word is that? I don't know what the hell will happen if the Napier adjunct gets his hands on this box, but I've been universally guaranteed that it'll be a Bad Thing."

"So say many of us," said Arithmos. "But not all; you know that. The spinning Bones at first helped you by moving you to new safe locations as your previous setting was compromised, but those numbers that are not on your side have managed to grab hold of them and keep them spinning."

"So what do we do to get out of this?" asked Billy.

Arithmos seemed to shrug. "Your only option may be to dump the Bones and run."

Dom shook his head. "Napier wouldn't leave me alone when I didn't have the Bones, so he sure as hell isn't going to just wave goodbye when I leave them behind. He doesn't even have to worry about me getting a head start this time, since any direction I choose will have something standing guard."

"So what do you suggest?" asked Arithmos. "We're keen to help, but the numbers that can serve you will be limited."

"Can you follow me?" asked Dom. "I got a whiff of something when I came in, and I wanna check it out."

"Put your hand on the wall," said the numbers. Dom did so, and they crawled up along his arm and in under his clothes. The numbers tickled and scratched as they settled into place, and he winced, resisting the urge to reach under his shirt and rub at them.

"Where to now?" asked Billy.

"I don't know, exactly. But I saw a flash of something when we came in. Did you see it?"

Billy nodded. "I thought it was just a light."

Dom grinned. "You were too busy worrying that we were being followed. It was numbers, and at first I put it down to something responding to the Bones. But since we saw that skeleton take its time even moving its toes, it had to be something else."

Dom felt a stirring under the collar of his shirt, and the numbers crawled up his neck and into his ear. "There are other numbers in here," said Arithmos, a whisper in his ear. "But none are of any consequence. They're old, fossils that left the ecology and chose to stay with whatever remained of their sources."

"What if one of those sources was in the Abbey now?"

"That's nonsense, Dom," said Billy. "Of course the sources are in the Abbey. There are plenty of dead bodies around, so their sources have *always* been here."

Dom nodded. "Right. I knew that." He took a step and then stopped, noticing suddenly that the people around him had suddenly slowed down. "What the hell?"

The crowds of tourists were still moving along, not just slowly but in slow motion, their speed reeled back like a gunplay scene in a John Woo movie. Standing in the middle of it all, Dom was still capable of normal speed, but for the moment he just stood there, open-mouthed and astonished. All was quiet now as well, the only sound Dom's breathing. The tourists slowed even more, until they were almost, but not quite, at a complete standstill.

Dom looked down to the Bones for a sign of anything different, but while they had been gradually losing their momentum since he'd first arrived in London, the difference didn't seem to be enough to explain this strange event. The numbers themselves still spilled off from the Bones at their usual speed, although as they reached out from where he stood they also slowed down, until by the time they met up with the almost frozen people grouped around him the numbers too had also come to a near stop.

In the distance, in a more open part of the old church, there was movement, normal speed. Dom watched as a number of priests or monks walked a procession towards the altar, each carrying a candle. As each got to his destination he bowed and then disappeared, snuffed out like the flame on his candle.

"I remember this," said Billy, his voice an awed whisper.

"You do?" asked Dom, immediately followed by Billy, voice this time quite different, asking, "What is it? Let me think for a moment."

"Your shadow has found himself again," said Arithmos.

"I've seen this very event before," said Billy, back to the first voice. "My God, I remember my name."

"What is it?" asked Dom.

"It's Blake. I'm William Blake."

"Jesus," said Dom. "The poet? Even *I've* heard of you."

Billy nodded his head.

"Are you shitting me, or are you for real?"

"He speaks the truth, Dom," replied Arithmos. "His memories have returned. Those numbers you saw when you arrived were the spark to remind the Shadow of who it was. This event we're witnessing with the priests is an echo, something he saw here when he was a man such as you. And now that he has returned, things must move on again."

With that, the box began to shake in Dom's hands, and with a jolt Westminster Abbey fell away from them.

Slick with sweat and rain and ocean spray, shivering from exhaustion and cold and yet also fearful she was about to overheat from the strain of the descent, Jenna finally sat down on the first stable rock she'd come across in over an hour. In front of her stood a cat, and as she watched, the animal reached out and laid a paw on a large rock that sat directly across from her and, like a stop-motion film taken over eons instead of years, the rock *eroded*, just peeled away layer after layer and stripped it bare to the elements of the numbers, until eventually the only thing that remained was a small pile of stones, pebbles now, and beneath that pile rested a weathered wooden box. And with that, the numbers were once again gone.

Jenna brushed aside the stones and picked up the box, looking at it closely, feeling the grain with her fingertips, admiring the beautiful and delicate scrollwork along the edges and the fine filigreed brass clasp that held it shut. She wanted to open it but the fear she felt for the safety of Dom and Billy was suddenly replaced by a deeper fear about what she was about to find. When she lifted the lid, what would happen? Was this piece of mojo really something that she would be able to work, as opposed to watching the numbers do their level best to keep away from her? And if so, what did that mean for her life? After these short few days of radical change there would likely be an even more extreme transformation, a change she wouldn't be able to undo.

As much as Arithmos had warned her, she knew that no matter what was said or shown to her she wouldn't be ready for what might happen when she used this artefact. But she also knew that she couldn't let that stop her, not with Dom and Billy in danger and not with her mother somehow a part of all of this.

She opened the box.

Inside was a simple coil-bound notebook, tattered at the edges and with faded printing on the worn leather cover, barely legible but apparently not in English. *Zweiter Band—Anmerkungen*, it read.

"What is it?" she asked, hoping beyond hope that Arithmos would be there to answer her question, but when she looked up the numerical being was still nowhere in sight. She couldn't imagine that it was affected by the presence of Napier, who she was sure had gone off after Dom and Billy, but did wonder if perhaps it was scared that she would now be able to do something new with the numbers, something that it wouldn't be able to handle.

Jenna peered closely at the notebook, searching for any numbers that might give her a clue as to what she would be able to do with it, but those few numbers she could see were almost unrecognizable, and, now that she was paying attention, acting in ways that completely flummoxed her. One moment a group of them would spew from within the confines of the book and immediately align themselves together in some strange fashion, and the next, those same numbers might disappear and then reappear just at the edge of her field of view, grouped now with other odd numbers but somehow unmistakably the same. And then that group of numbers would form into a cloud, each individual constituent bouncing about in the numerical equivalent of Brownian motion, but leaving bright glowing trails behind and then, once again, disappearing from view.

Disappearing from view but not, she found, from all of her senses. Something else about the coil-bound volume had triggered a new ability in Jenna, and suddenly she found herself able to keep track not just of actualities, but of *probabilities*. This was nothing she'd ever heard Dom or Billy talk about, and realized with a growing sense of wonder that her relationship to the numbers was really quite different than what her numerate friends experienced.

Numbers that disappeared had an infinite selection of points where they could materialize, and in the blink of an eye Jenna knew that she was now capable of tracking and processing an insanely large portion of this never-ending series, and also of narrowing down the possibilities—which, with any luck, would keep her from becoming completely overwhelmed.

Riffling through the pages, more and more numerical possibilities leapt out at her, and very soon Jenna realized that not only could she *keep track* of almost all of the boundless possibilities, she could now *control* them. She turned more pages, flipping back and forth through the notebook, and when she found her way to the inside of the front cover she saw a name that she recognized from something she'd once read: Heisenberg.

And with that, Jenna suddenly knew what she would do.

Darkness again. No weight, no feeling, nothing to sense, outside of his own feeling of being lost.

I don't know how all this spinning is going to help us get away for real, thought Dom.

There seems to be as much working with us as against us, replied Billy. *Eventually someone or something has to be able to stop Napier and Archimedes.*

Dom tried to laugh, but of course no sound came out. Inside his head he felt a mild chuckle instead. *Napier can get past two giants and he can turn numbers against us that had deliberately set out to work with us. I can't imagine anything can stop him right now.*

You still have the Bones, said Arithmos. *He can follow you, but so far he can't catch you. Besides, he currently resides years from now.*

Weight and light began to return. *Hold on a minute!* Dom tried to call out. *What do you mean?* "What the hell do you mean by 'years from now'?" His voice, returned to the physical realm, echoed back sharply to his ears.

They were in a small room, sitting on an uncomfortable wooden chair. A table sat beside the chair, a tall unlit candle in an ornate candlestick atop the table. Across the room, faded light blue curtains covered a window; the light behind the window shifted back and forth, fell briefly then returned to brilliance, like clouds were scudding across the sky at an unreal pace. Beside the window there was a plain wooden door with an old-fashioned brass knob.

Dom stood and walked to the window, pulled aside the curtain.

"Sonofabitch!" he yelled, and stumbled back a few feet before finding himself sitting down hard on the same chair.

Outside, peering in through the window, was a giant eye, bigger by far than that even of the Soutar, unblinking. It didn't shift its position to follow Dom's progress from standing to chair and back to standing, this time behind the chair, but he was sure that at least a small part of whatever possessed the eye was aware of his presence.

"I remember this, too," said Billy. "This is another memory from when I was still alive, in my own body." His voice was a mixture of thrilled and awed, and Dom could feel it too, like the layers were more quickly being lifted away from the hiding places of time.

The eye slowly blinked. Massive folds of wrinkled, timeworn flesh dropped over it, followed by a swath of grey and white hair. The eyelid and brow.

"You *remember* this?" Dom felt his voice approaching hysterics, and took a breath to get himself under control. This was worse than the giant cobblers at Cromarty; at least they had only paid attention to Dom when it was absolutely needed.

Billy nodded. "It's the eye of God, or so I called it." He looked around. "But if that's the case, then my younger self should be here."

"The Bones have flung us across the land," said Dom, "but do you think they can send us across time as well? Maybe we've gone deep into your memory instead."

The eye moved, up and down. Dom sensed that the head the eye was a part of had just nodded in agreement. He blinked in surprise, and in the fraction of a second that it took for that blink to be completed, what Billy said was God's eye had disappeared. Billy took charge of the body and rushed to the door, had his hand on the knob and was pulling it open before Dom could think to put a stop to things.

They were in a garden, and the trees were thick with angels.

Dom spun around, but the door, the room, the building they had been in, had all disappeared. They were surrounded by trees and flowers and, as a boundary, tall and carefully trimmed hedgerows, and on every branch of every tree perched angels.

Each one was lithe, very thin without being boney, and it seemed that each angel's body shone with a different colour from the next, a vast, winged prismatic array. Great feathered wings stretched out from their shoulders or else tucked up above and behind their backs. One feather, immense and perfect in its shape and whiteness, slowly drifted to the ground at Dom's feet, briefly dancing in the air as it was tugged by a warm breeze.

Dom looked up from the feather, saw that all the angels had their eyes on him, saw that those same eyes were hooded and dark in the harsh shadows caused by the high sun of noon. He finally forced some spit into his dry mouth, asked, "What the hell is this?"

Billy tucked a hand behind his neck and rubbed at a small pool of sweat that had gathered there. "They're angels, Dom. Just what they look like."

"Who the hell has memories of God looking in on him through the window and of a bunch of angels sitting on branches like something out of Hitchcock?"

Billy shrugged. "What can I say? I had a somewhat strange life. The numbers spoke to me in a rather different fashion, and what many of my contemporaries likely dismissed as drug-fuelled hallucinations or the ravings of a loon were, for me, very real events." He smiled. "You'll have to read some of my poems some day."

"There're hundreds of them," whispered Dom, looking at all of the angels. "Maybe thousands." Was this his next line of defence? Had spinning the Bones deliberately brought him to places where the number ecology would be able to at least try to protect him when Napier tracked him down? And would this hideously frightening flock of angels really be willing or able to protect him?

A figure approached them now, a human-shaped mass of numbers walking out of the hedgerow. Even from here, Dom was somehow able to tell that these numbers had nothing to do with Arithmos.

"Sir Isaac," said Blake, nodding his head. He smiled. "Still feeling as rational as ever?"

"Don't be so smug, Blake. The Mysteries I studied may have proved to be a fruitless dead end, but I stand here, safe amidst the Heavenly Host, while you seem to be on the run." The numbers shimmied and swirled, then walked a circle around Dom. "In fact, I'm here, and you're in the body of a much smaller host who seems unaware that the end is soon to come."

Dom felt his eyes roll. "Spare us any talk of God's return, Sir Isaac. He seems more than content to maintain an anchor in the Garden."

Somehow, Dom could tell that the shifting storm of numbers had just raised an eyebrow. "Who said anything about *God* returning? You're only here as a temporary respite from your own Armageddon."

Another figure emerged, this one from the shadows cast by the wings of the angels. It was tall, almost reptilian in appearance, and carried a large metal bowl in one hand. Its body was mostly reddish-brown, its skin scaly, pointed ears set low and aimed backwards on a large, bumpy head.

"The Ghost of a Flea," whispered Billy, likely for Dom's sake. The numbers that Billy had called Sir Isaac, and Dom had guessed were Isaac Newton, turned and bowed low, then stepped back.

"I need blood for my bowl, Blake," growled the creature, waving its bowl at them, its tongue flicking out a foot or longer. "Shall I have yours?"

Billy shook his head. "Today you are nothing but a manifestation of my mind, Ghost. And besides, I think Napier would prefer to take me himself."

The creature leered, flicked its tongue. "Who says Napier doesn't speak through me this day?"

"If Napier spoke through you, this would have ended much earlier," replied Billy. "I don't know why the numbers have chosen to show me this, but I know it is nothing controlled by our persecutor."

"It was enough to fully bring you back to yourself, Blake," said Newton. "And now that that has been accomplished, perhaps it is time for you to leave again." There was a great whoosh from overhead as, in unison, the angels in the surrounding trees flapped their great wings, and the roiling air plucked Dom from his feet and into darkness.

Any fears about how long it would take to learn what she needed to learn were quickly allayed when Jenna realized that, outside of where she stood right now, time did not pass. More accurately, it did pass, but only when she paid attention to it. When focused on the task at hand, learning how to harness these new numbers and the strange new abilities they gave her, the world around her slowed to a crawl and sometimes even stopped completely. Several times, still not used to this situation, she forgot herself and looked up with a start, worried that she was leaving Dom and Billy in grave danger, and the world would pick up where she had left it, for the briefest of moments seeming like it wanted to dash madly to catch up to her, waves crashing forward with a renewed intensity and birds darting through the sky at almost dangerous speeds, but then something about the numbers would grab her attention again and she would turn her gaze back to them, and once again the world would slow down and finally, if she hid from it long enough, stop.

There was a lot to learn, and even with all the time she knew she had, there wouldn't be enough. At best, she would have to leave here and march into battle to protect Dom and Billy and even the whole world with limited knowledge and abilities and just hope for the best.

"You can't do that," said a voice.

Jenna turned. Out of the corner of her eye she saw the world briefly try to start again before crashing to a sudden halt as her attention zeroed in on a new group of numbers, like Arithmos, only more dynamic, even unknowable, shimmying and shaking like they were caught in a curiously localized earthquake. "Can't do what?" she asked.

"You must stay until you have mastered this new world you are about to enter."

She shook her head. "I have to go soon. You know that."

The numerical creature appeared to shake its head. "If you stay long enough, you will be able to do all, including bending time on purpose, rather than simply as you've been doing up until now, by accident."

"What do I call you?" asked Jenna.

The numerical creature seemed to think for a second, and then replied, "You may call us Quanta."

Jenna shook her head. "Well then, Quanta, I'm sorry but I'm getting too tired to concentrate," she protested. "Soon I won't be able to keep all my attention on the numbers, and then time is going to go on as it always does. When that happens, I won't have much of it left to save Dom and Billy." It was true: she knew as she spoke that the more tired she became, the more difficult it was to concentrate on what she needed to learn, which meant that she was turning her focus more and more to the world around her. Soon, time would travel as fast as it was meant to, and if she didn't get moving soon she wouldn't be able to do anything to save Dom and Billy. And her mother.

"We worry about what will happen if you leave now, without taking the proper time to align yourself and your abilities with this new universe we have presented to you."

Closing her eyes and casting out her new senses, she could just detect a hint of panic emanating from far away, panic she knew was coming from Dom. After the briefest flash of her own panic, Jenna steeled herself and frowned at the numbers. "They need my help, and I'm going. Are you with me or not?"

Quanta seemed to heave a great sigh. "With you, of course. But may we recommend a course of action that might go a short distance to aiding both of us in our goals?"

They were back in London, and the Bones were still spinning. To his right was the Thames, and across the river sirens still wailed. To his left was a building that looked old, albeit in remarkably good shape.

"The Globe," whispered Billy. "I remember reading with my previous host that they had rebuilt it."

From over the edge of the wall that led down to the river they could hear the clatter and roar as metal lions with mooring rings stuck in their mouths came back to life. "Inside the theatre," said Arithmos, suddenly beside them. "We think we know how we can end this."

Dom turned and ran, hoping to hell that bringing all of this to an end didn't include offering him up as a sacrifice. In the distance he heard a booming roar, and people around him screamed and scattered, blessedly none of them running for the building.

A security guard tried to grab him as he ran past the ticket seller, but he reached into his pocket and grabbed the puck, skated past the man and up some stairs, through another door and out into the theatre itself.

"Psalm 46," said Billy, looking up at the sky over the centre of the theatre, away from the roof hanging low over the gallery where they stood.

"What?" There were no people in here. No metal or stone creatures, either, thankfully.

"I often thought that Shakespeare was a numerate." He looked down and gestured at the stage, which Dom saw was crawling with numbers. "In the King James Bible, the forty-sixth word of Psalm 46 is 'shake' and the forty-sixth word from the end is 'spear.' I always thought he might have noted that and perhaps even set it down someplace. An attempt at becoming an adjunct, although I've never heard of him being anywhere."

"Nice synchronicity," said Dom. "But the chances of finding an artefact like that are pretty slim, aren't they?"

Arithmos arose from the teeming mass of numbers on the small stage below them. "You must come down to me," called the numbers. "Now!"

Dom didn't pause to think about what might require the urgency he heard in Arithmos' voice. He jumped over the railing and dropped to the ground below, calling up numbers to soften the blow of the fall. On the stage, Arithmos briefly shimmered, static overriding its presence, but when Dom dismissed the numbers they rushed back to rejoin the body of his numerical companion. "Sorry," he called.

"It was understandable," replied Arithmos. "Now please, onto the stage."

All around them now were roars and calls, as well as screams and calls for help from people outside of the theatre. The sky overhead was swiftly turning black with numbers, both from the spinning Bones and from flocks of numbers that came from every direction to join in. With one last frightened look above, Dom pulled himself up to join Arithmos on stage.

"Oh my," said Billy. "I can taste the numbers, the history here." He stepped across the boards of the stage, testing its limits, swinging his arms wide. He tilted his head back and shouted, "I hope good luck lies in odd numbers. 'There is divinity in odd numbers, either in nativity, chance, or death!'"

Dom rolled his eyes. "That one of your poems?"

Billy shook his head. "It was Shakespeare. Mind you, he also wrote, 'Rumour doth double, like the voice and echo, the numbers of the feared.' Not quite as reassuring, I think."

"'A victory is twice itself when the achiever brings home full numbers,'" said Arithmos, and Dom could swear he heard some humour in its voice.

"I get it," he answered, nervously tapping his right foot. "You're both better read than me. Maybe I could quote some baseball stats instead of a play some dead guy once wrote."

Billy grinned in return, but said nothing.

In the meantime in the sky above, gryphons and dragons were fighting off all manner of other flying beasts, as well as numbers that had coagulated into deadly, angry forms. But they were horrendously outnumbered, and soon the last of the defenders broke into thousands of tiny pieces and fell from the sky. Numbers and animated statues alike now swarmed the floor of the theatre, and Dom flinched as he reached for the hopelessly tiny help the puck might bring, but all of them stopped dead at the foot of the stage.

"How is this possible?" asked Dom, shouting to be heard over the roar of the swarm of creatures and numbers at their feet.

"It's the stage itself," replied Billy. "The numbers in the boards are somehow able to resist Napier's call."

"Yeah, but . . ." said Dom, willing his body back to the centre of the stage. Billy had marched them right to the edge, daring one of the hissing and roaring multitude to reach across and tear him, them, to pieces. "I'm pretty damn sure that the boards that make up this stage aren't the same ones that made the stage when this theatre first existed."

"The numbers lay fallow for hundreds of years, Dom," said Arithmos, surprisingly still intact. "When the Globe was rebuilt, they sought it out. All they wanted was their original piece of the ecology, old wood or new."

"If they're a part of the ecology, then how is it they're not turning against me?"

"They may yet," replied Arithmos. "When Napier and his ilk arrive. But for the moment they're content to stay in place. A sure sign that Shakespeare was a numerate, I would say. Even over the centuries he's managed to exercise control over them."

There was a new commotion in the middle of the metal and stone beasts, followed by a loud crash. Dozens of them fell to the ground, and from out of the middle of the swarm stepped Jenna.

The distance between Jenna and Dom was infinitesimally small, she discovered. She could almost reach out and touch him, but held back, still unsure of what she could do, more unsure of what she *should* do. Whatever it was that had been causing him trouble—Napier or something fashioned by Napier or his numbers—seemed to have left off, and although for the moment he seemed little more than a hazy blur to her, she could tell that he was safe, or at least as safe as he could be under the circumstances.

Instead of going right to him, then, she continued to forge a path in his direction, a passage that was as circuitous as possible. And circuitous not just in physical distance but in time as well. The further she travelled the easier it was to focus on learning from the numbers and to use less of her attention on the actual travel. Less focus on the travel and therefore her surroundings meant less focus on time, which paradoxically meant that less time actually changed for her. Soon enough she found she had gone almost the entire length of Britain, from the Point of Stoer in Scotland to the outskirts of Cambridge. The numbers swirling around her showed that she'd walked almost 500 miles to this city north of London, but she could just as easily have walked from one end of the USU campus to the other; she felt no exhaustion or hunger at all.

Jenna stood at the side of a now-busy road, surrounded on all sides by suburbs, surprised to find herself there so soon. "Heisenberg spent some time here not long after the war," said Quanta. "But we first took special notice of him when he came to lecture in St. Andrews in Scotland. That was when he presented us with the notebook, for safekeeping and for the possibility that one day someone would arrive who could control the numbers he and his people had unleashed onto the world."

"I can't find him," said Jenna, frowning and waving off the history lesson. "Where's Dom? Where's Billy?" She looked briefly to the numbers and then turned attention back in the direction of the unseen London skyline. "Do you know where they are?"

"We don't," was the reply. "And if we actively try to look for him, we'll only bring on Napier's attention. Patience is the key now. Wait for them to show themselves."

"But these numbers I've been shown, this quantum view of the world, that's another way." Jenna squeezed together her fists in frustration. "How can something like that bring on Napier's attention? Why is it that suddenly I find myself here and close to Dom and suddenly I can't see him anymore?"

"All of this time learning from us and still you don't understand," said Quanta. "This is why we were worried about you rushing in too quickly. Without a complete knowledge of the gift you've been given and the responsibilities it imparts, anything you do will be dangerous, to you and to everyone else."

Jenna responded with a curt nod. "Anything I do will have consequences that reach beyond what normal mathematics is capable of dealing with, I understand," she said. "I also understand that if Napier is allowed to regain control of his bones, not only does his own body come back, but then the change in his own control of numbers will make things all the worse. For everyone: numerates, regular people, and for numbers too. Right?"

The numerical being—so different from their previous companion, differences that she wondered if any other numerate would even be able to sense—paused for a moment, and then seemed to nod its head, a rush of numbers tumbling up and down, disappearing and then reconstituting in multiple locations, once even to the point that it seemed to be casting a numerical shadow as well, or perhaps a faded doppelgänger, a momentary replica from somewhere and somewhen else. "We are willing to admit that you could be right, as small as that chance is," said Quanta. "Although we feel you could deal with Napier well enough sometime further into the future, there is no guarantee that he would allow you to live that long once he got word of your existence."

"Get him now, while he's still in my mother's body and not hanging onto the Bones, or run and hide and hope that he doesn't find me before I'm able to handle the new and improved version." With some hesitation, the numbers nodded, and Jenna pressed on. "But that's less important to me. Right now, the only idea is to save Dom and Billy. Everything else is secondary."

The numerical being broke apart and flashed through the air and into Jenna with a great rush and briefly staggered her, and as it did so it spoke one last time, directly into her mind: *In that case, we are here and at your service.*

And then, at that very moment, there was an enormous explosion of numbers deep in the heart of London, reaching up to the sky like the roiling, angry cast-off of a negative image nuclear bomb and dark enough to cast the day into an angry and horrible shadow, and Jenna knew where she needed to go.

Just as Dom noticed Jenna, a horrific grinding noise rattled the air, the sound of a buzz saw cutting through thick layers of rusted metal accompanied by teeth, not nails, scraping along a blackboard. Dom flinched, but when the noise had stopped he saw that all the statuary beasts had come to a halt, some in mid-step; the two still flying overhead plummeted to earth. The stone one crashed through the roof above the seats before falling in smaller pieces to the ground, its metal cousin crumpled and dented close by.

Numbers still swam through the air, ferociously trying to attack them, but whatever mojo the stage offered was holding up well for them. Dom looked down at the box in his hands, saw that the Bones had stopped spinning. Numbers from them rushed off in a horizontal vortex towards Jenna, but instead of running into her or even dodging around her, they dissipated in seemingly random sequences, and then some even seemed to reappear, although in a much more mellow mood than they had been an instant before, floating aimlessly off into the sky.

"Dom!" shouted Jenna, gesturing wildly.

Dom waved back, then felt a blinding pain in his head and staggered to his knees, the theatre spinning past his eyes. He put a hand to the back of his skull, felt the rising lump and the wet smear that told him he was bleeding, then closed his eyes when he realized which hand he was using.

He wasn't holding the Bones anymore.

Arithmos reached out and touched his wounded skull.

J enna ran from the encroaching spotlight and numbers, turned around to see Dom spin the Bones. A swirling, sparkling tornado of numbers completely engulfed him for a moment, and then dropped away, and Dom was no longer there. The spotlight wavered and then also disappeared, but the numbers with it did nothing of the sort, instead turned their attention to her, racing over the grasses and heather in her direction, steam rising from the heat of the attention of numbers and sunshine, those numbers light enough to be prone to its effect momentarily tumbling upwards in the rising heated air. Jenna stumbled and caught herself, ran hard in the direction Arithmos had told her to go.

The numbers came hard at her, but at the last second they dissolved, seemed to jump in one direction or another or even both—it was so hard for her to tell—and then, after one horrifically frightening moment in which they all seemed to multiply into a seemingly infinite series, they were all gone. Jenna blinked in surprise, then followed the path at a slow jog for as long as she could keep it up, before finally settling into an easy walk, dictated partly by exhaustion and partly by the weather and the state of the path.

Eventually more numbers rose up from nowhere, but these ones made no move towards her, only came into being and then faded away once she had passed them, to be replaced by similar numbers further along. Signposts of a sort, she hoped, marking the trail for her.

After twenty minutes or so she saw that the numbers no longer showed her the main path, and instead led her off trail and through heather and over rocks. She looked around, saw no sign of anyone following, and trudged off the trail to follow the numbers, uphill at an angle that, while not terribly easy, was at least not straight up. On the trail or off, there was not much of anything she could see; the rain was no longer coming down and the wind had finally died, but clouds had descended low enough to brush against the ground. The sense of isolation she felt was complete. Even the sounds of the wind and the waves and the seabirds were muffled, so distant that she sometimes feared she had slipped away and into another world.

Finally, though, she came to a small pile of stones, the largest of them about the size of a decent hardcover dictionary, with the last set of numbers resting atop of them. A wet and cranky-looking black and brown cat sat beside the rocks, licking at the edge of one paw and watching her approach. She stopped and squatted down about twenty feet away from it, unsure what she was to do now.

The cat stood and pawed at the stones, and they broke apart, each piece turning itself into a constituent group of smaller pieces, until eventually all of them had crumbled into nothing but dust. Then it stepped back, and she stood and cautiously approached, having no idea what she might find.

Al of this Dom had seen, but now he was back in his body
again, blinding pain in the back of his skull as Billy tried
to pull him up to his knees. "What's happening?" he
asked.

"You're back?" asked Billy. "You were knocked unconscious."

Dom tried to shake his head, wincing in pain at the motion. "I
wasn't. I was in Jenna again, but this time it was earlier, just after
we parted."

Billy started to say something, then stopped. "Never mind right
now. We have trouble."

But before Dom could react, he found himself spinning away to
Jenna's past once again.

J enna reached down into the dust where the cat had pawed, and the cat itself stepped around to the other side of the crumbled rocks, always keeping a careful eye on her. After a few seconds of searching she pulled out a wooden box about the size of a video cassette.

"We have, over the centuries, taken to storing artefacts in various safe places," came a voice from behind her. Startled, she turned, hands in front of her face and ready to fight or, more likely, to run. But then she relaxed; it was Arithmos. "With some of these artefacts, we've had no idea what would ever be done with them, if there would ever be anyone who could successfully *and* safely use them." It gestured at the box. "This is one of those items. Truth be told, we never expected there would be a time where this artefact would be unveiled."

She looked at it. The wood was rough, unvarnished and not sanded. Instead of hinges, two pieces of leather were tacked to the body and to the lid, and it was held closed by a length of ancient string. "*Safely* use it?" She didn't like the sound of that.

"We've watched you from the beginning of this odyssey of yours," said Arithmos. "How could we not notice how unable we are to interact with you? At least, in terms of the mathematical ecology as most numerates understand them."

The clouds were lifting, and Jenna looked out to the ocean, to a tall jutting rock that thrust up out of the water and to seabirds that wheeled around it, unknowingly creating patterns that buffeted in the air behind them. She was suddenly struck by a sense that she was on the top of that rock, leaning over the edge and balanced precariously as she looked down into a new form of chaos.

"You know why?"

Arithmos seemed to nod. "We believe so. Open the box and discover for yourself."

She hesitated. Even touching the box brought about all sorts of unbidden images, so clear and at the same time so bizarrely indistinct. There was change in this box, somehow she knew, and she wasn't so sure it was change she would be able to keep in check.

"Without this artefact and the abilities it brings out in you, we know for sure that Dom and Billy will not be able to last the next twelve hours," said Arithmos. "Napier has grown to the point where he is far too strong. Which means that Napier will get his hands on his Bones, an event that will likely result in the extinction of the numerical ecology as we know it, to say nothing of major changes to the non-numerate world."

"How so? What exactly is it that Napier will do?"

"Even as an adjunct, Napier is too powerful. Once reconstituted, everything changes. He'll have proven that he is no longer mortal, and will have control of all numbers. You need to know that mathematics lies at the heart of the very existence of the world and of the entire universe, even for something as intangible as the forward motion of time. Eternity for Napier will be however he sees it, but we can assure you that for us it will feel like a very long time. To say nothing of what changes he makes will be wrought on humanity."

Jenna shook her head. "But I can feel something similar in here," she said, and shook the box in her hands at the numbers in front of her.

Arithmos shrugged. "What happens if you succeed, if we are indeed right about not only you but the artefact you hold, is that we are freed completely, not reduced to slavery ever again. There may be pockets of time and space where this does not happen, but we believe that it will work in our favour."

"Provided I'm able to use this and somehow figure out how to stop Napier."

The numbers slowly nodded. "Provided so, yes."

Jenna untied the string, a difficult task with the knot being so old and her fingers chilled and tired. But finally she managed, and opened the lid. Inside were some papers loosely bound into a book, each imbued with numbers that didn't run away from her, instead seemed to see who she was. They rose through the air at an almost languid pace, touched down on both of her shoulders, then reached in and tickled her mind, gave her hints of what could be, what might be, what would be.

She smiled, and behind her the cat hissed, for a moment almost impossibly appearing to be both dead and alive. And then at that very moment, Jenna seemed to *multiply*, to be everywhere at once. Learning, finally finding what it was she was meant to discover.

N ow Jenna found herself fighting her way through the crowd of numbers towards the doorway, the time she'd spent learning and gathering her resources gone in the blink of an eye, and her journey from the hillside at the Point of Stoer to here at the Globe had even shifted her backwards in time, if only by a fraction of a moment. The numbers above and around her, those that didn't seem committed to the coming battle, seemed to confirm that backwards slide in time for her newly tuned senses. It was like a universal clock that all this time had surrounded her, before this moment always invisible.

Napier, Archimedes, and her mother were approaching, but she couldn't yet get a handle on the direction. For this the numbers were too scrambled, too many siding with them, whether or not it was voluntary.

She entered the theatre, and all the strange mystical creatures she had seen as the new type of numbers had dropped her back into this world, this small sliver of space and time, stopped moving, frozen into unfamiliar positions. In response, the numbers that had been spilling from the Bones in Dom's hand gathered themselves back up into a tight ball and flung themselves towards her, a tight angry tornado of numerical hornets looking to sting Jenna to death.

She didn't even blink. The new numbers that accompanied her smeared reality, and the numbers forced into action by Napier's Bones were suddenly everywhere and everything else.

But in that moment a woman—her mother, she was sure, even though it had been so long since she'd seen her—appeared out of nowhere, dropped onto the stage and, before Jenna could warn him, cracked Dom on the back of the head with a large club shaped from numbers.

Dom rolled over to look at the woman. She definitely resembled Jenna, but the shadows that overlapped her body seethed and skittered, played harshly on her face. She held the Bones in her left hand.

"It's about time I caught up to you," she, or rather, Napier said. She reached up and pulled some numbers from the air, flung them down in a pattern that pinned Dom to the stage and left him gasping for breath, the weight on his chest almost unbearable.

"And you!" she called, looking now across the theatre at Jenna, while Dom struggled to free his hands, looking for any mojo he could use to get them out of this. "Family or no, you'll have to be punished for helping them." She sent more numbers Jenna's way, a horrendous torrent of them, but every single one of them crashed to the ground between them, numerical shards of glass that had run into an invisible barrier.

She frowned, then shook her head and spun the Bones. Instantly the creatures that surrounded the stage came back to life. "Deal with her," she said, pointing a finger in Jenna's direction.

Dom and Billy found some numbers embedded in the stage, numbers that were still not under Napier's control. They used them to get out from under the crushing weight of the numbers that held them down, and, still with some difficulty, stood.

Dom was back with Jenna again. He tried to look to see what was happening on the stage, but he had no control over what she did.

Every creature called up again by Napier attacked Jenna, but a simple wave of her hand was enough to halt their progress. Every single stone and metal creature stopped in mid-step, and the numbers that accompanied them continued to disappear or to become something else as they attacked Jenna, spinning off into uncertainties and fluctuations as the numbers found new universal laws to observe.

She reached the stage and pulled herself up, in time to see Billy, in Dom's body, rush her mother. She closed her eyes and put her hands back down onto the stage, felt the flow of numbers, looking for the right sequence.

The numbers in the stage were still unwilling to go to work for Napier, that much was obvious. The wood under Napier's feet buckled and twisted now, although the host, Jenna's mother, was doing well keeping her—their—balance.

Back in his own body again, Dom was thrown off balance as he, as Billy, ran after Jenna's mother. More numbers came after him, trying their best to pin him back to the stage, but with Billy's help he was able to find sequences he could use to fend them off. Although Napier's numbers were tough, they had the advantage in that already Napier's mind seemed to be on other things, and the numbers could do no more than try to hold their own; they were not set forth to behave autonomously, and so each one could be batted away.

Napier was concentrating on the Bones now. Dom knew that the body was Jenna's mom and that Archimedes was in there as well, but it suddenly seemed obvious to him this was all Napier. Instead of spinning them into random numbers and equations, which had only kicked Dom and Billy randomly across the Britain, the adjunct was cautiously turning one Bone, and then another. As he did so, numbers hovered overhead, waiting their turn to interact with the Bones and create whatever it was Napier was after.

Dom sat up, fingered the copper wire still around his wrist, then sought out other numbers in the frantic ecology that surrounded them. Ignoring the momentary pang of guilt, he pulled down a rain of formulae, and bolstered the attack with a small wave of imaginary numbers that had found their way to the theatre.

The first attack buffeted Napier, and the second hit him hard enough to almost make him drop the box of Bones. Jenna's mother looked up, rage written across her face, but before she—Napier—could counterattack, Dom grabbed hold of Barylko's puck and skated across the newly frozen surface of the stage, knocking the Bones from her hands.

The box went flying through the air, and Napier and Jenna's mother fell to the stage, the ice having caught them by surprise. Dom spun around and moved to catch it, but a new series of numbers dropped in his path at shoulder level, and he had to fall to his knees as he slid to avoid being shredded by the razor sharp edges that Napier had given them. The box dropped to the ice and skidded to the far corner of the stage, the Bones all of a sudden spinning again. Once more, Dom found himself in blackness, off to yet another random location.

They were on a small hill overlooking the ocean. Jenna's mother stood on the beach down below them, the Bones at her feet. Numbers rose from her head and body in a twisting, raging storm and fell hard towards Jenna, only ten feet away. Jenna's response was almost negligible; some strange numbers rushed from her fingertips and her forehead and kept her mother from reaching down for the Bones, but she did nothing that Dom could see to fight off the numbers attacking her head on. Instead, the attacking numbers just dissipated, motes of dust in a powerful wind, before they got to her. The roar of the numbers overpowered any sounds of wind and waves, and made it difficult for Dom to think about what he could do to help.

For a brief moment again he found himself in Jenna's head, but this time she whispered, seemingly right in his ear, "Not now, Dom. Go back to your own body, and I'll explain later."

Back and looking through his own eyes again, he jumped forward to help, but before he could get close sand and gravel exploded around Jenna's mom, a tall curtain of earth that surrounded her and would not return to the ground. An identical wall of sand jumped up to surround Jenna, and then, slowly, each curtain leaned in towards the other, until the two were almost parallel with the ground, enormous, ferocious sandblasters. Jenna stepped out from the midst of her own curtain, smiled at Dom, then lifted a hand and stepped back into the midst of the dry conflagration, towards her mother. Rocks and sand curled around and over her, none touching her, the most damage being a slight ruffling of her hair.

"Jesus," said Dom, coming to a halt.

"No doubt," replied Billy. "I've seen much in my life, but never such as this."

Both curtains of sand dropped down to nothing, and Jenna's mother frowned, and then took the opportunity of the silence to reach down and grab the Bones. New numbers were conjured, and Dom made to call up his own numbers to try and stop them, but Jenna held up her hand and shook her head. He stopped, aware of something in her eyes that he hadn't seen before.

Napier had the last Bone in place. For a moment that seemed to Dom to stretch on forever, everything seemed to stop: birds out over the water hung in mid-air; waves reached out and waited for gravity to return; the few clouds that had been rushing across the sky came to a halt. Silence hung ominously over everything.

And then with a crash of renewed sound the world sprang back to the present, and the sudden onslaught of numbers turning back towards Napier was both awe-inspiring and hideously frightening. Dom watched as the shadows within began to split off from Jenna's mother, as both Napier and Archimedes coalesced into solid masses of numbers, then smoothed out and filled themselves in, becoming real bodies. Now both Napier and Archimedes seemed real, living people again, no longer shadows inhabiting an unwilling hostess.

Instantly, the blue sky turned pitch black, even though the sun still shone overhead. Static charges flashed and noisily crashed and broke up overhead, fuzzy motes of brilliant whiteness like temporary splashes of white pollen on black felt.

Jenna's mother and the Archimedes shadow both stumbled back, and Napier reached up and called more numbers down onto Jenna, but everything he threw at her went astray, many of the numbers just seeming to give up interest as they approached her, others finding themselves in places that they hadn't intended to be.

"I'll kill you if I have to twist your neck with my bare hands!" yelled Napier over the angry buzzing and crashing, his accent thicker than before, his voice shaking with rage and exhaustion; the storm of numbers he was controlling would have wiped out Dom by now, and likely, any other numerate. Napier had very short hair and a thick, long goatee, and he wore a black robe with a slightly soiled white ruff around his neck. His face was contorted with rage, and his prominent ears were flushed bright red.

Jenna spread her arms and tilted her head to one side. "You're welcome to try," she answered, also yelling to be heard over the noise of the crashing numbers. "But it won't do any good." She flicked her eyes to the ocean, sad smile on her lips. "We have visitors."

Everyone turned to look, saw that a large pod of dolphins had come ashore, all of them eerily calm, and even from here, Dom could tell that they all had their eyes focused on Napier. The shadow—no, now a man, no longer an adjunct—seemed to count them all, then grunted in surprise and dismay. He attempted several attacks on them, but all of the numbers again just petered out.

"Cetacean math and our math are not the same things," said Jenna's mom, now standing so close behind Dom that he jumped in surprise. He turned, prepared to fight her, but she put a gentle hand on his arm and shook her head. "They've come for you, Napier."

"You control us no longer, John Napier," called Archimedes in thickly accented English, standing not far behind Napier. He smiled nervously, a short, dark-haired and somewhat plump man in a loose-fitting yellow robe and sandals, fretful numbers dancing around his head, anxious to protect him.

Napier himself made to conjure up a new attack, but Jenna silently stepped forward and laid her hands on the Bones. A shadow eased out from inside of her, and replicated itself over and over and over again. And suddenly the numbers that surrounded them were not only doing things that Dom had never before seen, but things he never even would have thought possible. They were disappearing and reappearing in random fashion, some of them copying themselves before his eyes and others changing from one form to another and back again as he watched them.

The sky changed then, no longer black, but suddenly a spectrum of colours, and Dom got the idea that it wasn't changing from one to the other but rather was all of them at once, as if he could see each and every possible colour at the same time. He turned to look back at Jenna and saw that the same was happening with her, that he could see two, a dozen, a hundred, even a million different Jennas, all at the same time, shifting and sliding in through and around each other, all of them with one hand on the Bones and the other reaching for Napier himself.

The former shadow winced and ducked, but if one hand missed, even if twenty of them did, others found their mark. Suddenly Napier was himself an impossible number of alternates, each one grimacing in agony as the numbers that had helped maintain his existence abandoned their positions.

Napier, all of the Napiers, screamed with rage, with fear, and fought back with everything he—they—had, an explosion of numbers rising from the ground, falling from the sky, spilling from the sea, all collapsing in on him as he sought their help. He waved his arms and built up impossible-seeming torrents of formulae, a last-ditch attempt to save himself and defeat Jenna, and Dom was momentarily thrown to his knees by the rampaging winds and shaking earth, but every Jenna still stood, now implacable. With one last flurry of motion, an angry swarm of numbers jumped from the top of Napier's head and skittered across the beach to the dolphins, and each dying animal opened itself to accept the numbers.

Napier collapsed and at the same time Dom felt a wrenching sensation inside his body, but behind where Napier had stood Archimedes stayed in one piece, the final numbers that Dom only just now noticed had tied him to Napier shedding away from his body and dropping to the beach. "Thank you," he whispered, and several Jennas turned their attentions from the dolphins long enough to nod in response.

"By God," said Billy, his own accent stronger now. Dom turned, alarmed to hear his voice come from somewhere else and saw that the poet was standing beside him, now in his real body as well, slightly dumpy, with receding grey hair and thin lips. He was smiling.

"What the hell just happened?" Dom looked to Jenna, to as many of the Jennas as he could focus on, and saw that many of them were now walking across the beach to join the dolphins. He felt inside, looking for the numbers he had carried as his shadow, but felt nothing; they were gone, and Blake really was an ordinary person standing beside him instead of nesting inside his head. Dom looked around now, and realized that, aside from those that accompanied the Jennas, he couldn't see any numbers. It was like he'd spent all of his life in the jungle and suddenly found himself in the deserts of Mars, the world around him airless and lifeless. Not really paying attention to what he was doing, he reached out and took Jenna's mother's hand, then staggered along after her as she walked to join her daughter—daughters, since there were still uncountable versions of Jenna on the beach—followed closely by Blake and Archimedes.

One Jenna stepped ahead of the others, and by the time they'd reached her, the one he was now thinking of as *Jenna Prime* was on her knees, stroking one dolphin's snout and whispering to it. The animal seemed to lean into her, and a string of indeterminate numbers leapt from her to it and then to all the other dolphins, a lacework of numerical electricity, and then all of the dolphins, sixty-seven of them, were dead.

She stood, tears in her eyes, and first hugged Dom, and then her mother. As Dom watched Jenna with her mom, the light around her seemed to shift and crack into crazed patterns, bending around her like a refraction through water, making her look like a living Hockney collage. "What the hell is happening?"

"It's all the same," said Jenna.

"Different," she said, standing a few feet away from herself.

"Changing," said another version.

"Infinite."

"Impossible."

"Probable."

"Continuous."

"And more, as I reach back and forth across time." She closed her eyes. "I can't collapse the wave front," she grunted. "Can't get out of here." Behind her, the dead dolphins came to life, swam back out to the ocean, at the same time festered and rotted where they lay. The sun blinked and wavered, and new stars poked through the bright sky. Clouds scudded in all directions at once, and in the distance strange and marvellous beasts strolled along the horizon, seeming to walk on the very ocean, impossibly tall and thin, stretched like a monster child's rubber playthings.

Jenna's mother stepped forward. "I don't pretend to understand this new world of numbers you've called forth, but you brought down Napier when Archimedes and I and many others could never resist him." She gently took her shoulders and looked into her eyes. "Jenna, you're my daughter. I'm so very proud of you for what you've accomplished, and every bit as sorry for what I've done to you. But you've shown great strength in dealing with everything I threw at you. You can deal with this as well." She leaned forward and kissed Jenna Prime on the cheek.

Sweat broke out on Jenna's forehead, the strain pushing hard at her. "I can," she finally whispered. All around, the seemingly infinite versions of Jenna folded in on Jenna Prime, and then she stood alone on the beach, the sun now out and shining behind her head like a halo. She smiled and held out her hand to Dom, who, with a modicum of hesitation, reached out and took it.

"What the hell just happened?" he asked.

"All these years after the birth of quantum mathematics," said Jenna's mother, "there has been no one who could control those numbers like a numerate could control the standard numerical ecology."

"No one until me, it seems," said Jenna. She squeezed his hand. "All I needed was an artefact to give me the final key. Whatever I had that made the numbers avoid me unless I concentrated on getting them, it was something I was born with."

Dom looked around, trying hard to see numbers. But he was like a blind man now. "So what happened? Where did the numbers go?"

"Nowhere and everywhere. The artefact I have came from a physicist named Werner Heisenberg. It helps me control the numbers like I was never able to before, but now that I've activated it, the ecology will never be the same. His Uncertainty Principle and other aspects of the quantum universe are going to rule parts of our world on a macro scale now, and I'm afraid that it won't be just numeracy that sees the change."

"Wait," said Dom. "Is this something to do with why I kept popping into your head?"

Jenna nodded. "Quantum entanglement, Dom. There was something about our relationship, from the moment I first saw you. Any time I tried to use numbers, there was a brief moment of entanglement, a melding of your numerate ecology and my unheeding perception of the quantum world that dragged us together, and then after I was given the artefact and began to use it, we melded for longer periods, from further distances apart."

Dom shook his head, not understanding this at all. "Then how come I wasn't in your head at the end there?"

She smiled. "Because I'm in control now."

Jenna looked back to the dead dolphins on the beach, and then removed on old, creased piece of paper from her back pocket and placed it on the sand; part of the artefact that had been in the box, Dom realized. As she smoothed it out, new numbers slowly rippled outwards, disrupting the grains of sand around it, and as Dom watched, the sky began to shift again, sideways and backwards, and a seemingly infinite amount of sand seemed to multiply itself, every grain prepared to introduce him to the new universe.

ACKNOWLEDGEMENTS

A lot of time and research went into writing this novel, and as with anything that requires so much digging around in history, I am greatly indebted to a large number of people for their aid and counsel, and to an equally-large number of people who stepped up with wonderful ideas and criticisms.

First and foremost, I must thank my wife, JoAnn Murphy: yes, when we got married the thought did occur to me that it might be useful for an author to be married to an academic librarian, and she was indeed a help when navigating my way through old museums and libraries in Scotland and England, but in the end it was just a great thing to have her for company in the U.K. while tracing the path of my heroes and villains.

This book would not exist without my old friend Wayne Malkin, who first showed me a picture of Napier's Bones and who uttered the magic words that would launch the central conceit behind this book. Thanks also go to Frank Wu, who sent me the cool artwork for a concept that ended up being edited out of the novel, Kevin Hutchings, Associate Professor of English at the University of Northern British Columbia, the staff at the College Heights Starbucks in Prince George, where much of the book was written, and Judy Green in the Special Collections Library at the University of Alberta.

For offering wise words of criticism and support, George Murphy (my father), Douglas Smith, David Hartwell, Nalo Hopkinson, Donald Maass, Holly Phillips, Jena Snyder, the late, great Phyllis Gotlieb, and of course my wonderful and insightful editor Sandra Kasturi and publisher Brett Alexander Savory.

Jay Caselberg in London and Charles Stross in Edinburgh were kind to me when I was in their respective cities (note to Jay: never forget the homicidal midget). Stephen Dodson, proprietor of Languagehat (www.languagehat.com), one of the smartest and most interesting blogs I read, was invaluable and very patient in helping me with translations. As with any other expert advice I was given, if mistakes are found they're mine and mine alone.

At Napier University in Edinburgh, Eric and Chris were a huge help, taking me on a tour and printing off all sorts of information from the university records. I wish I had remembered to get their last names. In the university's library, Liz Butchart took wonderful care of me and came up with excellent reference material.

I was apparently too busy to ask for their names, but I also received tremendous help from people at the National Library of Scotland in Edinburgh, at Lambeth Palace Library in London, and the individual (name lost on a long-dead computer) whose membership in a nature society led me to the wonder of the Ballachuan Hazelwood. If nothing else came out of this project, the fact that I got to lose myself—literally—on Seil Island for a few hours was a once-in-a-lifetime experience. Finally, I am indebted to the Canada Council for the Arts for their generous support in helping me complete this project.

ABOUT THE AUTHOR

Derryl Murphy's stories have appeared in a variety of magazines and anthologies over the years. He is also the author of the ecological science fiction collection *Wasps at the Speed of Sound* and, with co-author William Shunn, of the ghost story *Cast a Cold Eye*. He has been nominated three times for Canada's Aurora Award, and anticipates that someday he'll be nominated and lose again. He lives on the Canadian prairies with his wife, two sons, and dog, and vaguely remembers the day when he thought this whole writing thing would be glamourous.

978-0-9812978-9-7

978-0-9812978-8-0

978-0-9812978-7-3

TIM LEBBON

PHILIP NUTMAN

SIMON LOGAN

**THE THIEF OF
BROKEN TOYS**

CITIES OF NIGHT

**KATJA FROM THE
PUNK BAND**

978-0-9812978-6-6

978-0-9812978-5-9

978-0-9812978-4-2

GEMMA FILES

DOUGLAS SMITH

NICHOLAS KAUFMANN

**A BOOK OF
TONGUES**

CHIMERASCOPE

**CHASING THE
DRAGON**

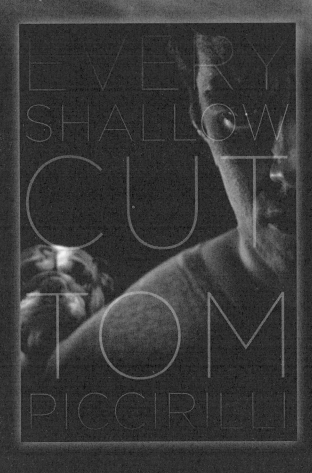

EVERY
SHALLOW
CUT
TOM
PICCIRILLI

COMING MARCH 15, 2011
FROM CHIZINE PUBLICATIONS

978-1-926851-10-5

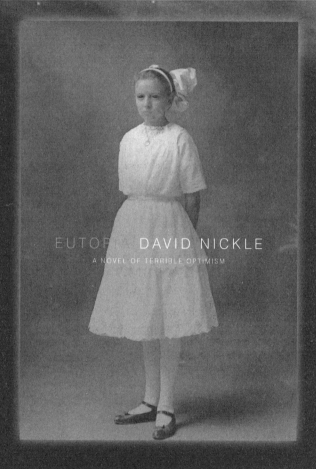

EUTOP   DAVID NICKLE
A NOVEL OF TERRIBLE OPTIMISM

COMING APRIL 15, 2011
FROM CHIZINE PUBLICATIONS

978-1-926851-11-2

THE DOOR TO
LOST PAGES
CLAUDE LALUMIÈRE